LIVING THE DREAM AT PUDDLEDUCK FARM

DELLA GALTON

Boldwood

First published in Great Britain in 2024 by Boldwood Books Ltd.

Copyright © Della Galton, 2024

Cover Design by Alice Moore Design

Cover Photography: Shutterstock and iStock

Every effort has been made to obtain the necessary permissions with reference to copyright material, both illustrative and quoted. We apologise for any omissions in this respect and will be pleased to make the appropriate acknowledgements in any future edition.

A CIP catalogue record for this book is available from the British Library.

Paperback ISBN 978-1-83518-514-8

Large Print ISBN 978-1-83518-510-0

Hardback ISBN 978-1-83518-509-4

Ebook ISBN 978-1-83518-507-0

Kindle ISBN 978-1-83518-508-7

Audio CD ISBN 978-1-83518-515-5

MP3 CD ISBN 978-1-83518-512-4

Digital audio download ISBN 978-1-83518-506-3

Boldwood Books Ltd
23 Bowerdean Street
London SW6 3TN
www.boldwoodbooks.com

For Rhian Rochford, with my love

1

Stepping into the cake marquee was like stepping into another world: a hot, sweetly vanilla-scented world, lined with trestle tables, covered with white cloths, on which arrays of gorgeous-looking cakes were laid out. The closest table held Victoria sponges, golden topped and sprinkled with icing sugar, cellophane wrapped, but each with a thin triangular slice missing.

Phoebe Dashwood took a deep breath and let out a contented sigh. 'Cake heaven,' she said to the man beside her and he squeezed her hand.

'I'll say.' His blue eyes crinkled with warmth. 'Looks like we should have come earlier. We might have got a taste.'

'I think you have to be a judge for that, Sam,' Phoebe teased.

'I could be a judge. I love cake.'

'On that basis, most of England could be a judge. I too could be a judge. I adore cake.'

'Yeah, that's true. I wonder how you get to be a judge. Hey, look at this Battenberg, all on its own.' He pointed to the marzipan-adorned cake, which had a red rosette pinned to its cellophane wrapping. 'Do you think it won because it was the only entry in its category?'

'Maybe. Although I'm sure it was delicious too,' Phoebe added, in case its baker was anywhere in earshot.

It was Thursday 27 July, the last day of the New Forest Show; a three-day affair held annually at Brockenhurst, Hampshire, and one of the biggest summer events in the South of England calendar. There weren't many people in the cake marquee now the judging had been done, which they hadn't realised when they'd wandered in.

Sam Hendrie smiled, and Phoebe glanced at his familiar, strong profile and felt her heart shift with love for him. She had known that face her entire life. Known the way his dark hair curled slightly at the nape of his neck when it needed cutting, the slight dip in his chin, his quick smile. They had grown up together, their mothers being best friends. She had watched Sam become a man, and he had watched her become a woman. But until three weeks ago, Phoebe had never imagined they'd end up in their own love story.

A sudden flurry of movement at the other end of the marquee interrupted Phoebe's musings and both she and Sam glanced towards the exit. Something was going on outside. There were shouts, the sounds of a fracas, and the few people who'd been inside were hurrying out to see what was happening.

Sam and Phoebe followed. They were just in time to see a riderless horse, reins and stirrups flying, cantering at speed towards the marquee, which was close to the edge of the showground and encircled by the trip hazard of dozens of guy ropes.

Before Phoebe could react or even take in fully what was happening, Sam stepped into the horse's path, his hands out in front of him, and deftly caught the flying reins, so that the horse, which Phoebe realised now was more of a pony, had no choice but to jerk to an untidy, breathless, skidding halt, although not before

Sam was tugged along for a few paces with it. There were a few 'oohs' and 'aahs' from the people closest as both man and horse finally came to a standstill.

'Hey, little fellow. Steady on there. What's the rush?' Sam's voice was breathless, but his whole demeanour was quietly calm, in sharp contrast to the pony, which was soaked with sweat. Its chestnut flanks heaved with exertion as it sidestepped fretfully on the dusty grass, showing the whites of its eyes, while Sam slowly shortened the reins until he was close enough to run his palm along its coat with long smooth strokes. One of the pony's plaits had come loose, Phoebe saw, and was dangling down untidily on its neck.

'There now. It's OK. It's all OK.' Sam kept talking and the little horse, a child's show pony, Phoebe guessed, finally responded to Sam's voice and calmed down enough to stand still.

A small crowd had gathered. Phoebe took a step closer to Sam and his charge, the shock of what had just happened hitting her. Sam had stepped straight into the animal's path. She knew he'd done it deliberately. He knew horses. He had his own, Ninja, a flighty Thoroughbred, but it was still pretty dangerous, and she could feel the slight tremble in her stomach at the thought of what might have happened if the pony hadn't stopped.

'Well done,' she said quietly. 'That was brave.'

'Calculated. They won't deliberately mow a person down.'

'But they might inadvertently,' Phoebe murmured, glancing around them. The sky was a hazy blue with a few scribbles of white cloud. Summer was at its best and the showground was teeming with people, families with children, dozens of dogs on leads, and old people on mobility scooters. Phoebe shuddered to think of the chaos that could have happened if Sam hadn't intervened to stop the bolting pony.

'We're not far from the equine ring,' Sam said, glancing around.

'We should probably go and find this little fellow's owners. Did you notice he's got a cut on his off fore?'

Phoebe nodded, feeling herself go into professional mode, as she leaned to look at the front leg properly. A trickle of blood ran down his white sock, but she was relieved to see the cut didn't look serious enough to stitch. 'Let's take him back. We can see if he's lame. There'll be a vet ringside, I'm guessing, but I'll point it out.'

The crowd around them, eager to be part of the drama, showed no sign of dispersing. 'He's cut himself,' a woman called. 'He needs a vet.'

'I am a vet,' Phoebe told her. 'He'll live, but we'll make sure his owner is aware.'

'Is that your animal?' A man in a deerstalker with a very red face was striding towards them. 'It ran straight through my prize marrows. Put a hoof through my best one. Total write-off. You'd better be insured. My marrows are magnificent. Or at least they were before that beast ran amok.'

'He doesn't belong to us, we just caught him.' Sam shot him a pacifying look. 'You'll need to take up any damage issues with the owner.'

'Oh, I shall.' The man fell into step beside them, still muttering about his mutilated marrows.

Phoebe and Sam exchanged glances. Phoebe was trying not to laugh; mostly, she knew, because of the aftermath of adrenaline, but the look of outrage on marrow man's face was comical too. He and a few other curious onlookers had joined them in the trek across the showground and the crowds parted obediently to let the small procession through.

There was a slight breeze shifting through the tops of the trees that lined the ground. Otherwise, it would have been unbearably hot and the smells of frying burgers, hot pies and coffee percolating from stalls with long queues reminded Phoebe that they'd arrived just after eleven and it was long past lunchtime. They'd both had a more active role at last year's show – Sam had been showjumping and Phoebe had been on a rabbit rescue mission – but this year they'd wanted to be 'proper tourists' with no dramas. So much for that!

Half an hour later, Phoebe and Sam had reunited the pony with his tearful eight-year-old owner, Holly, and her anxious father. Apparently the pony, Hal, had been spooked by an escapee pig and had bucked off his rider and bolted from the ring halfway through an egg and spoon race. It turned out the ringside equine vet was treating the pig, which had also somehow got injured whilst escaping from its pen, and so Phoebe ended up treating Hal's cut foreleg, checking he wasn't lame, and giving advice to Holly's grateful parents.

She and Sam escaped while they were calming down the deer-stalker marrow man, who had been slightly mollified by Holly's mother's offer of a slice of her prize-winning Battenberg and her father's wedge of compensatory cash. It had also turned out they had a friend in common from the allotment because Holly's grandad had a plot there too. There weren't many locals who didn't have a few links in the community. Six degrees of separation, or more like three degrees of separation, applied to practically everyone in the New Forest, once they got chatting.

Phoebe and Sam were now sitting at a wooden picnic table, sipping coffee.

'So much for a relaxing day out,' Phoebe said, eyeing Sam over her recyclable paper mug, which might have been eco-friendly, but was too hot to be finger-friendly once she'd dispensed with the paper serviette it had come with. She put it down swiftly on the table. 'Although I guess it's a lot less dramatic than last year when you and Ninja crash-landed halfway through the jump-off and you got carted off in an ambulance.'

'That's true.' Sam met her gaze. 'Although it was almost worth crashing to see you racing into the ring to reach my side. Your face was a picture.'

'That's because I thought you were dead!'

Sam grinned. 'It'll take more than a little tumble off a horse to kill me. I'm as tough as old boots.' He picked up his coffee and then put it down sharply again. 'Ouch. That's hot.'

'Very tough,' Phoebe teased, and offered him a serviette. They both laughed and she added, 'Besides, it was hardly a little tumble. You could have been dead. Rupturing your spleen isn't a minor thing. I'm surprised that accident didn't put you off horses for life.' She paused before adding thoughtfully, 'Do you ever get anxious now when you're riding?'

'Not when I'm riding, no. But when I'm competing – yes, maybe a bit.' He sipped his coffee. 'Not too much, though. It's not as though I can lose my spleen again, can I? That's gone forever.' He clicked his tongue.

Phoebe shook her head in mock disapproval of his levity. 'Is that why you haven't competed as much lately?'

'Maybe a bit. It's also because I've had too many distractions.' He reached across and touched her face. 'You being the main one, Phoebe Dashwood. If you'd have told me a year ago that we'd be sitting here together like this, I wouldn't have believed it.'

'Me neither.' She leaned into his touch.

'You don't regret it, do you? Giving up the lord of the manor for a lowly shopworker?' His eyes, as blue as the summer sky above them, sobered a little, as he held her gaze.

'Sam, don't you ever do yourself down. There is nothing I regret about our relationship.' She could hear her voice, half fierce, half husky with emotion. 'And there is nothing lowly about working in your mother's shop.'

His eyes warmed and she wondered whether the tiny threads of insecurity she occasionally saw in him would ever entirely disappear.

Maybe it wasn't surprising. Barely a month ago, Phoebe had been dating Rufus Holt, the son of a real-life lord. His father owned Beechbrook House, which was in the heart of the New Forest, as well as a lot of the surrounding land and cottages. Phoebe's grandmother, Maggie Crowther, owned Puddleduck Farm next door. The Holts and the Crowthers had a long and chequered history, but these days they rubbed along OK and Maggie rented most of her grazing land from Lord Holt.

Puddleduck, once a dairy farm, was now an animal sanctuary, and recently Phoebe had fulfilled a long-held dream to set up her own veterinary practice, Puddleduck Vets, in an old barn on the land.

Phoebe's relationship with Rufus, which had looked so good from the outside, had never worked. They had never even consummated their relationship. But Phoebe hadn't told Sam this detail. It was a secret she would probably keep. Neither she nor Sam were the type to divulge the minutiae of failed relationships.

'The only thing I'm starting to regret, Sam,' Phoebe said now, 'is that today is turning into a busman's holiday, what with you catching escapee ponies and me patching them up. That's pretty much what we do at home. Perhaps we should have chosen a different place to spend our precious week off.'

'Yeah, we should probably have gone abroad. We could have been sunning ourselves on some beach. White sand. Palm trees. Exotic cocktails.'

'You'd have worried about Ninja,' she said, picturing Sam's Thoroughbred horse. 'Not to mention Snowball.' Snowball was Sam's fluffy black cat. Sam was almost as dotty about animals as she was.

'And you'd have worried about Maggie and Eddie and whether Puddleduck Vets was coping OK without you.'

'You know me so well.' Phoebe had a very soft spot for her feisty seventy-five-year-old grandmother, who'd recently announced she was marrying Eddie, her former farmhand. They were getting married in early December. Also, this was the first time since Puddleduck Vets had opened that Phoebe had trusted her staff to run it without her, and had gone off on a proper holiday, even if it was more of a staycation.

'Why don't we head off and I'll take you for dinner at some flash eatery in Southampton?' Sam suggested. 'Hopefully we'll be safe from marauding horses and pigs there.'

'I'd much rather go to a country pub. How about The Huntsman on the edge of Burley? We can pick up a nice bottle of wine to take back to yours afterwards.'

'I'd much rather do that too. And I seem to remember there's no phone signal at that pub so we can't get disturbed.'

'What are we waiting for?'

* * *

By the time they'd finished their meals at the pub – steak and chips, as they were on holiday – and had picked up the wine, it was gone eight and they were both yawning.

Sam had been right about The Huntsman having no phone signal. But they were barely a mile into their homeward journey when both of their phones tinged simultaneously. Sam was driving, but Phoebe hooked hers out from her bag.

She fully expected to see a message from her assistant vet, Max Jones, who was holding the fort. She'd told him it was absolutely fine to call her if she was needed. But it wasn't a message from Max.

It was a notification of a voicemail from her mother. There was also a text. That was odd. Louella Dashwood rarely texted.

Phoebe glanced at it, frowning. The top line said:

Hi love, are you with Sam? Can you get him to call his dad?

Phoebe opened the message swiftly.

It's nothing to worry about, but Jan's had a funny turn. I'm with her now at the hospital.

She frowned.

'Trouble?' Sam asked, flicking her a glance.

'Mmmm. Apparently my mum's with yours at the hospital.'

'What's happened?' His fingers tightened on the steering wheel.

'I don't know. She said it's nothing to worry about. Could we pull over when you get to a convenient place? We can phone them and find out what's happening.'

2

A few minutes later, Phoebe had spoken to her mum and Sam had spoken to his father, both of whom were at Salisbury District Hospital A & E, and Sam and Phoebe were now piecing together the events of the evening.

Jan Hendrie had been on her way to a hotel in Salisbury for a school reunion – she'd gone on the bus, so she could have a glass of wine and the family car was in the garage anyway – when she'd been taken ill with chest pains and the worried bus driver, encouraged by a couple of concerned passengers, had driven her straight to hospital.

Ian Hendrie, carless, had phoned Phoebe's parents to ask them for a lift and hence had involved the Dashwoods.

'Pa said she's having tests,' Sam told Phoebe. His suntanned face had gone a little pale. 'They think it might be her heart. Ma's not old enough to have heart problems, surely. She's only fifty-nine.'

'Anyone can have heart problems, although you're right, your mum isn't the obvious candidate.' Jan Hendrie was slim, didn't smoke, and as far as Phoebe knew had always been fit as a fiddle.

She squeezed Sam's hand across the Subaru's handbrake. 'She'll be OK. Try not to worry. Shall we go to the hospital?'

'Yes. I think we should. They might be there hours. You know how long hospitals take to do stuff. Then at least Louella can go home. I can give Dad a lift back later. And you can go back with Louella too. There's no sense in all of us waiting up there.'

'I'll wait with you, Sam. I don't mind a late night. Anyway, we're getting ahead of ourselves. We don't even know what the problem is yet.'

'Thanks.' He gave her a swift look of gratitude and again her heart softened.

Sam was great in a crisis. Very calm, very methodical. Phoebe watched him tap the hospital postcode into Google Maps on his phone before starting the car once more and pulling out smoothly into the line of traffic.

It hadn't been very long ago that Sam had rescued her when she'd ended up in a ditch on a quiet back road in the forest, having swerved to avoid a deer. She hadn't been badly injured; she'd head-butted her Lexus's steering wheel, and had ended up with two black eyes and a sore nose, but the car had been well and truly stuck. Sam had ridden in like a knight in shining armour on a white charger and rescued her.

Well, actually he'd ridden in on Ninja, and had insisted she ride the horse back to Brook Stables, which had been barely ten minutes away across the forest, while he walked alongside them, carrying her vet bag. He'd also insisted on driving her to the minor injuries unit to get patched up and checked over. Then he'd taken her home, run her a bath and made her hot chocolate and done everything a good friend would do.

The bruises on her face had faded but there was still a faint soreness where she'd bashed her nose. Yet Phoebe knew that despite the pain and shock of driving her car into a ditch, she would always remember that day with huge affection because it was the day she'd realised that Sam meant so much more to her than just a friend. It was the day the denial had finally dropped from her eyes. Phoebe had always loved Sam. But that had been the day she'd actually fallen *in love* with him.

* * *

Sam didn't once break the speed limit as he cut expertly across the back roads of the forest. He knew this area like the back of his hand.

He was praying Phoebe was right and it wasn't too serious. He was close to both his parents, but to Ma particularly because they worked together side by side in Hendrie's Stores. You couldn't, strictly speaking, call it a family business, in the sense that his father was a chippie – the shop couldn't sustain all three of them – but it did pretty well. As a village stores it was the centre of the community in the small market town of Bridgeford on the banks of the river Avon where they all lived. Hendrie's was usually pretty busy and having the post office there too made it more so. No way could Ma have managed it alone.

In another life, Sam would probably have based his career on being a full-time riding instructor – he taught kids at the weekends and some evenings at Brook Stables because he couldn't have afforded to keep Ninja there if he hadn't also worked for them. But he wouldn't have abandoned Hendrie's Stores. Loyalty kept him there.

His mind raced ahead – even if Ma had suffered from a very mild heart attack, she was going to have to take it easy for a bit. It wasn't possible to cope for long in the shop without her. They had a temp in this week for his holiday cover, but Jan was the mainstay of Hendrie's: endlessly cheerful and utterly tireless.

Sam couldn't do more hours there than he already did, so they might have to employ someone on a more permanent basis. Where on earth were they going to get the money to do that? The spiralling cost of living had meant that everything had gone up lately. They were pushed to the limit as it was.

He stole a glance at Phoebe, who looked deep in thought. He had loved her for so long. He had known she was the woman he wanted to share his life with for so much longer than she had known she wanted to share her life with him. But relationships took up time too. Earlier he'd joked about them holidaying on a tropical beach somewhere, but he'd known deep down that a tropical beach was a far-off fantasy.

Who'd get up at the crack of dawn every day to look after Ninja if he didn't do it? He certainly couldn't afford to pay Brook Stables to keep his horse at full livery. His mind ran on in endless circles. Whichever way he looked at it, Ma being taken ill couldn't have been worse timing.

They drew into the hospital carpark just before ten. Sam parked while Phoebe went and got a ticket from the machine and then they were racing, hand in hand, into the building.

It wasn't too difficult to find Sam's dad and Phoebe's mum. They were both sitting on the uncomfortable plastic seats in the crowded A & E department. The noise levels were high. Stress and tension pervaded the small space like a bad smell.

Sam patted his father's shoulder and Phoebe hugged her mother and then they stood in an anxious square, communicating in short sentences and head shakes.

'No news yet,' Louella told Phoebe. 'They've been a while. They must be doing a thorough check.'

'And you can't tell us any more about what happened?' Sam asked his father.

'Not really. I know she got herself in a state over what to wear.' He shrugged and glanced between Phoebe and Sam. 'I don't really know why she went. She hasn't seen any of them for years.' His eyes, the same blue as his son's, clouded. 'I wish I could have taken her in the car. I would have done if it hadn't been in the blasted garage.'

'I doubt it would have made a difference, Pa.'

'No.' Ian Hendrie looked unconvinced. Phoebe's heart went out to him.

'Here she is,' Louella exclaimed, glancing suddenly across the room towards a door. 'Isn't that her, Ian, with the doctor?'

They all looked, and Phoebe saw she was right. A bemused Jan, dressed uncharacteristically smartly in a blue dress and a cream linen summer jacket, which now looked a bit creased, had just come out of a door, accompanied by a man in scrubs. 'Gosh, yes,' Phoebe gasped. 'That has to be good news. She looks fine.'

Ian couldn't seem to believe his eyes. He shook his head, and Sam patted his shoulder again. 'Let's go and meet them, Pa. Find out what's what.'

Phoebe and Louella stayed where they were and a few moments later they saw Ian and Sam in a huddle with the doctor. All of their faces were grave, but Phoebe was sure she was right. The news couldn't be too bad if they were letting Jan leave so soon.

Ten minutes later everyone, including Jan, was outside again in the car park. They stood in a pool of neon beneath the hospital floodlights in the cooling air, and Jan herself was reassuring them. 'I definitely didn't have a heart attack. They're completely sure about that. I've had every test under the sun.'

'But it must have been something,' Ian said. 'Why aren't they doing more tests? Have they booked you in for more?'

'No, love, I've told you. They're letting me go with a clean bill of health. They said it was an anomaly.'

'What do they mean "an anomaly"? What is that anyway?'

'A freak incident.' Jan's face was flushed. 'I don't know. I'm not a doctor. Will you stop haranguing me? I'm as mystified as you are. All I can tell you is that I'm very relieved that it wasn't a heart attack.' Phoebe saw her exchange a look with Louella, who looked as though she was about to say something, but stopped when Jan gave a swift shake of her head.

'Now can we please go home? I'm very tired and I'm sorry to have caused all this fuss and bother. Why are you all even here? What are you youngsters doing here? I'm sure you've got better things to do than hang around hospitals.' She tutted.

Ian started explaining that their car was in the garage, in case she'd forgotten, and that Louella had kindly given him a lift, and was hopefully going to give them both one back home again.

'Of course I am.' Louella rattled her car keys. 'Whenever you're ready.'

Phoebe glanced at Sam. 'Back to Plan A then?' she suggested softly.

'Sure.' He stepped towards his mother, pecked her on the cheek and said gently, 'You take care of yourself, Ma. I think you should have a day off tomorrow. I can cover the shop.'

'No, you can't. You're on your annual leave. You and your Phoebe are supposed to be off enjoying yourselves. Weren't you going to the New Forest Show?'

'We've been. Today was the last day.'

'Oh. Yes, I see.' She nodded, looking defeated and suddenly very tired.

Phoebe noticed for the first time the dark circles around her eyes. It was weird that the hospital hadn't found anything wrong. Every instinct Phoebe had was telling her that all was not quite right, whatever story Jan was telling them. She fervently hoped that she wasn't holding anything back in some misguided attempt to prevent them worrying.

Phoebe stepped to Sam's side. 'Sam's right. I think you should take it easy. We'd only be cutting our holiday short by a day or two. Your health's more important. I've got stacks of paperwork to catch up on before Monday anyway.'

Sam caught hold of her hand, squeezing her fingers in a silent signal of thanks.

'We'll see, then,' Jan said. She gave a little shiver – that summer jacket looked quite thin – and then put a very determined smile on her face. 'Now that you've sorted my life out for me, can we please all go home?'

3

It may have been an abrupt end to their holiday, Phoebe thought, but forfeiting the last two days with Sam so he could help out at Hendrie's and make sure his mother was OK had definitely been the right thing to do.

They'd had a really late night on Thursday, talking about Jan and speculating on what could be wrong. Sam agreed his mother certainly wasn't telling them everything.

'Ma's never been very good at being ill. Or at least admitting she's ill, if that makes sense. She's very stoic about everything to do with health, which isn't very helpful.'

'Like mother, like son,' Phoebe had teased. 'I don't think I've ever known you have a day off work either.'

'I had two weeks off last summer.'

'Only because you were in hospital, getting your spleen removed. And that was an accident. Accidents don't count.'

Sam had laughed and kissed her to shut her up. Then they'd finally gone to bed, and it had been quite a while before they'd gone to sleep.

It still blew Phoebe away how compatible they were in bed.

She'd spent years convinced there was no chemistry. She'd been so wrong.

In the morning, she'd been vaguely aware of Sam dropping a kiss on her forehead before heading into the kitchen, making himself breakfast and then bringing her in a cup of tea prior to leaving for work.

He'd worked Saturday too, and they'd met for a quick drink on Sunday. But Sam had told Phoebe he hadn't got any further with what was really going on with his mother. 'There's no point in pushing her. Hopefully she'll tell me when she's ready,' he'd added with a sigh.

It was now Monday morning and Phoebe had just got into work at Puddleduck Vets. It was just gone eight, an hour before her first appointment would usually be scheduled, but she discovered that Jenna, her vet nurse – a kind, very sensible motherly type, who was in her late forties, but who looked much younger – was already behind reception.

Jenna was deep in discussion with Max, who, at thirty-two, was the charmer of the practice, at least where women were concerned. Max wasn't your traditional charmer; he had a Roman nose and sandy hair, but he wore Ralph Lauren shirts beneath his scrubs and sounded a lot like Hugh Grant. Phoebe sometimes wondered if he was even aware how attractive their female clients found him. He certainly didn't seem to be, and he definitely didn't exploit it. Max was also a brilliant young vet and although he'd only joined the practice back in February, Phoebe already trusted him totally.

Max and Jenna both stopped talking and glanced up guiltily when Phoebe opened the plate-glass door and strolled towards reception. Her oversensitive radar pinged madly. 'I'm getting the feeling I've walked in on something. What's going on?'

'Um, nothing,' Max said.

'He means nothing to worry about.' Jenna blushed. 'It's just a few small things. Quite literally, actually.' She glanced down and at the same moment Phoebe heard a mewling and the sounds of scuffling coming from behind reception.

She reached the desk in two strides and peered over. There was a cardboard box on the floor full of newspaper and four white puppies. Very new puppies, by the look of it, as they still had their eyes tightly closed.

'Where on earth did they come from, and where's their mother?'

'Someone left them by the side gate first thing,' Jenna told her. 'I'm in early because I promised to phone a customer, so luckily I saw them. Maybe they were meant to be dropped off at the Puddleduck Pets entrance, but they dropped them off at ours instead. We thought Maggie might know about them. We were just going to fetch her.' She sighed and added, 'No mother unfortunately. Although there is a note.'

Max handed Phoebe a piece of paper, torn from a pad, which only had a few words scrawled on it in black ink.

Three days old. Mother dead. Please look after.

There was no name or signature.

'And that was it?' Phoebe shook her head in exasperation. 'What is wrong with people? Do they really not care?'

'At least they brought them here,' Max said. He was always unerringly positive. 'So they must have cared a little bit.'

'Yes, I suppose that's true.' Phoebe knew he was right. It could have been worse.

The practice door opened again and Marcus, Phoebe's receptionist, came in wearing a short-sleeved shirt and smart trousers. Despite being the youngest member of the team, at twenty-nine, he'd only recently got out of the habit of wearing a suit and tie to work. Marcus was a strange mixture of formal and funny, honest and a rule-breaker. Marcus cared passionately about animal welfare and had carried a torch for Natasha, who was the sanctuary's young manager, for months before finally plucking up the courage to ask her out. They were now an item, much to everyone else's delight, as the two animal-mad youngsters were clearly made for each other.

Jenna brought Marcus up to speed about the puppies and in no time he was behind reception, crouching down to coo at them. 'I'll keep an eye on them, no worries. They are gorgeous.'

'They should probably be in quarantine, seeing as we don't know where they came from, or what killed their mother,' Phoebe warned. 'They shouldn't be behind reception. Just in case.'

'They all look pretty healthy,' Jenna said. 'I've checked them over. But in the absence of a mother, they are going to need feeding.'

'I can do that,' Marcus said instantly. 'I think we've got some formula in stock. One of the breeders wanted some not long ago and I over-ordered. I could set up a crate for the pups out the back. Then I can keep an eye on them.'

His eyes were alight with enthusiasm. Phoebe didn't have the heart to say no. 'OK, I guess we can do that, as a temporary measure. I'll have a word with Maggie as soon as I've done my morning appointments. What time is my first appointment anyway?'

Marcus consulted the computer. 'Not till nine thirty. We thought you might need to ease back into things slowly, boss.'

'And have a catch-up on what you've missed,' Max said.

Phoebe dragged her gaze from the puppies and flicked a glance at each of her small team, all of whom were looking at her with varying expressions. Max was wearing a rather forced smile, Jenna's eyes were guarded and Marcus looked hopeful.

Phoebe realised guiltily that she hadn't even said thank you to them for holding the fort in her absence. She'd just marched in and started firing questions at them and berating them for doing what they did best – caring.

'I'm so sorry,' she said. 'Let's rewind and start today again. What I should have said as soon as I came in was thank you for looking after everything while I've been off galivanting. I bought you fudge,' she added, extracting a box from the tote bag she'd brought in with her, 'from the New Forest Show. And for anyone who doesn't like fudge, there's shortbread.'

'Also from the New Forest Show,' said Max, peering to look. 'And New Forest chocolate biscuits,' he added. 'And New Forest ginger beer.'

'A bit of a theme going,' Jenna remarked. 'Did you actually go anywhere else? I thought you were doing day trips.'

'We didn't really go anywhere else,' Phoebe said, not wanting to confess they'd actually spent their first couple of days either in bed or watching episodes of *Loose Women*. It had been surprisingly easy to get Sam hooked on *Loose Women*.

'I'll get the kettle on as soon as I've set up a crate for the pups,' Marcus said. 'How often do pups need feeding anyway?'

'Every four hours,' Jenna told him. 'Including all through the night.' She clicked her tongue. 'You might regret offering to be a puppa mumma. Or puppa papa, I should say.'

'I won't,' Marcus said staunchly. 'I love dogs. What kind of dogs do we reckon they are anyway?'

As he spoke, the door opened again. This time it was Maggie. She stood in the doorway with her hands on her hips. 'They're dalmatians,' she said, clearly having heard Marcus's question. 'Are they here? I was wondering where they'd got to.'

'So they *are* something to do with you,' Phoebe said, relieved.

'We were hoping they might be.' At least *she'd* been hoping they might be; Marcus already looked disappointed.

'I had a phone call from a concerned member of the public.' Maggie crossed to the counter and peered into the box. 'She found them at the roadside apparently. She wouldn't leave her name, but I told her to bring them in.'

'Ah,' Jenna said, 'poor little mites. I don't suppose she knew what had happened to their mother?'

'Apparently not.'

'Lovely of her to take the trouble to bring them in, though,' Max said.

'Yes, it was,' Maggie agreed cheerfully. Phoebe looked at her in surprise. Her grandmother usually had plenty to say about people who dropped off animals, claiming they had simply stumbled across them and didn't know their history, but since her engagement to Eddie she seemed to be wearing rose-tinted glasses.

'And you're back from your travels too.' Maggie's hazel eyes, so like her granddaughter's, fixed on Phoebe. 'Did you and Sam have a lovely break? You must come and tell me all about it later. We've got lots to catch up on.'

'Wedding plans,' Phoebe ventured. She was dying to hear all the latest developments about Maggie's wedding, although she suspected she was the only one who was. After all, most of it had already been planned. They were having a church ceremony, the reception would be at Puddleduck Farm, and the honeymoon some kind of cruise. But it had become a standing joke amongst friends and family, not to mention everyone at Puddleduck Vets, that Maggie had talked about nothing but weddings, whether it be dates, cakes, guest lists or outfits, since Eddie had proposed to her three weeks earlier. Mind you, as the pair of them had originally wanted to get married in November – barely four months away – this had subsequently been switched to 21 December, then switched again to 2 December – it wasn't exactly surprising there was a lot to organise.

'Wedding plans, among other things, yes.'

Everyone groaned in mock despair and Marcus gave an exaggerated yawn.

Maggie ignored them and looked at Phoebe hopefully.

'I'll be up as soon as I finish work,' she promised.

'Thank you, love. I need some advice on table settings. Things weren't anywhere near as complicated when your grandfather and I tied the knot. There's far more choice, these days.'

'Those puppies don't look very much like dalmatians,' Marcus said, gleefully changing the subject. 'They're pure white.'

'The spots don't appear till they're a week to ten days old,' Maggie told him with authority. 'They sound hungry. I'll shift them up to the house if you like, Phoebe, I'm sure you don't want them cluttering up your reception.'

For a second, the two women's eyes met and a soft look passed between them. Maggie might sound a bit dismissive about the pups, but Phoebe knew her better than that.

Maggie adored dogs and had a kennel full to prove it. Phoebe knew she struggled not to add more to the two who already lived with her in Puddleduck Farmhouse: Buster, an elderly black Labrador, and Tiny, a daft enormous Irish Wolfhound. Both of whom had been abandoned by their original owners.

The four baby dalmatians might very well end up in the sanctuary kennels when they were bigger, but in the meantime they'd no doubt be carted up to the farmhouse to live by the Aga while Maggie and Eddie pandered to their every need.

'We can look after the pups here during the day if you like?' Phoebe offered. 'I know Marcus is up for the job – he's already volunteered.'

'Absolutely, Mrs Crowther,' Marcus said instantly. 'I'm totally up for it.'

Maggie flicked a glance at him. 'Thanks, love. It'll give me a chance to get a crate sorted out. Eddie can come and get them later.'

The phone started ringing, even though they didn't officially start for another half an hour, and Maggie left them to it. Phoebe caught up with Max and her list of appointments. She had a feeling it was going to be a very busy day.

* * *

She was right. By 5 p.m., Phoebe had seen three dogs with kennel cough – there was currently a spate of cases – a cat with an ear infection, another with a furball problem and another with arthritis. She'd also called at a dairy farm to see a cow with mastitis.

Puddleduck Vets had focused on small animals when they'd started but, under the mentoring of her previous boss, Seth Harding, who had a practice on the edge of Southampton, Phoebe also went out to farm animals. The two practices also helped with each other's out-of-hours cover.

Phoebe loved all aspects of her job. But she was glad she had no call-outs tonight and could catch up with Maggie, as planned, to discuss table settings. Maggie had chosen an animal theme and she'd whittled it down to a choice of three.

'Ducks, donkeys or dogs. Eddie got me some samples.' She produced a handful of coloured wooden shapes and spread them out on the farmhouse table.

Phoebe picked up the nearest one, which was a clip with a white duck on top, and studied it for a moment. It looked exactly like a novelty clothes peg.

'Where did Eddie get these samples?'

'I think he said the hardware shop. Why?'

'Because I think this might actually be a clothes peg.'

'I must admit I did wonder.' Maggie gave a rueful shake of her head. 'They'd do, though, wouldn't they, to hold the name cards by people's plates?'

'Or we could check out actual animal table settings. Shall we look on your laptop?'

They had a quick break to feed the dalmatian pups which were, as Phoebe had predicted, in a crate not far from the Aga. Tiny and Buster, their attention caught by the tiny yelps and the smell of food, came to supervise.

But a few minutes later, Maggie was oohing and aahing over a selection of duck, donkey and dog table settings. 'These are much nicer.'

Then she frowned.

'What is it now?'

'I still can't choose.'

'Then don't choose. Have all three? We can pick whether people will be a duck, a donkey or a dog. That could be excellent fun.'

Maggie snorted with laughter. 'Thank you, darling. I'm so grateful.'

'It's my pleasure, Gran.'

'But not grateful enough for you to start calling me Gran. You know it makes me feel old.'

'Sorry! Wait... Hang on a minute, I thought you'd decided on a buffet reception here at Puddleduck. We're not having a sit-down meal – right?'

'That's right, we did.'

'So why do you need place settings?'

'Um, good point. I don't suppose we do. We were just ticking things off the wedding planner list that Eddie got online.'

'So we've just spent an hour making decisions about clothes pegs, when we didn't need any – um – clothes pegs anyway!' It was

Phoebe's turn to shake her head in mock disapproval, and then they both started laughing again.

Phoebe was still smiling when she finally left for home with a promise to bring Sam round for supper as soon as possible. Maggie adored Sam. All of the family did. And they were thrilled the pair had finally become a couple.

There was only one thing that bothered Phoebe. She wasn't the only one who'd been on the rebound. Sam had just split up with a woman he'd loved, but whose parents hadn't approved of him. Both Sam and Phoebe had turned towards each other for comfort in their hour of need. They'd both been at their most vulnerable.

Phoebe occasionally wondered what would have happened if she hadn't driven her car into a ditch, and if Sam hadn't rescued her. But she squashed these thoughts down firmly every time they surfaced. Lots of people had rebound relationships that worked perfectly. Her doubts felt like a very small cloud on a very bright horizon.

4

At Hendrie's Stores, Sam's day had also flown by. He'd persuaded his mother to take Monday off too, and despite her protestations that she was perfectly fine, she'd agreed. Fortunately the temp, Hannah, a sweet but mature teenager, had been happy to stay on for an extra day.

'I can stay as long as you like,' she'd told Sam. 'I'm starting uni in September and I'm saving up. I don't want to be saddled with a student loan for the rest of my life.'

'What are you studying?'

'Zoology, I'm hoping to get a job with animals, maybe in an environmental context. I'd really like to go into film – be the next David Attenborough.' She'd flicked back her hair and her eyes had lit up with enthusiasm.

'Sounds amazing,' Sam had said, knowing that jobs like that would be few and far between and the competition would be intense, but not saying anything. Who was he to tread on someone's dreams?

It was now just before closing time and Sam was serving Vera Walker, who'd long ago been renamed Vera Talker by everyone who knew her because talking was the thing she did best. Vera could talk the hind legs off a donkey, and very probably the front legs too, Sam thought, donkeys being very apt because Vera was currently in mid-flow about a spate of donkey thefts that had apparently been happening in the New Forest.

'Who'd want to steal a donkey? It's not as if they're much use, are they? Unless you use them for rides on the beach. I used to love that when I was a girl, riding a donkey along the sand with the sea air blowing through my hair. Of course, I was a bit slimmer in those days. I couldn't ride one now. I'd flatten it.' She chuckled loudly and patted her ample tummy.

Sam nodded politely, and handed her the bag with its few items of shopping he'd just cashed up and packed at the till. Two potatoes, a bag of carrots, an onion and a copy of *New Forest Views*, the free magazine. Vera never bought much, but she came in a few times a week.

Sam thought she had finished the story, and he was about to say something, but Vera was far from finished, so he did what his mother did and let her words ebb and flow over his head, not really listening until she mentioned his name suddenly and looked at him keenly.

'I'm surprised you didn't hear about it, Sam. What with you being a horsey man, and all.'

He frowned. 'The donkey thefts? No, I didn't hear about that.'

'Not the donkeys. We've done donkeys. Keep up. The pony. The one I was just telling you about that got dumped in the New Forest.' She didn't draw breath, so he couldn't have answered if he'd wanted to.

'As I was saying, all sorts of rumours have been circulating about where it came from. But no one can catch it apparently. The agisters tried at the weekend, Liam Barker was telling me it's in good condition too. Liam's Colin Barker's son, you probably know

Colin Barker, he lives out Brook way. That's where you keep your horse, isn't it? Up at Brook Stables. I'm sure he knows Marjorie Taylor. Liam said he thinks it's been well looked after.'

Sam's ears pricked up at the mention of agisters, who were responsible for supervising the day-to-day welfare of animals that grazed the New Forest. But the trouble with Vera was that it was difficult to get a word in edgeways because she didn't often pause for breath. Even when it appeared she was asking you a question, she didn't stop for an answer. The only way was to actively interrupt and even then you had to talk over her because she didn't really want to listen to anyone else, so intent was she on whatever story she was telling.

Sam's ma had once remarked that it was usually lonely people who talked like Vera did. But Vera was married to a meek-mannered man called John, who, on the rare occasions that he came into the stores, said very little.

Probably because he couldn't get a word in edgeways either, Sam thought, taking a deep breath and deciding to do what his ma often did, which was to come out from behind the counter – there was no one else in the shop, Hannah having left a few minutes earlier – and slowly guide Vera to the door.

'So did they catch the pony in the end?' he asked, taking a few steps ahead of her towards the exit.

'I don't think so.' She swung her string shopping bag and trotted to keep up. 'It's probably been stolen, they're saying, and then dumped because it was too hot to handle. The thief probably thought it wouldn't stand out much in the forest – you know, that it would blend in with all the other ponies. Which of course it wouldn't. To anyone with any local knowledge.' She huffed disparagingly. 'People do some dumb things.'

'They do.' Sam had reached the door and now he opened it. 'Sorry, Vera, but I need to close up. Great to chat, though.'

'Yes, I always like chatting to you, Sam, you're such a good boy. How's your mother? Is she ill? I noticed she wasn't here...'

Sam opened the door a little wider so the chimes jingled. 'I really must close up. Ma's fine. I expect she's cooking her tea.'

Vera finally took the hint and exited, and Sam locked up with relief. He hoped his mum was fine. He hadn't had the chance to check on her since lunchtime. The shop had been chock-a-block with customers all day. He ran up the back stairs to his parents' flat, which was above the shop. His father was out on a kitchen refurbishment at Lyndhurst and had said he might be late, but he heard female voices from the lounge as he passed. Mum had company then. Good.

He was about to go in when he caught a snatch of conversation through the half-open door. 'It was terrifying. I couldn't breathe.'

He hesitated and then cleared his throat loudly before opening the door. His mother and Louella, who turned out to be her visitor, had their heads close together and they jumped guiltily when they saw him. On the table were two mugs and a plate on which was a scattering of chocolate biscuits.

'I'm just about to put the kettle on. Anyone need a top-up? Is everything all right, Ma? Only I couldn't help hearing...'

'Everything's fine, Sam,' his mother said – a little too brightly in his opinion – before carrying on swiftly, 'I feel like a right fraud sitting here drinking tea and eating choccie biscuits. I'm working tomorrow. No arguments.'

Sam glanced at Louella, who was nodding in agreement.

'I don't think it can hurt.' Louella's cheeks were pink. 'After all, the doctors have given her a clean bill of health.'

They were definitely hiding something, Sam decided, but if Louella was happy with it – and she obviously knew more than either he or his father did – then he supposed he was happy too.

'I'll let Hannah know we don't need her then, if you're sure?'

'I'm totally sure.'

He didn't argue. No doubt Ma would tell him in her own good time what was going on. And she looked a lot better than she had on Thursday night at the hospital.

'I'll get off then,' he said, and went across to peck his mother on the cheek. 'Night, Ma. Night, Louella.'

Sam was about to reverse his old Subaru out of its parking space at the back of the shop when he heard his name called. He looked up to see Louella, who must have raced to catch up, hurrying across the paved area towards him.

'Sam, I'm glad I caught you.' She looked out of breath and clearly had something on her mind. He lowered the glass and she flicked a glance up at the flat a little guiltily, as if she were worried Jan might be looking out of the back window and see them.

'I don't want to betray a confidence, but neither do I want you and your father to be worrying yourselves sick.'

'OK.' Sam waited patiently. It was obvious Louella was in a quandary. He'd known her as long as he'd known Phoebe and she definitely wasn't the gossiping kind. She'd always been straight down the line. Compassionate, kind and honest, traits she had passed on in spades to her daughter.

She leaned into the car. 'Physically, your mum is absolutely fine. I just wanted to reassure you.'

'Physically?' Sam queried, meeting her gaze. 'But...?'

'The doctors seem to think it was a panic attack.' Louella looked uncomfortable. 'They're much more common than people think, but... it can be a difficult subject still...'

'And she didn't want to tell us,' Sam finished.

He knew what his mother was like. She and Louella might be best friends, but Louella, who'd worked as a primary school teacher for years at the local school, had always been the more outgoing and confident of the two women. Ma was happiest behind the counter of Hendrie's, chatting with customers like Vera. She wasn't one for going out much. Not even with his father. They hadn't been on holiday for years because she didn't like flying and she rarely even went for a coffee with anyone except Louella.

'I think she'd rather pretend it hadn't happened. But that's not why I'm telling you. I just wanted you to be aware in case it happened again.' Louella gave a deep sigh. 'It was a long time ago, but your mother had postnatal depression quite badly.'

Sam nodded. He was vaguely aware of that. A distant, half-buried memory tugged in his mind. Something that one of his aunts had once said. Ma's sisters didn't live locally. They had a smallholding in Wales, and their parents, Sam's grandparents, lived in Spain and rarely came back to England.

'I'm worried she might be heading for some kind of relapse,' Louella went on, her eyes anxious. 'Going to the reunion was obviously an ordeal for her. I know she doesn't want me to make an issue of it, but I had to say something.'

'I'm glad you did.' Sam met her worried gaze. 'You're a good friend. I'll keep a close eye on her.'

'As will I,' Louella promised, looking relieved. 'And I might be wrong. Hopefully the panic attack was a one-off.'

'Fingers crossed,' he said, 'and thanks again.'

Sam's head swirled with contradictory thoughts as he drove home, fed Snowball, got changed into his old yard clothes, although he doubted he'd ride tonight, and headed to Brook Stables. He needed to get an update on what riding lessons had been pencilled in for him. Saturday afternoon was his main teaching time, but he did a lot more in the school holidays and during the sunny light evenings.

Louella's words replayed in his head. He didn't know whether to be relieved or disturbed that his ma had experienced a panic attack. It was better than a heart attack obviously, but it was still a thing –

quite a big thing from what he knew about panic attacks. And he'd learned a little more about them in the last few years, because Brook Stables were an advocate of riding for wellbeing, which was aimed at promoting people's self-esteem through connection with horses, and Sam was one of their instructors.

His mind flicked unwillingly to Rufus Holt, who until very recently had been dating Phoebe. Sam knew the man independently because he'd taught his son, Archie, to ride. The first time Archie had come for a lesson, Sam had realised Rufus was scared of horses. But it hadn't been until much later that Sam had learned about Rufus's PTSD, which had been brought on by witnessing his wife die in a riding accident and had subsequently been triggered by horses.

Sam didn't know much about either PTSD or postnatal depression, other than the fact both of them could involve panic attacks. He wished his mother would trust him with whatever was going on for her, but that wasn't the way things were done in his family. Feelings weren't something that got discussed. Particularly negative feelings.

He got out of his car at the stables, greeted a couple of people just leaving for a hack – the yard was hardly ever empty whatever time he rocked up – then he tried to put the subject out of his mind. Hopefully Louella had been right, and it had been a one-off attack, brought on by going to an event Jan was nervous about.

Hopefully it wouldn't happen again.

* * *

It felt good to be back in his regular routine, grooming and feeding Ninja, chatting to other livery owners and coordinating lessons with Marjorie Taylor, who owned and ran the place. Sam never got tired of the soundtrack of the stables: the clop of metal shoes on the tarmac yard, the snorts of horses, the rattle of buckets and the scents of leather and horse were all things that felt like part of his soul.

Although he had to admit it was going to feel odd not being with Phoebe 24/7. He had loved the few days they'd spent as a live-in couple last week, but making love, living on pizza and binge-watching inane TV already seemed far away. A part of someone else's life. Little more than a beautiful memory.

Reality had crashed in when he and Phoebe had been hurtling towards Salisbury hospital. Sam was a fan of reality usually, well, he was a fan of most of it, and he liked his routines. But even at Brook Stables, which for years had been his second home, the knowledge that he probably wouldn't see Phoebe again until the end of the week made Sam ache with a longing that he couldn't shake off.

5

At Beechbrook House, Rufus Holt was also aching but for entirely different reasons. His aches were physical, the result of being hunched over a computer in his home office for most of the day. Recently, he'd made a decision to spend less time inside and more out and about on the estate or seeing tenants like his father had always done, but it wasn't working out very well.

He was about to have a formal meeting with Emilia, Archie's Swiss-German live-in nanny, which he was dreading. He was now sitting behind his antique walnut desk, where he'd been working all afternoon, waiting for her to arrive.

He'd asked if they could meet at close of day, although he hadn't set an actual time, which had possibly been a mistake. He hadn't wanted it to be so official, even though it was a formal meeting. He was about to tell Emilia that her services were no longer required.

He should have done it weeks ago, but he'd been putting it off. Emilia had been working for him for five years; ever since he'd lost Rowena, Archie's mother. She hadn't been the first nanny he'd employed to look after his son, who'd been six at the time, but she'd been the best. And she'd been with them ever since.

Archie was now eleven and he was due to go off to boarding school in September. There was no possible reason for Emilia to stay on at Beechbrook. Rufus knew he should have given her notice when the schools had broken up for summer in the first week of July. There was a three-month notice period in her contract.

Rufus hadn't given Emilia her notice then just in case Archie had decided to come home from summer camp where he was scheduled to be for another week. But there was no sign of that happening. Archie was having a whale of a time.

However, there was no reason to put it off any longer. Rufus had been paying Emilia to do nothing for nearly a month already and he couldn't justify letting it drag on indefinitely. The estate was doing well at the moment, but as his father was fond of pointing out, they couldn't afford passengers. Rufus knew his father was hoping that Emilia would agree not to work out her notice period.

Lord Alfred Holt had done very little himself lately. He had a heart condition and so Rufus had taken on most of his work. Rufus was happy about this, his father would be seventy next year; it was high time he retired. Rufus planned to employ someone else to help him on the administrative side. But he couldn't justify the extra expense unless he freed up some funds and Emilia was the obvious choice.

Other than cooking for him and Archie, which she still did out of habit, even though Archie wasn't here, there was very little for her to do, a fact that had been underlined when he'd seen her sunbathing a few times lately in a far corner of the garden. Once, he'd seen her sunbathing topless, although he knew she had never done that when Archie was around. For a start Archie, who was never backward in coming forward, would definitely have told him. Fortunately, Emilia hadn't realised that Rufus had seen her, so he hadn't had to say anything to her, which he would have found mortifying. He'd mentioned it to Harrison, his estate manager, though, and Harrison hadn't made very much of it.

'Topless sunbathing's very common in Europe,' he'd said with a grin. 'So she probably thinks it's OK. And she's fairly easy on the eye, isn't she? Not that I'm interested,' he'd added hastily. 'I am well and truly settled.'

Rufus knew that was true. Harrison and his partner, Tori, were expecting a baby in December and Rufus had never seen him so happy.

The two men were much more than employer/employee. They'd gone to the same public school and had been close friends for years. Harrison's partner Tori was also, coincidentally, close friends with Phoebe Dashwood, the woman Rufus had been dating until recently. It had all felt rather incestuous, Rufus had thought, not that he was seeing Phoebe any more, they'd both been too entangled with their jobs for a relationship.

A soft knock on the door interrupted his musings but before he'd had the chance to call a greeting, Emilia came in. As usual, she was dressed casually, in a short dress that showed off her bronzed legs, but her shoulder-length hair was not in its characteristic ponytail. Instead, it framed her face in soft blonde curls. Had she just styled her hair?

Rufus blinked. 'Hi, Emilia, thanks for coming.'

'Good evening.' She strolled over and sat in one of the visitors' chairs on the other side of Rufus's desk and crossed her legs. She was so petite, the chair with its leather-studded arms dwarfed her. 'You are looking very serious, Rufus. There is a problem, ja?'

'Not a problem, no.' He leaned forward and said earnestly, 'I've always been very happy with everything you've done.'

'This is good.'

'It's very good.' Rufus took a deep breath. He'd rehearsed this a dozen times. And he wasn't sure why he was so nervous. He just needed to man up and say it. 'As you know already, Archie is off to school in September, which means that I'll no longer be needing your services.'

'I know,' she said unexpectedly. 'I will need to finish my service at Beechbrook House.'

'That's right.' He breathed a sigh of relief. All that worry and she was already aware. Of course she was aware – she was an intelligent woman and Archie had been excited about going to his new school for months. He'd been talking about it and looking forward to it much more than Rufus had, as it happened. Of course Emilia had known.

'I will finish here in November – on the 1st,' Emilia said, looking up at the multicoloured wall planner, which looked out of place between the ancestral portraits in their gilt frames. 'This is when my three-month notice ends.'

'Well, yes, it is, but you don't need to stay until November, Emilia. I don't expect you to work out your notice period. I will pay you until then, of course.'

'It's not a problem to work this notice,' Emilia assured him with a quick smile. 'This is very nice place to live.'

'Er, yes.' Rufus realised suddenly that he couldn't force her to go. Full board was part of her terms of employment. He should have pre-empted this. Why would Emilia want to pay rent elsewhere when she had accommodation here? However, her whole family lived in Geneva, so he'd half expected her to jump at the chance to go home early. Not that she'd been back to Geneva lately. Even when she'd been on leave, she hadn't left Beechbrook often.

'I will not be in your way,' she said, standing up. 'I can continue to cook for you if this is what you wish?'

'You don't need to do that,' he said quickly.

'I know, but I like to do this.' Her eyes sparkled. 'Then you can get on with your endless working, ja. And I can see Archie before he goes off to his big school. I can say goodbye to him and give him a big hug.'

Rufus couldn't really argue with that. Of course she would want to say goodbye to Archie – and Archie would want to say goodbye to her. He might complain about her loudly from time to time, but Rufus knew that his son was fond of Emilia. She had been more than just a nanny to him. She hadn't replaced Rowena. No one could have done that, but she had gone a long way to making sure that the loss of Archie's mother was more bearable.

Emilia jumped to her feet. 'I must get dinner ready – will Lord Alfred be joining you?'

'I expect he will. Yes.'

Emilia hesitated at the door, and then looked back at Rufus. 'You do not see Phoebe the vet any more – is this right? You have finished your acquaintance.'

Rufus swallowed. Emilia rarely asked him anything personal. Almost all of their conversations centred around Archie, even when he wasn't here. Occasionally she talked about work because that was a subject that was openly discussed in the house too, but she had never mentioned Phoebe before.

He saw no reason not to tell her, though. Archie would tell her, once he found out, which he would next time Rufus saw him for a proper chat. Rufus was hoping to play that down; Archie had hit it off with Phoebe from the start.

'I'm not seeing Phoebe any more, no.'

Emilia gave a quick nod of acknowledgement, and didn't say anything else, but she looked pleased. Or was that his imagination? Rufus knew the two women had never really seen eye to eye, but what difference could it possibly make to Emilia?

'I will make the dinner, ja.' She disappeared and the door clicked shut behind her.

Rufus let out a sigh of relief.

He supposed it didn't really matter if she stayed on until the end of October. Financially it made no difference. At least they had finalised the date of her leaving, which meant he could think about employing someone to help out in the office.

He got up, stretched his arms above his head and followed Emilia out into the hall but instead of going deeper into the house he turned left, let himself out of the front door and went outside into the cool blue evening. He needed a stroll to clear his head.

A few minutes later he was walking along the edge of the lavender fields that ran either side of his quarter-mile drive down the slight slope to the walls that bordered the estate. The lavender was like a rolling purple sea and its scent was all-pervading. Rufus took a deep breath, and thought that from now on lavender would always be the smell of summer.

According to the experts Rufus had employed, the lavender was now at its very peak and would be harvested this week. Their first eco crop, which was to be made into essential oil that would in turn be made into upmarket skin products. He had negotiated a deal with an artisan cooperative, and although this was only the first stage of the process, Rufus was pleased that so far the venture had been a success.

But right now, his head ached and Emilia's mention of Phoebe had unsettled him. Since they'd decided to go their separate ways, he'd tried not to think about her. Rufus was very good at compartmentalising. Putting the various sections of his life into separate boxes and locking them up when they weren't needed. *Archie, Dad, Work, The Past, Other.* Phoebe was currently in the box marked *Other*. He hadn't managed to get her into *The Past* box yet. He had simply switched her off and focused on work. He was also very good at burying his feelings with work and, by God, it wasn't as though there wasn't enough of it.

Rufus was also a lot more anxious about Archie going off to

boarding school than he wanted to admit, even though he knew Archie was really looking forward to it. Rufus wasn't sure whether his anxiety was coming from the fact he didn't want to lose Archie or the fact that he had such bad memories of school himself.

He should probably book in another session with Bartholomew Timms, his father's golfing companion and Rufus's on/off therapist. Bartholomew was a strong advocate of talking therapy. Rufus had been starting to agree with the man – at least in principle. But talking about difficult subjects was something he and his father had always avoided at all costs. And lifetime habits were very hard to break.

He didn't regret ending his relationship with Phoebe, if you could call it a relationship. It had been the wrong time, and Phoebe had been the wrong woman too, certainly as far as his father was concerned. The fact that she was, to all intents and purposes, a Crowther would have always been an issue where Dad was concerned. But Rufus had been fond of the beautiful vet, and ending their alliance had saddened him deeply.

6

Phoebe's plans to meet Sam for a drink on Thursday night were thwarted when she had a call-out to a difficult calving at Middlebrook Farm, a big dairy farm on the edge of Burley. To her relief, it wasn't a call-out that ended in her doing a caesarean in the middle of a field, which had happened once before. She and the dairyman finally managed to deliver the calf normally and both mother and baby were soon bonding well, the calf finding her legs in the straw of the stable where she'd been delivered and the cow nosing her baby with interest.

Phoebe glanced at her phone as she left the farm. She had promised Sam she would call by and see him if she wasn't too late, but it was nearly nine and the truth was she was totally exhausted and in dire need of a shower.

Sam had sent her a text which in typical plain-speaking Sam style simply said:

If you're tired go straight home – I'm pretty tired myself – it's been a full-on week. XX

Phoebe decided to take him at face value, and she went straight home to Woodcutter's Cottage. It was Murphy's Law that the call-out hadn't happened on Tuesday or Wednesday when Sam had been teaching at Brook Stables. Wasn't there an old saying? 'Life is what happens when you're busy making other plans.'

That was certainly the case with her and Sam, Phoebe thought, biting her lip as she parked outside her home. The same thing had happened with her and Rufus – they simply hadn't had time for a relationship.

She squashed down this disturbing thought as she let herself through the green front door and into the coolness inside. That was the beauty of cob walls. They kept the cottage cool in summer and warm in winter. The two-up, two-down seventeenth-century thatched cottage didn't belong to her. She rented it from her best friend, Tori, but it was exactly the kind of place she'd have bought herself if she'd been in the market for a house.

Woodcutter's had a large decked area at the back and a garden, although Phoebe didn't spend a lot of time in either space, and it also had its own parking. Its seclusion was what made it a very desirable property. It was tucked away at the end of an unmade road. Phoebe adored the privacy, but if she looked forward into the future, she'd probably end up buying a bigger house than Wood-cutter's.

Tori was going to need a bigger house than Woodcutter's too, Phoebe thought, thinking about her friend as she washed up the dishes from last night's tea and this morning's breakfast in the Belfast sink. Tori was having a baby, which was due in the third week of December, and as far as Phoebe knew, she and Harrison, her partner, still hadn't settled on a place to live.

Tori lived in a first-floor flat in Bridgeford, not far from where Sam had a maisonette, but it was nowhere near as big as Sam's and Tori had already decided it wasn't suitable for a baby. Harrison currently lived in the gatehouse of the Beechbrook Estate, which was lovely, not to mention free accommodation, but wasn't much bigger than Woodcutter's either.

Phoebe left the washing up to drain, dried her hands on a tea towel, and went into the lounge, the only other downstairs room. She had an urge to phone Tori and catch up now. It wouldn't be too late to speak to her friend, who owned and edited *New Forest Views*, the local free magazine, and often worked late on deadlines.

To Phoebe's delight, Tori picked up on the second ring.

'Hey, stranger. You're never going to believe this, but I had literally just picked up the phone to call you. Telepathy or what?'

'Synchronicity,' Phoebe said. 'Well, I was going to ask you how you're doing and how Bump is – are you still calling her Vanessa Rose, or has that changed since we last spoke?' She grabbed a cushion, settled back on her sofa and drew up her legs. 'What were you calling me about?'

'Well, to answer your questions in order: I'm blooming, apart from flaming backache. Yes, we're definitely calling her Vanessa Rose, after my grandmother. And I wasn't calling you about anything in particular.' Tori giggled. 'No, that's a lie. I was mainly calling to ask how it was going with Sam. I didn't like to disturb you on your hols in case you were in bed or something... Love's young dream and all that...' Tori was the eternal romantic. She had known Sam as long as Phoebe had, the three of them – four if you included Phoebe's younger brother, Frazier – had grown up together, and had spent much of their childhood on Puddleduck Farm, back in the days when it had been a working dairy farm, run by Maggie and her late husband, Farmer Pete.

Tori had predicted when they were all still children that Phoebe and Sam would one day become an item, and she'd been dropping increasingly heavier hints ever since, or at least she had until Phoebe had surprised everyone by dating the lord of the manor.

'Our holiday was last week,' Phoebe pointed out. 'But thank you for your consideration and yes, we did spend most of it in bed.'

She was almost deafened by Tori's squeal of excitement. 'Oh, that is so brilliant! I am absolutely thrilled to bits for you both. Finally, finally. What's it like? I don't mean the bed bit, that's your business obviously, besides, you already told me he was eleven out of ten. Enough said.'

It was Phoebe's turn to giggle. Yes, she had done that. In the first euphoria of spending a fabulous night with Sam, she'd sent Tori a one-word text, the number eleven typed out, and Tori had known exactly what she'd meant. But they hadn't discussed it since then.

'I mean the whole friends to romance thing,' Tori went on. 'How does that feel?'

Phoebe paused. Tori was actually the only person in the world who had an inkling that she and Rufus hadn't got past the dating stage. She had once confided in her, but then she'd led Tori to believe things had improved on that front and Tori had never asked her again.

'What is it?' Tori said. 'You're not still worried about the whole rebound thing, are you?'

'Um, no. Well, maybe a bit. We did both move straight on from relationships, didn't we? Neither of us really had time to process what had happened with our exes.'

'I guess that's true, but it's not as though you moved into a brand-new relationship, is it? You just moved the friendship thing on a notch. A bedpost notch – so to speak.' There was another giggle in her voice.

'I hope we're not just notches on each other's bedposts,' Phoebe said quickly. 'No, don't worry, I know we're not. I'm certainly not worried about that.'

'Then what are you worried about?' Tori's voice grew a shade more serious. 'You and Sam are made for each other. I've always known it. Everyone's always known it, honey.'

'I know that too.' Phoebe tried to gather her thoughts. 'I haven't seen Sam since Sunday. We had to finish our holiday early too – his mum had a funny turn.'

'Oh dear, what happened?'

Phoebe told her and she made sympathetic noises. 'I hope she's OK. Keep me posted.'

'I will, thanks. I guess it's just that last week we were a full-on couple – hey, remind me to tell you what happened at the New Forest Show in a minute – and this week it's the total opposite. It's not because we don't want to see each other. It's just that Sam has two jobs already, not to mention a horse, and I have the practice, which is not nine-to-five by any stretch of the imagination. I was supposed to see Sam tonight, but I had a call-out.'

'Couldn't you still go round? You could spend the night together. Harrison and I do that sometimes when our jobs get too full-on.'

'I was going to but then we'd have a really late night and Sam gets up at first light to see to Ninja before work.'

'Hmm, yes, animals are a full-on flaming commitment. We don't have that problem.'

'I think babies are more of a commitment,' Phoebe pointed out drily.

'Ah, yes, but we'll be living together when Vanessa Rose arrives. In fact, with a bit of luck we'll be living together this time next week. We went to look at a house to rent in Bridgeford yesterday and we both loved it. We're picking the keys up on Monday.'

It was Phoebe's turn to squeal. 'That's brilliant news! Why didn't you tell me straightaway? What's it like?'

'Hang on a sec, I'll WhatsApp you a link with the details. There you go. Done. Have a look at it now and tell me what you think. I'll hold on.'

Phoebe heard a ping. She took the phone from her ear, opened the link and scrolled through the photos of a pretty semi-detached with a large back garden full of trees. It was spacious inside too. The kitchen had a breakfast island and there were three bedrooms.

'That looks lovely, but I thought you were planning to buy somewhere.'

'We've decided to rent until we get married. We could also do with the interest rates stabilising a bit. Harrison's pretty savvy financially and he thinks that's going to happen next year.'

They chatted for a while about house prices and areas that were affordable – there weren't many in the New Forest – and ways of getting a good deal, most of which involved buying a run-down place and doing loads of work yourself, which they agreed could actually be really exciting as then you could really make a place your own.

There was another pause and then Tori added softly, 'Rufus didn't say a word about you two splitting up to Harrison. That's odd, isn't it?'

'In view of how locked down Rufus is, not really. I doubt he's even told Archie. If he has, Archie hasn't mentioned it. He's at pony summer camp with his friend, Jack, and he sends me photos and videos of them out riding. Mind you, he's never really done much in the way of actual messages.' She sighed. 'I do miss Archie.'

'Sorry. I shouldn't have brought them up.' Tori's tone changed. 'Let's get back to you and Sam. Maybe living together is the solution for you guys too. Then at least you know that whatever else happens, you'll wake up and have breakfast together every morning.'

'It's a bit early for us to be thinking about living together,' Phoebe replied, although the thought of waking up with Sam every day was appealing. She yawned. 'Talking of Sam, I need to send him a bedtime message. Otherwise he might think I don't care.'

'He won't think that,' Tori said confidently. 'He knows he's got the girl. By the way, did the New Forest Show thing involve a runaway pony and a heroic couple who not only stopped it mid-bolt, but fixed its cut leg?'

'I wouldn't have put it quite like that, but yes... how on earth did you hear about it?'

'I'm a journalist. Not much gets past me.' Tori left it a beat and added, 'I had a stand at the show for the mag. I didn't go, but Laura, my trusty assistant, was there every day. She entered the Cake and Bake and she just happened to have a conversation with the woman who won the Battenberg category. Laura wants to do a write-up. A nice human-interest story that our readers will love.'

'About the Battenberg win?'

'No. About an heroic local couple. Come on, Pheebs. It's so much more interesting than who won Young Farmer or the Rural Diversification category. Not that those things aren't important, of course.'

Before Phoebe could answer, she added quickly, 'It would be great PR for Puddleduck Vets.'

'Like we need any more publicity. I'm too busy already.'

'Puddleduck Pets then.' Tori was relentless, which was what made her such a good editor. 'We could feature some of the animals that need rehoming on the same page. I bet there are loads.'

Phoebe thought about the dalmatian puppies, who were doing really well. Maggie, Eddie, Marcus and Natasha were all taking turns to do the night shift.

'If you must, but no pictures of us,' she said. 'Night, lovely. It's great to catch up.'

'Night, Pheebs. I'm so pleased you and Sam are an item.'

When Phoebe finally pressed disconnect, she saw a message Sam had sent an hour ago. Had they really been talking that long?

Night sweetheart, I'm off to the land of nod. Phone on silent now. Sweet dreams. XX

She hadn't even answered his last message, Phoebe thought guiltily, sending a heart emoji back.

She needed to make more of an effort. She couldn't bear it if she and Sam split up for the same reasons she and Rufus had split. Or at least one of the same reasons, which was that they couldn't squeeze enough quality time for each other into their hugely hectic lives. She realised it wasn't the first time this disturbing thought about history repeating itself had flashed into her mind.

7

On Friday, Phoebe had a call-out to Anni's Alpacas at Buckland Farm. Phoebe still felt jolted every time Anni's number flashed up on her mobile. Back in March, they'd had problems with anaemia in their alpaca herd, and it had taken Phoebe ages and the intervention of another vet to get to the bottom of it. Thankfully, since then, the herd had been in tip-top condition.

Phoebe had got close to Anni during the few weeks it had taken to get to the root of the problem. As well as being a friend of Maggie's, Anni was a fascinating character. She had Romany heritage. Madam Kesia, her grandmother, had once told the fortunes of the rich and famous as well as the not so rich and famous on Scarborough seafront and although Anni insisted she hadn't inherited the gift, she could read tea leaves with unerring accuracy. She had seen heartbreak ahead in her own life just before she'd lost her favourite alpaca. Then, when she'd read Phoebe's tea leaves, she'd given her a pretty accurate estimation of her love life and predicted the success of Puddleduck Vets. She'd even seen Tori's pregnancy in the leaves. Phoebe, who had never put that much stock in fortune telling, now saw it in a whole new light.

To Phoebe's huge relief, Anni hadn't mentioned alpacas when she'd texted her. She'd said she had a problem which was urgent, but not serious, and would be grateful if Phoebe would fit her in quickly.

Phoebe was relieved when Anni greeted her at the door of Buckland Farmhouse, smiling broadly. Her black ringleted hair was pinned off her face in a clip today and she looked overheated. 'Hello, lovie, I think I may have called you out on false pretences. It's not quite as urgent as I thought.'

'It's not a problem, it's always nice to see you.' Phoebe met the older woman's dark smiling eyes. 'It's not Reuben, is it?'

Reuben was one of the farm cats and the only other animal Anni had registered with Puddleduck Pets.

'No, it's not Reuben. It's not an alpaca either, it's Quackhead.'

'Er... Quackhead?'

'Yes. Quackhead's a duck. He turned up about six weeks ago by the pond in the bottom field. He was half-starved, poor little mite. He'd injured his beak and couldn't feed properly so I shut him in the barn and kept an eye – well, basically I fed him canned tuna and gave him a paddling pool of water to splash about in until he recovered.'

'Wow,' Phoebe said, thinking that Anni would never cease to surprise her. She and Nick had their work cut out looking after their herd of alpacas, who were their retirement project, without looking after injured birds. They ran the place on a shoestring with no help because they couldn't afford any.

'When I told Nick I was going to rehabilitate a duck, he instantly coined the name Quackhead and started calling me Nurse Anni. Nick's always had a strange sense of humour...' She rolled her eyes. 'We have a grandson, Rocco, who had a few problems with crack cocaine a while back and had to go into rehab – he's all right now, thankfully.'

While they'd been speaking, they'd been standing in Anni's large hallway which was filled with pictures of her family; framed portraits of handsome men, glamorous women and sloe-eyed children, all of whom bore a strong resemblance to Anni. Phoebe assumed they were her children and grandchildren. She'd never met any of them in person. Although it was a relief to hear the errant grandson was on the mend.

'I've got fond of Quackhead,' Anni continued. 'He's a quacker, a cracker. God, I'm at it now. Anyway, he's a character – just like our Rocco.' She paused. 'Similar temperaments in some ways. Charming once you know them, but pests if you don't. He goes after the birds. Flapping and screeching like a thing demented. Quackhead, I mean, not Rocco.' She smiled fondly. 'Rocco loves the ladies. I think that's how Quackhead got injured, though. Going after the wild birds, he's more like a goose than a duck. He's a Muscovy. They can be quite territorial.'

'OK. So what do you think's wrong with Quackhead now? Has he had a relapse?' The words were out of Phoebe's mouth before she had a chance to edit them.

'Don't you start!' Anni rolled her eyes again. 'And no, he hasn't had a relapse. He's got himself stuck.'

'A stuck duck,' Phoebe repeated. 'Where?'

'In a truck.'

Phoebe blinked, no longer sure whether this whole thing was some kind of elaborate joke. 'You're telling me you have a duck stuck in a truck?' she said slowly. 'A duck called Quackhead!'

'Precisely. Or at least I thought he was stuck. It's easier if I just show you. Follow me.'

Feeling slightly mystified, but very intrigued, Phoebe followed Anni through the hallway and old-fashioned farmhouse kitchen and out into the sunshine at the back of the farm. The first few days of August had been hot and the weathermen were predicting temperatures of 27 rising to 30 for the rest of August too.

Blackberries were already ripening in the hedgerows around the farm and the ground felt hard beneath the soles of their shoes.

Anni led Phoebe towards an old barn with its doors flung open to the elements and much of its roof open to the sky where the wood had rotted through. Inside, the air smelled of old hay and dust. Tucked in the far corner of the barn, in a spot that was thankfully cooler, was a rusted-out ancient vehicle. It had peeling red paintwork and a rusty old section of cutting machinery on the back that didn't look as though it would ever be fit to cut anything again.

'Nick says he's going to do it up one day and then it will be worth something.' Anni kicked one of the huge tyres and scoffed disparagingly. 'I'll believe that when I see it. The useless piece of old rubbish.'

It was hard to tell whether she was talking about Nick or the ancient machinery. Phoebe decided it would be prudent to keep quiet. This whole situation was surreal enough already.

Before either woman could say anything else, they were distracted by a raucous squawk and Phoebe realised there was a large duck perched up inside the cab of the truck. Mostly white, it had a distinctive red head and black patches on its back. Anni was right about it being a Muscovy, but it wasn't often you saw one looking ready to drive off – all it needed was a chauffeur's cap.

How it had got in was a mystery, as the cab was completely enclosed and there was still glass in the windscreen and windows. Anni walked towards the driver's door, with Phoebe following. When the duck saw Anni, it waggled its tail feathers, a movement Phoebe's grandmother had told her meant ducks were happy, and waddled across the passenger seat to greet her.

Phoebe followed, fascinated.

'Hello, Quackhead.' Anni made a chuck-chucking sound and

the duck put its head on one side and squawked again and waggled some more.

Phoebe didn't think she'd ever seen such an obvious display of affection. Not even the puddle ducks at Maggie's were so tame. Quackhead clearly knew what side his bread was buttered on... that's if ducks had butter on their bread.

Then the duck spotted Phoebe and in an instant its whole demeanour changed. Screeching madly, it launched itself towards the quarter light window in the door and in the next instant its head and long neck were through a gap and Phoebe realised that the quarter light did have some leeway and wasn't completely shut.

She stepped back instinctively as the vicious-looking beak snapped open and shut a few inches from her face. Quackhead clearly wasn't anywhere near as pleased to see her as he was to see Nurse Anni and was showing his displeasure vocally. Behind the glass, his wings flapped madly in a flurry of white.

'That's what he was doing earlier,' Anni said. 'Nick came in with me to see what was happening and he had a hissy fit. The duck was none too happy either.' She turned and winked at Phoebe, her tanned face screwed up in amusement. 'I'm joking. It was Quackhead that had a hissy fit. Nick wasn't very pleased, though. Having a duck setting up home in his truck and crapping all over the seat did not impress him one bit.'

She clapped a hand over her mouth. 'I shouldn't laugh. Nick prefers four-legged animals, anyway, the thing is, when Quackhead here had finished seeing off the enemy he got himself stuck in the quarter light. I was scared of moving him because he'd cut his neck on a jagged edge. You see that bit underneath? And then he couldn't seem to back out, although he did eventually, obviously.'

Phoebe looked cautiously at the underside of the duck's neck and spotted the cut. 'Sure. But how did he get in there in the first place? Were the doors open?'

'No, they're locked. Nick lost the keys years ago, which is one of the reasons he hasn't got started on the project. He says he's got to drill the locks out.'

Phoebe frowned. 'Could Quackhead have got in through the quarter light? It doesn't look big enough.'

'I think he must have done. I think he must have flown up onto the shelves alongside and then banged into the glass hard enough to get the old mechanism to shift. I'm guessing he was attracted by the wing mirror that's propped up on the seat.' She sighed. 'I blame Nick for leaving it there. Quackhead must have seen his reflection and maybe he thought it was another duck and attacked it. That would be true to form. Anyway, what I reckon happened is that the mechanism opened up enough for him to get in but now it's jammed solid.'

As she spoke, Anni gently shoved the duck's head and neck back through the small gap and tried to pull the quarter light outwards, but as she'd said it was jammed solid and wouldn't budge.

'I'm sorry to have wasted your time, Phoebe.'

'You haven't. We still need to get him out so I can have a proper look at that cut.'

'Yes, but I'm sure you've got better things to do than get ducks out of trucks. I'm just going to have to smash the window, aren't I, whether Nick likes it or not. I can't leave Quackhead in there much longer. He'll get dehydrated.'

'I've got half an hour. Before you smash the window, have you tried WD-40 on the hinge mechanism?'

Anni brightened. 'I think it might be too far gone, but it's worth a try, I suppose. For the sake of harmony, it would be good if we could do the least damage possible – to the duck or the truck.'

While Anni went to fetch the WD-40, Phoebe took another cautious look at Quackhead's neck. Blood was still oozing from the cut. That probably wasn't helping the duck's mood any. Birds usually went into shock when they were injured, and it was the shock that was more likely to kill them than the initial injury, but she decided to keep this to herself for now. Quackhead didn't look like he was in shock. There was definitely a malevolent expression in those mean beady eyes.

'Don't worry, mate. We'll get you sorted out,' she said cautiously. At least he didn't try to fly at her again.

Anni reappeared with a can in her hand and sprayed it liberally over the hinged mechanism. 'Wriggle it a bit,' Phoebe suggested from a safe vantage point. 'Maggie swears by that stuff. She says it's a miracle cure for rust.'

While they waited for the oil to do its job, they talked about Maggie's forthcoming nuptials.

'Is she still planning on getting hitched at the beginning of December or has that been changed again?'

'Not yet.' Phoebe held up crossed fingers. 'I think that date might stick. Maggie's never liked December much, and she says it will liven it up.'

Anni chuckled. 'That's something to look forward to then. I must get Nick to dig out his suit and give it a dusting. The last time he wore that was for our Harley's naming day but that's got to be ten years ago. Oh, I do love a good wedding.' She gave the opening mechanism a sharp tug and it moved. 'Hey, did you see that? It's working.'

Quackhead was now huddled on the seat and had fluffed up his feathers in the way birds do when they're either cold or ill. Phoebe hoped he wasn't going into shock. He was still keeping an eye on her, but he hadn't tried any more direct attacks.

'How's your love life going?' Anni asked Phoebe ultra-casually as she sprayed on more WD-40. 'You chose the right one in the end, didn't you?'

'I think so.'

Anni nodded approvingly. 'It's so hard to know. Although I think it might be easier these days because couples don't have to decide so young. I mean let's face it, choosing a life partner is the biggest decision you ever have to make and you're expected to do it when you're still wet behind the ears. I think they should shove up the age of consent to eighteen like it is in some states of America and no one should be allowed to tie the knot until they're at least thirty-five. At least not without the written consent of their parents.'

Phoebe snorted with laughter. 'A bit harsh. What if their parents aren't around?'

'A wise elder then.' Anni was undeterred. 'Someone like me. I can tell straight away whether a couple has a long-term future.'

'By reading their tea leaves?'

'No, by looking at them. It's obvious when you're as perceptive as I am. I can predict it to the year.'

'Can you really?'

'Maybe not to the year, but I could give you a pretty accurate estimation. Don't just take my word for it. We'll do an experiment at the wedding. There'll be young couples there, won't there? You point them out and I'll tell you if they've got a long-term future.'

Phoebe thought about Tori and Harrison. She'd never been able to work out why Tori was so besotted with the morose estate manager she was planning to marry. On the other hand, she'd have hated to know if their future was doomed from the start, especially as they were having baby Vanessa. She looked uncertainly at Anni, and the old lady must have caught her look because she coughed lightly and said, 'OK, I won't tell you if I think you don't really want to know. Credit me with some sense. But I've been right about more couples than you'd ever guess. Ha!' she exclaimed, as the hinge mechanism suddenly gave up the battle and moved enough for her to open the old quarter light window. 'There we go. I think that's it.'

A short while later, they had freed the wary Quackhead from his prison and also discovered he was actually a 'she' and had laid an egg to prove it.

'Maybe that's why she went into the truck,' Anni said in amazement. 'So much for my enhanced perceptive powers.'

'It's hard to tell the sex of a duck,' Phoebe said as Anni cradled the bird on her lap, and held her beak firmly shut while Phoebe cleaned the cut and administered some antibiotic powder. Luckily it didn't need stitching, and she seemed none the worse for her experience.

'Should I keep her in the barn for a bit do you reckon?'

'Yep, it's back to rehab for Quackhead,' Phoebe said, trying not to laugh. 'But she should be right as rain in a week or so. Joking aside, perhaps she went into the truck because she was looking for a mate. You don't see a lot of Muscovy ducks round here.'

'Yes, maybe it's time she had her freedom. Would it be OK to just release her near some other Muscovy ducks – assuming I can find any? I hate the idea of her getting injured again.'

'I'm not sure, but Maggie would probably know. She's good with ducks. Shall I get her to phone you?'

'I'll phone her,' Anni said. 'Now are you sure you won't stay for a scone and a cuppa?'

'Thanks, but I'd better get on,' Phoebe told her reluctantly, as she headed for her Lexus. 'Maybe next time.'

As she drove away, she could see Anni in her rear-view mirror, waving goodbye.

God, she loved her job. The animal characters were amazing, but she'd recently realised that something else she hadn't expected had happened when she'd made being a vet her vocation. She loved the human characters too.

8

Phoebe and Sam arranged to meet on Saturday evening in their local, The Brace of Pheasants, for dinner.

'We both have to eat,' Sam had pointed out after a phone chat about work getting in the way of their social life. 'We can at least do that together.'

'I'll be there at six, come high or hell water,' Phoebe promised and when she arrived on the dot, she saw Sam ordering drinks.

The pub was busy with locals who'd popped in for a pie and a pint, and after they'd ordered pies themselves, they found a table in the middle of the room and sat opposite each other.

'Hello, stranger.' He caught her hands across the round table. 'I just about remember what you look like.'

'Sorry, Sam. It's been one of those weeks.'

'I'm just as bad. The world, his wife, and their kids have wanted a riding lesson this week.'

'We'll have to have a holiday.'

'We only just had one.'

'I know, but the New Forest Show feels like a distant memory.'

She sighed. 'Someone dumped a box of dalmatian puppies at the gate on Monday. Their mother had died apparently.'

Sam's face softened. '*101 Dalmatians* was my favourite film when I was a kid.'

'I know. It was mine too. Luckily there were only four in this box. They're the cutest little things. They must have only been a few days old. Their spots hadn't even come through.' She showed him a picture of the pups with their white coats and pink little tummies. She'd been taking pictures daily and on the latest one you could see the shadows of spots coming through.

'Oh my God, they're cute. Do you think we're too busy for a dalmatian?' His eyes danced with amusement.

'Stop right there, Sam Hendrie.'

'What? Maybe we could co-parent one?'

She couldn't tell if he was joking or not. But suddenly the idea of co-parenting a puppy with Sam seemed like the best idea she'd ever heard.

'Do you think we really could? I've wanted a dog forever but I keep telling myself I'm too busy.'

'We're both too busy. But then again, our lifestyles are pretty compatible for a dog. You could teach it to be a practice dog. It could greet all your canine clients and help them to relax at the vets and I could take it riding with Ninja.'

Before they could get any deeper into this fantasy, the waiter arrived with their pies. Sam handed Phoebe a knife and fork wrapped in a green serviette from the pot in the middle of the table.

'Let's talk about it some more when the pups are bigger. Who's looking after them? Don't pups that young have to be fed every four hours?'

'Maggie and Eddie are sharing the job with Marcus and Natasha. Thank goodness for committed people.'

For a while there was silence as they tucked into their food.

Phoebe hadn't realised she was so hungry. When she was on call, it was impossible to keep to regular mealtimes. She just grabbed a snack when she could. It was lovely to be able to sit down with Sam and have a meal.

She'd always thought the easy companionship they shared wouldn't translate into a romance, but she'd been so wrong. The easiness was part of the reason it worked.

As they ate, Phoebe told Sam about Quackhead the duck and then had to apologise when he almost choked on a mouthful of pie. 'Please warn me next time you're going to tell me a funny story. Then I can swallow first.'

She laughed. 'Sorry. I should tell Tori, she's always looking for amusing stories for the mag.'

'I doubt she'd be allowed to print that.'

'She heard about your horse rescue at the New Forest Show. She asked if she could put it in the mag as a human-interest story. I caved in under pressure. I hope you don't mind.'

'Like that would stop her. How's she doing, anyway? Apart from working too hard by the sound of it.'

'She's fine. Blooming, I think the word is. Who'd have thought it would be Tori who got all grown up and settled down first?'

'You're forgetting Frazier.' Sam washed down his last mouthful with a sip of his drink. 'Married with twins, who'd have guessed that!'

'Yes, but my little brother was always an adult ahead of his time. I thought it would be you that settled down first.'

'I was waiting for you. Which makes me sound a bit sad and desperate.' Sam laid his knife and fork neatly on his plate and leaned back in his chair. 'I wasn't really waiting. As soon as we were teenagers, I knew our lives would take different paths. I wasn't surprised when you went to London and became a high-flying city vet.'

'I much prefer being a country vet. London never felt like home.' Phoebe finished her pie too and took a sip of Diet Coke. She was on call, but keeping her fingers crossed she wouldn't be called out. 'How's your mum doing? No more funny turns, I take it?'

'No. Have you spoken to your mum this week?'

'No. Why?'

Sam's eyes sobered a little. 'Because she came over to see Ma on Monday and I overheard them talking in the lounge. It was a panic attack Ma had.'

'Blimey.' Phoebe felt a little jolt of shock. Jan Hendrie, who'd always seemed the epitome of cheerful composure, was the last person she'd have expected to suffer with panic attacks. 'Oh, Sam. Your poor mum. How did they find out? We thought something was up, didn't we?'

'I don't think anyone at the hospital told her specifically it was a panic attack, but she's had them before.'

'Oh, my goodness. I didn't know. When?'

'Ma had postnatal depression after she had me.' He grimaced. 'I remember my Aunt Grace mentioning it once. Years ago. That's one of the reasons they didn't have any more kids. It was quite bad apparently.'

'You've never told me that before.' Phoebe felt a twinge of sadness that he hadn't trusted her with it.

'That's because I wasn't even sure it was true. Aunt Grace was fairly tipsy when she told me. It was never mentioned again. Ma's certainly never mentioned it and as far as I know, she's never had a problem since. But your mum obviously knew about it or she wouldn't have said anything. Besides,' he added ruefully, 'I didn't like the thought that my arrival was so traumatic for Ma that it somehow sent her off the rails.'

'I'm sure that's not true at all. I don't think even the medical profession know what causes PND. But it certainly wasn't your fault.'

'It wouldn't have happened if I hadn't been born. That's for sure.'

It was hard to argue with that. Phoebe wished suddenly that she wasn't on call. She would have liked a proper drink. She would have liked to have gone back to Sam's and shared a bottle of wine with him and talked about family secrets and how they could help Jan. The pub, which had seemed lively and warm a few minutes before, now felt overcrowded and noisy.

Phoebe also wished Sam had told her sooner. He'd carried this around with him all week while she'd been blissfully ignorant.

'What are you thinking?' Sam asked.

She told him and he held her gaze.

'I wanted to tell you face to face, Pheebs, that's why I didn't mention it before. And I haven't been walking around worrying about it. I'm glad Louella said something because it means that I can keep an eye on Ma, but as far as I can tell she's fine.'

'Does your dad know?'

'I guess he must know she had it before, but he certainly hasn't said anything about this time. You know what my parents are like. They find it hard to talk about "feelings".' He mimed inverted commas in the air around the word 'feelings' and Phoebe nodded. Jan and Ian Hendrie were lovely but they'd always been much more reserved than her family.

'I don't know how you turned out to be so well balanced, Sam Hendrie.'

'I think that's the nicest thing you've ever said to me.' His voice was half joking, half serious and he leaned over his plate and put his hand over hers.

Phoebe felt a rush of love for him. A tenderness so deep that her throat ached. He was such a strange mixture: practical and down to earth as well as gentle and eloquent, hugely stoic and massively perceptive, and at the core of him was an integrity and unselfishness he'd had since they were children.

She wondered if that was partly why he hadn't told her about his mother having PND. Or perhaps he really had been worried it might have been his fault.

They finished their drinks and Phoebe stacked their plates on the edge of the table for the server. 'Shall we go back to yours, Sam? We could chill and watch TV.'

'Please, not more *Loose Women*,' Sam groaned theatrically.

'You know you love it.'

'Or we could just have an early night?' He flicked her a glance. 'If you're not totally worn out.'

'That sounds like much more fun. I'll keep everything crossed that I don't get a call-out.'

'I'm not sure you can keep everything crossed,' he said with innuendo. 'Not all night.'

Phoebe caught his look and the chemistry sizzled between them. How had she ever thought there was no spark?

She jumped to her feet and tugged him to his. 'What are we waiting for?'

They were almost at the door when it opened, and two familiar figures appeared. Rufus and Harrison. Phoebe caught her breath. She'd known she would bump into him sooner or later – they lived and worked so close to each other – but it was still a shock. For a second, their eyes met. Rufus looked as startled as she felt, but he recovered himself very quickly.

'Good evening, Phoebe.'

'Hi,' she said, and acknowledged Harrison with a nod. She heard Sam, who was a couple of steps behind her, also murmuring greetings and then they were through the door, which Rufus was still holding, and out into the summer evening.

She and Sam exchanged glances.

'Is that the first time you've seen him?'

'Yes. But it's fine. Really, Sam, I don't think there are any hard feelings either on his part or mine. It's all good.'

It was true, she realised. It had been a surprise to see Rufus, but she had felt no animosity. No pain either, come to that.

Sam held her gaze for a second before looking satisfied and they headed to their respective cars and drove in convoy back to his flat.

Thankfully Phoebe had no call-outs. St Francis of Assisi, the patron saint of animals, must have been on their side and Phoebe woke up in Sam's king-size bed the following day in the honey-coloured half-light of dawn and rolled over on her side to look at Sam. He was lying on his back, one hand flung behind him, snoring softly.

The duvet covered his bottom half from the hips downwards but not his top and she could see his chest, lightly sprinkled with hair, and his flat taut belly, honed from all the physical exercise he did. A thin red scar ran vertically down his abdomen. A permanent reminder of the accident he'd had last year. Sam had told her the scar would fade but for Phoebe, suddenly, in that moment it was a reminder that even when you were blissfully happy and doing what you loved most in the world, life could still throw you a curve ball.

9

Rufus was dealing with his own curve ball in the shape of his son, Archie.

On Saturday, he had picked him up from summer pony camp where he'd been with his mate, Jack. Archie was not in a very good mood.

On the plus side, this was because he'd had such a brilliant time and didn't want to go home.

'I don't see why I have to come home now at all,' he'd said, the second his father had collected him. 'There's loads of the holidays left.'

'You've got to come home because there's a lot to get ready for school, and also because I'd like to spend some time with you. And also...' Rufus went on because he could see that Archie clearly wasn't impressed with either of these reasons and was about to interrupt, 'because you've got a selection of guinea pigs and rabbits to look after, or had you forgotten?'

'Emilia's looking after them,' Archie said, his face mutinous. 'She likes looking after them. She told me.'

'That doesn't mean she's going to look after them indefinitely.

You promised you'd rehome them all before you go off to school in September. You're going to need some time to do that.'

'Phoebe will help me,' Archie said confidently. 'She's very good at rehoming animals because it's what her grandmother does professionally. So it won't take long.'

Rufus winced. He needed to tell Archie that Phoebe was no longer going to be a part of their lives. But he knew he needed to pick his moment for that and it certainly wasn't now while he was driving the Mercedes back to Beechbrook between patches of dried-out heathland dotted with yellow gorse. It hadn't rained for days.

'Emilia is going back to Switzerland when you become a boarder,' Rufus said because he was pretty sure that Archie was going to find that the least traumatic piece of news he had to tell him. 'She needs to get ready to go home and she wants to say goodbye properly to you.'

Not that Emilia had shown any sign at all of getting ready to go home, Rufus mused, which wasn't really surprising as she wasn't planning to leave for another couple of months.

'Why does Emilia have to go?' Archie's voice dropped into sadness.

'Because she'll no longer need to look after you,' Rufus explained patiently. 'Once you go off to school, Emilia will have nothing to do. We've been through this already, son.'

'But she looks after you too. She cooks all the meals.'

'But the main reason she lives with us is because she looks after you. She only cooks for your grandfather and I because she's cooking for you.' Emilia had taken over the whole household's catering a year or so ago and Rufus, who'd felt relieved at the time, because it saved him a job, hadn't objected too much. Emilia was a very good cook, even if she did insist on batch cooking wholesome Swiss dishes most of the time so they never ran out of what she called 'excellent, nourishing food' and Rufus occasionally dreamed of the old days when he managed to justify a pizza or a ready meal if he was too busy to cook.

Archie had lapsed into silence, which hopefully meant he was coming round to the idea of saying goodbye to Emilia.

'Besides,' Rufus added, 'Emilia has her own family in Switzerland. She wants to go back and live with them.'

'I bet she doesn't,' Archie said just loudly enough for Rufus to hear. 'She doesn't like any of them very much.'

This was news to Rufus. 'Did she tell you that?' He shot a glance at his son, who was now playing with his phone, in the passenger seat beside him.

'She's told me it loads of times.' Archie's cheeks had gone a little pink. 'She had a big bust-up with her parents and her sister's a verrücktes huhn.'

'A what?'

'It means crazy chicken. Emilia taught me it. She's taught me loads of words.' His face went even pinker.

Rufus decided not to ask what kind of words. By the look of it, there probably weren't many polite ones.

'Archie, this isn't up for discussion. Emilia was only employed to look after you. You know that.'

'S'pose.' Archie bent his head over his mobile and Rufus didn't say anything else. Perhaps he shouldn't have brought it up as they were on the way home. Perhaps it had been a bit tactless. Archie had had so many changes in his short life. Rufus hated the fact that he'd be going through so many more soon, no matter that most of them were really positive ones.

An hour later, Rufus turned the Mercedes beneath the giant sculpture of a stag that straddled the gateway of Beechbrook House and they drove up the long driveway between the lavender fields. Harvesting had begun and there was a machine crawling slowly up the far corner of the field. A black dot of a beetle traversing a purple sea. For a while, Archie was distracted asking questions about that.

'Once we get unpacked, you can go and have a proper look. You can ask the farmer as many questions as you like. Maybe have a ride in the tractor. Would you like that?'

'No, thanks. I'm going to see my mini pigs.' Mini pigs was the name Emilia had always used for Archie's guinea pigs – and neither Rufus nor Archie had ever bothered correcting her, because it seemed a much better fit than the correct English version.

'Whatever you like, son,' Rufus said peaceably.

He parked the car, but before he had time to even get out, the main door of the house opened and Harrison appeared.

His friend's face was stern and Rufus felt a prickle of trepidation run down his spine. He hoped there weren't more problems with the harvesting. Yesterday they'd had so many hitches he'd thought they'd never get it done.

Harrison was hurrying across to the car. 'Hi, Rufus. I've been trying to get hold of you. Have you not had your Bluetooth on?'

'I thought it was on.'

Rufus felt around in his back pocket, realising that the familiar shape of his phone wasn't there. Come to that, he couldn't remember when he'd last seen it. He shrugged. 'Sorry. I'm not sure where my phone is. Are there problems?'

Harrison inclined his head, then bent to greet Archie. 'Hi, Archie. Good to see you.' He turned back and shot Rufus a look. 'Can we go in the house?'

'Yes. Of course.' Rufus didn't like the sound of Harrison's voice. Clearly this was something more serious than a problem on the estate if he didn't want to speak in front of Archie.

Fortunately, Archie was distracted. He'd opened the hatchback and was heaving his rucksack out.

Rufus leaned in to pick up his bigger case. 'I'll bring these in if you want to shoot straight out and see the animals.'

'Thanks, Dad.' Archie smiled for the first time and Rufus felt a wash of relief. His son seemed to have regained his usual sunny disposition. That was one thing less to worry about. Neither had he yet played his trump card, which was that he and Harrison had found a couple of possibly suitable ponies for Archie and they needed to arrange a time to go and look at them. He'd been saving this piece of news so he could offset, hopefully, some of Archie's disappointment when he heard that Phoebe was no longer going to be around. She had at least promised she was happy to stay in touch with Archie and that he was welcome to go to the animal sanctuary as much as he wanted.

As Archie ran ahead of him into the house, Rufus turned back to Harrison. 'I take it you didn't want to speak in front of the boy.'

'That's right.' Harrison's eyes went a shade darker. 'Your father's been taken ill again. The ambulance left here half an hour ago. They've taken him straight into Salisbury hospital. I was going to follow in my car, but I wasn't sure where Emilia was and I thought you might need someone to keep an eye on Archie. So I held on here.'

'Thank you.' Rufus felt as though the sun had gone in. There was a coldness creeping around his heart as he looked at his old friend's face.

'What happened?'

'He collapsed. He couldn't breathe. His lips were turning blue. It was so lucky I came in and found him when I did.' Harrison shook his head. 'I thought the drugs were controlling his heart problem.'

'As did I. Thank God you were here.' Rufus could feel his own heart thumping in fear. 'I'm so sorry you couldn't get hold of me.' As he spoke, he was patting his pockets and he finally found his phone, which he saw was in sleep mode because the battery was low.

'I'll get off to the hospital now. I'll charge my phone in the car. Can you tell Archie what I'm doing without alarming him too much? Where is Emilia anyway? I thought she'd be here to welcome us.'

'I've no idea. I haven't seen her. But yes, of course I'll stay.' Harrison stepped forward and patted Rufus awkwardly on the shoulder. 'I'm sure your dad will be fine. They probably just need to change the drugs, yeah. Drive careful, eh. I'll keep an eye on the boy.'

'I will, and thanks again.' Rufus turned and headed quickly back to his car. The trouble with very old friends was that you could read every nuance of their expressions and he'd just seen something in Harrison's face that had told him he hadn't believed what he was saying about the drugs. Not for a second.

By the time Rufus had got to Salisbury hospital, his recharged phone had beeped back into life and he saw a message from Emilia which said:

What time are you collecting Archie tomorrow? I will make sure I am home?

So she had got the day wrong. That explained a lot. Rufus voice messaged her on his way to the coronary ward and explained where he was. Then he switched his phone back on to silent. He'd been told to wait in a private room while they found someone to come and talk to him.

The fear that rose in him every time he went near a hospital flooded through his veins. Hospitals didn't spark off his PTSD like horses did, but he still found them deeply unnerving places. He'd been in a waiting room like this when a doctor had come to tell him that his wife, Rowena, was never going to regain consciousness.

A trickle of sweat ran down his back at the memory, even though this room wasn't hot. Rufus paced up and down to keep calm. He always found movement, even pointless movement, soothing.

His thoughts tangled and jumbled as he paced. Having anyone here would have helped to take his mind off the hideous present. Surely his father would be all right. He was on medication – but what if he'd not been taking it? He must try not to pre-empt. If someone didn't come soon, he would go back to reception and ask.

This thought had barely taken shape when the door opened, and a female doctor came into the room. She was fair-haired, blue-eyed and chisel-cheeked and just for a second, she put him in mind of Rowena, but she didn't have Rowena's English rose delicacy, or her warmth. She wore a stethoscope around her neck, along with a cool mask of professionalism.

She crossed to his side. 'I'm Dr Annika Adreen. Hello, Mr Holt.' She had the faintest of accents. Scandinavian perhaps.

'Rufus. Please.'

'Rufus...' There was a fraction of a second's hesitation as she met his eyes. 'I'm so sorry to have to tell you this, but your father suffered a cardiac arrest in the ambulance on his way to hospital. The paramedics did all they could, but unfortunately they weren't able to resuscitate him.'

For a moment, Rufus couldn't do anything except stare at her in shock. He felt as though he were in a bubble of stopped time where he could understand what she was saying – she was speaking perfect English, after all – but the words didn't make sense. His breath quickened, he could feel the air rushing in his head, clogging his throat. His neck felt too hot. He clawed with one hand at the collar of his shirt, struggling to breathe.

The doctor was speaking, or at least her lips were moving, but he couldn't hear what she said. Then she stepped forward, as if she'd suddenly grasped what was happening and now he could hear her properly. 'Breathe in, breathe out, breathe with me. That's it. Just breathe. In and out. In and out.'

Rufus did as she said, feeling the panic attack recede as he did so, but it was a few seconds before his ragged breathing felt normal enough to speak.

'My father has... died?' It was a huge effort to get out the words. 'But he can't have died. He was fine earlier.'

The expression on her face softened, and time in Rufus's world, which had halted temporarily, now stuttered forward a couple of seconds.

'He had end-stage heart failure, which meant his heart was under huge pressure. I'm so sorry, Rufus.' Her eyes met his. 'Is there someone I can call to be with you?'

He thought fleetingly of Harrison, who needed to be with Archie, and then Phoebe. She'd have been a good person to have with him. But it had been a shock bumping into her in the pub last night. He couldn't call Phoebe.

He shook his head. 'Er, no. No one. I'm fine. Thanks.' He could feel his face flaming with embarrassment and stress.

'May I see my father? Where is he?'

Her eyes held his for a second, as though analysing the situation, before she said, 'Of course. Come this way, please.'

Rufus followed her across the room, which seemed to have narrowed into a tiny square box, its walls lined with chairs, and along a bland corridor where there were other people hurrying by. He could hear voices, but they sounded muted, and yet at the same time his surroundings looked crystal clear and sharp. He was aware of tiled floors, and pale beige walls that were dotted with posters and hand sanitisers, and the dry, sterile air smelled of nothing.

Rufus felt like an automaton putting one foot in front of the other as he focused on following Dr Annika Adreen along the corridor. His throat felt dry now and his hands were clammy, and he could hear his own heart thundering in his ears.

There wasn't any pain yet. He felt very disconnected, as if this whole scenario was happening to someone else. A complete stranger. Yet all the while there was a voice repeating a sentence in his head. *This is the last time I will ever see my father. The last time. The very last time.*

But it wasn't until the doctor pushed open the door of another room and Rufus saw his father lying very still on his back on a hospital bed that the enormity of what had happened finally came home to roost. Rufus moved on feet he could no longer properly feel towards the bed. His father's face was wax-white. His eyes were closed. Every line on his face had smoothed out. It was almost as if in death he had reverted from being an old man to a child once more.

10

Rufus left the hospital an hour later. The bubble of shock that had enveloped him when he'd heard the news was still around him. He felt as though everything he did was measured and slow and his brain was icy calm, as if nothing really mattered. He was moving through a chain of events that was almost predestined, so he couldn't move outside of them, even if he'd tried to. He was on a relentless soldier's march across enemy territory, getting closer and closer to the point where all hell would break loose.

It had crossed his mind that he should phone Harrison before he left the hospital, but then he'd seen a message on his phone.

Hope all OK. Emilia is here with Archie. I'm meeting Tori but you know where I am if you need me. H

Rufus had answered it with a thumbs up emoji. He would need to tell Harrison the sad news face to face but that could wait. Harrison worked long hours – far more than he was contracted to do – and Rufus knew he would be leaning on his best friend and right-hand man heavily over the next few days and weeks. Let him have tonight's normality because there would be precious little normality tomorrow.

Back at Beechbrook House, Rufus parked his car, and paused to stare up at the stone façade of his ancestral home. He had been raised here and had escaped briefly when he'd married Rowena. For a while, they'd lived in a normal house, or at least it was normal in comparison to Beechbrook House.

The old, golden-gabled farmhouse had been situated on the edge of Hampshire, with paddocks and stabling for the horses that had been his wife's passion, back in the days before horses had meant pain and terror for Rufus. They had been the happiest days of Rufus's marriage, if not his entire life.

They'd only come back to Beechbrook when it had become clear that Rufus needed to step up and take on more of the running of the estate. Even those days had been happy because Rowena had been the beautiful glue that had helped him and his father to become a family unit. The old lord, who came from a generation of traditional stiff upper-lipped, ramrod-backed men to whom duty was more important than anything in the world, had softened as he'd got to know Rowena and his only grandson. There had been Sunday lunches and laughter and even a fraction of movement towards the modern world, an acknowledgement that times and traditions had changed and maybe some of those traditions weren't all that bad.

Sadly, this had all changed again after Rowena's death. His father had reverted back to the man he'd been before. Austere and dictatorial, and unable to show his emotions, whether they were good ones or bad.

Instead of being united in grief by the woman who'd once united them as a family, it had seemed that a wedge of pain and denial had driven them even further apart than they'd been before.

Rufus had often wondered what would have happened between

him and Phoebe if his father had approved of her, which he never had. Phoebe Dashwood, with her hazel eyes, sharp intelligence and huge compassion, had come very close to breaking down Rufus's walls. The closest any woman had come since he'd lost his wife. He would have fallen in love with Phoebe if he hadn't put the brakes on. But he'd slammed them on at the last minute. This hadn't just been because their lives were so incompatible, which was what he'd told her. It was because he'd known that Lord Alfred Holt, so stuck in the past, would never have fully accepted Phoebe. Not because she wasn't of their class, but because of something that had happened a few generations back.

His great-great-grandfather had gambled and lost Puddleduck Farm and some land, which had once all been part of the Beechbrook Estate, to Phoebe's great-great-grandfather, who before that had been virtually penniless. A game of poker four generations ago had been the real reason that Alfred wouldn't have accepted Phoebe.

Rufus had, on occasion, wished he was more like Harrison, who'd cut off all ties with his own family long ago, because he'd wanted to be free to live the life he wished, rather than the life they wanted for him.

But he'd only ever contemplated this for a moment. He could not cut off his father. He could not abandon him. The core of duty and responsibility that ran through the middle of his father, like words through a stick of rock, ran through Rufus too. He could not deny his father a son nor a grandson and this was what cutting himself free of the family responsibilities would have meant.

Rufus gave a deep sigh as he forced his thoughts away from the past and back to the present. He was still standing outside in the gravel turning circle. He didn't want to go in. The weight of that responsibility and duty had never felt heavier than it did now as he looked up at the inscrutable paned windows of the house he now owned.

The setting sun reflected off them and into his eyes and he felt momentarily blinded. For a moment, he stumbled as he walked past the fountain with its ridiculous naked cherubs. He caught himself just in time and, realising suddenly that he was blinded by tears of grief, not sunlight, he swallowed hard. Then he straightened his shoulders again and, stiff backed, walked to the heavy old wooden front door.

He had to be strong for Archie. What use was a crying father?

He heard voices as soon as he entered the house. It sounded as though Archie and Emilia were in the lounge. The bright chatter of his son and the clear, clipped vowels of his nanny hit his ears. He set his jawline, fought for composure and pushed open the lounge door, where he hesitated in the doorway.

'Dad.' Archie shot off the nearest sofa and came to meet him. 'Brilliant news. Emilia is staying until I go to school. That's really good, isn't it? She's going to help me find homes for Elastigirl and Violet, in case Phoebe is too busy, and she's going to come and look at ponies with us when we find one. If that's OK with you, of course?'

His eyes were as bright as stars and Rufus would have given everything he owned not to have to take that look away. But this kind of news couldn't wait.

Emilia had already seen his face and she'd jumped to her feet, a questioning look in her eyes. Then, as Archie sensed his mood, the boy's face slowly changed too.

'What's happened, Dad?'

Rufus perched on the arm of the sofa, and he beckoned Archie to sit beside him. 'I'm afraid I've got some very sad news about Grandpa.'

'Is he dead?' Archie's face shadowed, as he met his father's gaze, and his shoulders slumped a little.

'Yes, son, I'm afraid he had a heart attack. It was very quick, he didn't suffer.'

'But I can't say goodbye.'

'No, son.'

'Did you say goodbye?'

Rufus thought back to the moments he'd stood beside his father at the hospital. His face had been so still yet also somehow more relaxed, as if all the lines of tension had been ironed out of him. Rufus had bent and kissed his forehead, fighting against not just pain but all the years of regret when such intimate contact had been discouraged.

'I said goodbye for both of us,' he told Archie now.

'That's good.' Archie clasped his hands in his lap and looked hard at his fingernails and it was a movement that almost broke Rufus. God almighty, was he really going to let his child grow up in the same way he had? Too inhibited in times of grief to even express his emotions.

No, he bloody wasn't. He shifted off the arm of the sofa and sank into the chair beside his son and he pulled him close. 'It's OK to be sad, son. It's OK for us to cry. It's a very sad time.'

For a second, Archie sagged against him and Rufus felt his small shoulders heaving and he held him tightly. His own throat was tight with painful emotions, and he wished for the luxury of tears that Archie had. He wished he could sob and sob but now that he wanted to cry, he couldn't do it. His eyes remained dry.

Rufus wasn't sure how long he sat there, holding his son. Nor was he sure when Emilia had decided to leave them to their grief, he hadn't heard her go, but the next time he looked up, she wasn't in the room and the door was closed.

* * *

Much later, having put his son to bed and promised that he'd stay close until he fell asleep, which he had, Rufus tiptoed out of Archie's room and went downstairs. The house already felt different. His father's presence was gone. It was 10 p.m. and even though their paths wouldn't have crossed at this time of night – they mostly saw each other for mealtimes and their weekly work meetings – the house felt totally empty.

And this was despite the fact that every inch of it, from its thick red carpets to its dusty old portraits and dark furniture, was a nod to a bygone era that his father had never wanted to alter. In fact, Rufus was pretty sure the furniture had been the same since his great-grandfather's day.

He wandered aimlessly through the spaces, from hallway to study, pausing to finger the arms of his father's favourite chair, the dents in the arms worn by years of use, then into the kitchen, where his father's favourite mug was upside down on the draining board. Rufus stared at it for a second.

He didn't have a clue what to do with himself. He didn't anticipate being able to sleep. Insomnia was a faithful companion at the best of times and there was no way he'd sleep tonight. He contemplated getting a whisky. He rarely drank much either, but wasn't a drink supposed to be good for shock? He went back into the lounge again and did a double take when he saw Emilia standing by the drinks cupboard.

She'd already opened it and had poured out a glass of amber liquid. She must have read his mind. Without a word, she crossed the room and held it out to him.

'Thank you.' He took the glass, sipped it and then downed it in one. What the hell, he didn't need to pretend in front of Emilia. She knew him well enough. While she'd been in his employ, she'd seen arguments between him and his father, heated discussions between him and Archie, and then earlier today, the grief. Emilia wasn't judgemental.

The afterglow of the fiery liquid burning its path down his throat seemed to focus him. Maybe that's why they said a stiff drink was good for shock. Deciding that this was the best thing he'd done since he'd got the news of his father's demise, Rufus went to the bar and poured himself another one. Alongside the bottle he'd picked up was another: his father's favourite Scotch. Half full, with a sprinkling of dust around its neck, testimony to how little his father ever let his hair down. Rufus flinched.

'Will you join me?' he said, turning back to Emilia.

'Just for one drink.' Her voice was soft. 'I am very sorry to hear of Lord Alfred.'

'Thank you.' He poured her a whisky from the same bottle that he'd poured his and took both glasses to the coffee table by the sofa where he'd sat with Archie earlier.

Emilia sat in the armchair opposite him, holding the glass with one hand while her other arm lay along the leather arm of the chair. They must have sat here dozens of times but tonight felt different. Perhaps because she didn't usually hang around when Archie was in bed. Even lately, when Archie hadn't even been here, Emilia hadn't spent much time with Rufus. He didn't know what she did in her free time – he'd never seen her with a friend, although he'd often seen her on the phone talking to them, her voice animated and giggling. It struck him that he didn't even know if she had a boyfriend.

'His death was unexpected, ja?' Her voice broke into his thoughts and Rufus blinked and then nodded.

'I didn't realise how sick he was. I didn't expect him to have a heart attack. I thought he had years left.'

It was true. Alfred hadn't been that old. He hadn't even reached his seventieth birthday and up until recently he'd been quite fit, playing golf, eating well, he'd barely drunk alcohol, he'd never smoked.

'I thought this too,' Emilia said. 'But death is not always fair, and never is it a good time to come calling.'

'No.' Rufus rubbed his temples. 'I didn't have time to say good-bye. My father died in the ambulance on the way to the hospital. I didn't have time to say the things I wanted to say.' The whisky must have loosened his tongue. Now he'd begun to talk, he couldn't stop. 'I should have been here with him at the house, I might have been able to do something to save him.'

'You would not,' Emilia said.

'But how do you know?'

She shrugged. 'Because I think that this is sadness talking. How do you say... *der kummer* – I'm sorry. I do not know English word.'

'Grief,' Rufus said, hearing his voice crack. 'The English word is grief.' He gave a small, involuntary sob. Then he put down his glass, empty again, and covered his face with his hands. 'I'm sorry. I'm so sorry.'

In an instant, Emilia was there. He felt her slight weight dip the leather seat beside him and then he felt her arm go around his shoulders, holding him, in the same way he'd held onto Archie earlier. 'This is OK. Not a time to say sorry. You must have this *trauer*. This is normal. It's OK.'

She carried on speaking, murmuring in a mixture of English and German so that Rufus was no longer sure what she was saying, but the sound of her voice was comforting and the touch of another human next to him was comforting too, and he no longer cared that it was Emilia. All he could feel was pain, his inhibitions released by the alcohol, and what seemed to be an endless wave of grief that poured out of him, unstoppable.

Rufus had no idea how long they sat there. Time seemed to

have tunnelled out into one long moment. He was aware only of being totally in the present, of Emilia's warmth, her voice, the soothing touch of her hands on his forehead as if she were comforting a child, and then finally of her stillness too. He thought fleetingly that she may have fallen asleep, holding him in her arms, but when he shifted slightly away from her so he could see her face, he realised she was not asleep. She was smiling.

'This feels better now. Ja?'

There was only the smallest question mark in her voice. She knew how much better he felt. He could see it in her eyes. Their faces were very close together.

'It does.' He couldn't believe the relief. He felt as if he had just washed out years of grief. Maybe he had. He couldn't remember the last time he had cried like this.

'Thank you,' he said, hearing his own voice come out a little husky. 'Thank you.'

In answer, she tilted her head up towards him and Rufus, as though drawn by an invisible thread, bent his head down towards hers and he kissed her. She tasted of whisky and sweetness, and very fleetingly, Rufus thought of Rowena, they'd occasionally drunk whisky together, but then he was back in the present. He wasn't kissing Rowena, he was kissing Emilia, and she was kissing him back. And it felt totally right. It felt as though it was the only sane thing to do – a progression from the release of the terrible grief he'd spent so long holding inside him, straight through to the life-affirming elemental desire to make love. It was such a shock to Rufus that for a few moments he held back, unsure that this was what Emilia wanted too, but she caught hold of his hands, drawing him back against her, and Rufus gave up trying to resist. For the first time in years, he gave in to the intensity of his feelings and fully let go of all of the resistance that had held him so painfully in the past.

11

The news of Lord Alfred's demise reached Phoebe on Monday evening when Tori phoned her to tell her.

'There'll be an official announcement in the press, in view of him being Lord Holt, but I thought you'd like to know first.' Tori sounded sad as she relayed what Harrison had told her about Lord Alfred dying in the ambulance on his way to hospital.

'Gosh,' Phoebe said. 'How awful for them. Thank you for telling me. Poor Rufus, and poor Archie.'

They talked a while longer about life, work, and baby news – Tori said she was feeling very tired, but that was to be expected – and they promised they'd catch up in person as soon as they could. They had the kind of friendship that could survive long physical breaks.

When Phoebe had been in London doing her vet training and during her first job, she'd hardly seen her best friend at all, but they always managed to catch up at whatever point they'd left off whenever they did actually meet again.

After she'd spoken to Tori, Phoebe's head was full of the Holts. She hadn't known the old lord very well. He'd always been polite, but conversations with him had felt superficial and stilted. Poor Rufus and Archie must be devastated. She wondered if it was appropriate to call and offer her condolences, but eventually she decided it wasn't and she sent a card instead.

It felt odd, giving it to Sam to put in the post box when she could have just delivered it by hand to Maggie's next-door neighbour – she went past the entrance to Beechbrook House every day – but she realised she didn't want to risk bumping into any of the Holts. It was too soon.

* * *

The funeral took place at the end of August. As Tori had said, there was an official announcement in the press, and Phoebe and Maggie sent flowers, from 'all of us at Puddleduck', but the paper had stated the funeral would be a private affair.

Rufus hadn't acknowledged either the flowers or the card Phoebe had sent. He would have inherited the title of lord when his father had died, and he was probably mired in a mountain of paperwork and protocol, so Phoebe wasn't really surprised.

There had still been no word from Archie either. Even the pictures of horses had stopped coming now. Maybe Archie was upset that she and his father had split up. He might even be cross. However he was feeling, Phoebe had no wish to add to his pain, even though her heart went out to the little boy who'd lost so many of his relatives in his short life.

Phoebe guessed she probably wouldn't see either of them again and, despite herself, she felt a sense of loss. Maybe Rufus had decided a clean break was better for his son as well as himself, and maybe he was right.

She knew she could have found out what was happening at Beechbrook House by asking Tori, but she didn't feel comfortable doing this. It wasn't really any of her business, after all. So she tried to put the Holts out of her mind. Rufus and all of his problems were part of her past. Sam was her future and she and Sam were very happy.

They had made a pact that no matter how busy they were, they would have a proper date night at least once a week – a date night that would be set in stone – and for the rest of the time they'd be flexible and fit in impromptu meetings whenever they could. They'd also accept the fact that sometimes they'd have to cancel arrangements and they'd try not to let it become an issue.

This was working well. They'd met for lunch in Bridgeford a couple of times when Phoebe had been able to get away. And Sam occasionally popped over to Puddleduck after he finished work at Hendrie's on his way through to see to Ninja.

One beautiful late summer evening, they'd even hired a horse from Brook Stables so that Phoebe could go riding with Sam. It had been brilliant, trotting through the forest, sunlight dappling the paths, with nothing to disturb the peace but the jingle of their horses' tack, the creak of the leather saddles, the muted thud of hooves and everywhere the sound of birdsong and the smell of the fresh forest air.

'There is nowhere in the world I'd rather be,' Sam had told Phoebe when they'd slowed to a walk once more, their horses blowing gently.

'Me neither,' she'd said, looking at his strong, handsome profile, as she lengthened her reins so the mare she was riding could stretch out her head.

'And there is no one I'd rather be with,' Sam had added, shooting her a glance.

'Same,' she had agreed, feeling a rush of love for him.

'Have you ever fancied making love alfresco?' Sam had asked her.

Phoebe had looked at him. 'In the forest? It would be a bit tricky with a couple of horses in tow.'

He had laughed. 'I didn't mean now. And it doesn't have to be in a forest. It could be on a beach or by a river?'

'It would have to be a very private beach or river,' she had said.

'But you wouldn't rule it out.'

'I wouldn't rule it out.' She'd felt a fizz of expectation.

She still felt a fizz of expectation every time she thought of that conversation. Sam never ceased to surprise her.

* * *

In early September, Maggie invited her whole family to a Sunday supper at Puddleduck Farmhouse to discuss wedding plans. It wasn't the first time they'd all been summoned to discuss wedding plans. Phoebe wasn't sure what else actually needed discussing at the moment. Maggie and Eddie had already chosen the venue, the same church Frazier and Alexa's twins had been christened at, and the reception would be at Puddleduck Farm – they had caterers coming in.

Phoebe and Alexa were bridesmaids, not that Maggie expected them to dress up like pink princesses, as she put it. Maggie was not wearing a traditional white dress; she was going in what she called sensible clothes. She hadn't quite decided on her outfit yet, which meant that Phoebe and Alexa hadn't organised theirs either, but apparently they would be wearing dresses that were elegant and simple and could definitely be worn again. Phoebe had left it at this for now.

Eddie and Maggie had also worked out the guest list, which was small with just family and closest friends, but hadn't yet sent the invites, as they'd had to be redone once already because of date changes.

Maggie, with help from her nearest and dearest, had also decided on music and flowers and – very importantly – which animals were going to attend the reception. Tiny and Buster would be there, of course, wearing their best collars, and so far Phoebe had managed to talk Maggie out of having the neddies along too. Donkeys weren't renowned for behaving themselves when there was food around, but Maggie wouldn't budge. The donkeys were coming to the reception. Phoebe guessed she should be relieved they weren't coming to the church.

Even the honeymoon was now planned. Eddie and Maggie were off on a Saga cruise to the Caribbean – a wedding present from Louella and James. Neither of them had ever been to the Caribbean and they were as excited as little children.

Phoebe was pretty sure that everything that needed organising (apart from the bridal outfits) had already been arranged. Or at least it would have been if Maggie hadn't kept changing her mind. It wasn't just the date she'd altered three times. The colour scheme, the food and the music had all been chosen and then discarded more than once.

Phoebe didn't mind about the backtracks and changes of plan one bit. It was lovely to see her grandmother so lit up about the wedding. When Farmer Pete had died a few months after they'd both retired, Maggie had been broken and depressed. Taking in animals to look after – initially it had just been Neddie, one of the donkeys – had given her a reason to carry on living. Phoebe was thrilled her grandmother was getting a second chance at love in her mid-seventies.

On the Sunday of Maggie's get-together, Sam picked Phoebe up from Woodcutter's and when they got to Puddleduck Farmhouse, Phoebe saw both her brother's and her parents' cars already in situ. She wondered if Frazier and Alexa had got a sitter or whether they would have the twins with them.

Judging by the peace of the house, as they went through the front door, which was unlocked, they'd managed to get a sitter. Phoebe was disappointed she wouldn't get to see her niece and nephew, although she had to admit it would be less chaotic without the toddlers.

'Is anyone home?' Phoebe shouted from the hall.

There was no answer.

'They must all be in the kitchen,' Phoebe told Sam, who was close behind her, carrying a bottle of wine they'd picked up en route.

But the kitchen was empty too – although it smelled of food and looked as though it had been only recently vacated. There was a plate of labelled up vegetarian sausage rolls, half of them gone, on the huge farmhouse table, and beside that an empty plate that looked as though it might have contained the more traditional version.

Alongside that was a plate of beef sandwiches, or more precisely a few bits of bread and butter that had been opened and the beef removed.

'That's odd, they've started eating without us.' Phoebe looked at the clock on the wall, which said six forty-five. 'We're not late, are we? I thought Maggie said seven.'

'I don't think any people have eaten anything.' Sam gestured towards Tiny, who was currently sprawled out on the flagstone floor by the Aga with what looked like an empty plastic container upended next to him. The giant wolfhound raised his head, licked his lips and wagged his tail, but didn't bother getting up to greet them.

'The little bugger,' Phoebe gasped, glancing back at the half-empty plates. Not that Tiny could be considered *little* by any stretch of the imagination. 'I wonder why he didn't finish the rest.'

'Probably because he'd had all the best bits. He's had all the beef out of the bread and he must have nicked half the veggie rolls before he realised they weren't meat. He's not daft, is he?'

Phoebe clapped her hand over her mouth. 'Jeez, you're right. Maggie is not going to be pleased. He hasn't touched the egg mayonnaise sandwiches either.'

'I don't blame him.' Sam wrinkled his nose. 'A thief with taste!'

'I'm surprised they left him alone with the food.' Phoebe hurried across to where the wolfhound lay and picked up the plastic tub, which was labelled 'Charlotte potato salad, Tesco finest'. It had been licked clean. She showed Sam. 'That's his favourite.' She shook her head and glanced back at the wolfhound. 'You are very naughty.'

Tiny thumped his tail in agreement and went back to sleep.

'Where are the dalmatian puppies?' Sam asked.

'They're in the barn. Are we still thinking of having one?'

'Would you like to?'

'My heart says yes and my head says we're too busy. They'll be ready to go soon, though, so I guess we should make a decision.'

She crossed to the stable-style back door. The top half was open and there was no sign of her family in the yard either. 'I'm going to see if I can find anyone. Do you think one of us should stay and guard the food?'

'No. I think Tiny's had everything he fancied.' Sam stared around the big farmhouse kitchen with its wooden worktops and nooks and crannies. 'Besides, it would be tricky to put it out of his reach unless it was on top of a cupboard. He's tall enough to reach all of the worktops.'

'Yep.' Phoebe shook her head ruefully as they both went out into the yard.

They walked past the barn, which had once been a milking parlour and now housed the animals that couldn't go anywhere else, like Saddam, a feral cat Maggie had rescued, and the occasional litter of kittens or injured creature. Beyond the barn, they navigated their way around a scattering of puddle ducks and geese. Phoebe kept a wary eye out for Bruce Goose, who had a habit of flying at your legs. She was relieved Bruce Goose wasn't on the guest list for the wedding.

Puddleduck Vets was deserted too. Not that Phoebe had really expected to find any of her family in the vet unit. But where on earth were they?

One or two curious cats looked out from the cattery block and a cacophony of barking began as they went past the kennel dogs, but the place seemed deserted of people.

It was most peculiar.

The small front field was currently home to the sanctuary's three donkeys, Roxy, Diablo and Neddie, all of whom were grazing peacefully in the evening sun.

Five Acre Field was empty. Maggie had recently fenced off a part of it so she could restrict the grazing – donkeys were prone to getting laminitis if they were on rich grass, but this way they could be moved around as and when the grazing got low, without too much risk.

Phoebe shielded her eyes to look across Five Acre Field, which rolled gently upwards towards the boundary of the Beechbrook Estate. A belt of woodland marked the boundary. It had been planted by the Holts to shield Puddleduck Farm from view. Maggie had once told her that the Holts had planted it so they didn't have a permanent reminder of what they had lost in a poker game. Out of sight was out of mind. Phoebe wasn't sure whether this was true. It hardly mattered any more. A few years ago, the Holts had bought back most of their original land from Maggie when she'd run into financial difficulties. To be fair, she hadn't thought she would need it once the dairy farm had sold its last churn of milk. But that had been before she'd realised the place would become an animal sanctuary. These days, Maggie rented back all the grazing land, as well as some of the land that housed the more modern blocks, from the Holts.

With her eyes still shielded against the evening sun, Phoebe saw a group of people gathered around something in a far corner of Five Acre Field. So that's where her entire family had got to, but what on earth were they doing?

She pointed them out to Sam, who screwed up his eyes in puzzlement.

'Shall we go and see?'

They climbed over the five-bar gate into Five Acre, but they hadn't got far across the field when there was movement in the circle of people. They heard raised voices and then suddenly a horse broke free of the circle and came careering in their direction.

Phoebe had a strong feeling of déjà vu. The horse seemed to be heading straight for Sam but unlike the one at the New Forest Show, this one wasn't wearing a bridle, but just a blue headcollar, so there were no flying reins to catch. It was a showy-looking bay with a dark coat and black mane and tail and it was in a tearing hurry. The sound of its hooves on the sun-baked grass was like thunder as it raced in their direction.

Sam met Phoebe's glance, then gave a slight shake of his head, as he stepped back out of the path of the horse, which then veered to the left of them and galloped towards the fence.

'That one wasn't stopping,' he told her breathlessly. 'That's a horse on a mission.'

He was right. The horse hardly faltered. It cleared the stock fence with a foot to spare and they both heard the clatter of hooves on concrete as it landed in the yard beyond, stumbled slightly before recovering and continuing out of sight.

Phoebe winced. 'That won't do its legs any good. But at least it shouldn't be able to get out of there. We shut all the gates, didn't we?'

Sam nodded. Like her, he'd been taught from an early age that an open gate could lead to animals escaping onto the road, which could cause mayhem, even though they were in cattle grid territory and the New Forest animals wandered at will day and night.

Phoebe saw her family were now hurrying towards them in a straggle, headed up by Maggie and Eddie, who, despite the fact they were the elders of the group and Eddie used a stick, were making the fastest progress over the uneven ground.

'I think we'd better find out what's going on,' Phoebe said to Sam, as they waited for them to catch up.

12

'Good grief,' Maggie said, puffing slightly as she reached them. 'The things I do for love.'

Frazier and Alexa arrived next, with Louella and James Dashwood close behind, and Phoebe saw both her mother and her sister-in-law were hampered by their outfits. Smart skirts and kitten heels. Not the best footwear for the uneven ground in Five Acre Field.

'Did you see her take the fence?' Frazier's voice was full of admiration. 'I never thought she'd do that.'

'Neither did I!' Alexa looked towards the fence in awe. 'I didn't even know horses could jump that high.'

'The highest a horse has ever jumped is eight foot one inches,' Frazier told them with authority.

Frazier's superpower was an almost photographic memory for facts. 'It was set by a Chilean rider in 1949 and it's never been broken.'

'Blimey.' There were gasps and murmurs from the rest of the party.

'Hopefully they wouldn't attempt that height now,' Phoebe said with a shudder. 'Sounds flaming dangerous!'

'Hear, hear,' Maggie said. 'But coming back to this century, we still need to catch that blasted mare. Although that should be easier in the yard.'

'What's she doing here anyway?' Phoebe asked, as they all set off again more slowly towards the gate that led back into the yard. 'I didn't know you had any horses.'

'I try not to take them. But it was urgent. And they said it was temporary.'

'Who did?'

'It's a long story,' Louella said. 'We were only halfway through it when Eddie came to tell us that the horse had escaped.'

'She jumped into Five Acre Field from the sectioned-off part,' added James. 'Isn't that right, Eddie?' He raised his voice so that Eddie, who had limited hearing, could hear.

Eddie nodded, although Phoebe was doubtful he'd heard anything as he launched into a tale about a mate called Colin who lived over at Brook.

They'd been walking as they'd been talking and were now back at the gate that led into the yard.

Maggie paused and rested her elbows on it. 'To cut a long story short,' she began, 'that mare has been wandering free in the forest for the last few weeks. Eddie's mate, Colin, one of the agisters, finally caught her this evening. He thinks she may have been stolen and then dumped in the forest when the thieves couldn't get rid of her. The thief probably thought she wouldn't stand out too much in the forest, but a horse like that sticks out like a sore thumb to anyone in the know.' She turned towards Eddie, held up a thumb and screwed up her face in pain. Presumably to indicate a sore thumb. Maggie and Eddie spoke in a mixture of British Sign Language (BSL) and their own improvised signs.

Eddie whistled through his teeth and shook his head, before adjusting his hearing aid slightly.

'Crazy thieves wouldn't know a Thoroughbred from a Thelwell.' He touched the top bar of the gate and then pulled his fingers away as if he'd burnt them and blew on them.

'Eddie thinks the horse was too hot to handle,' Maggie said, in case anyone hadn't got the reference. 'Or possibly just too difficult to handle. Judging by what we've seen so far.'

'Could she just be an escape artist?' Louella asked. 'Maybe she jumped out of her own field and ended up in the forest?'

Everyone looked at Sam, the resident horse expert.

'That's possible, but I'm guessing if that was the case, someone would have missed her. She's a nice-looking horse. I'd agree with Eddie that she's definitely part Thoroughbred. Looks in good condition too, from what I could see when she galloped past.'

'She was first spotted back in July,' said Eddie, who despite his deafness was having no trouble at all keeping up with the chat. Phoebe wondered if he occasionally pretended to be more hard of hearing than he actually was. Or maybe he only turned his hearing aid on when he needed to participate.

'They haven't been able to catch her,' Eddie continued. 'But they didn't mention anything about her jumping out of fields.'

'I'd put her in the sectioned-off field because the grass is too rich in Five Acre Field,' Maggie explained. 'Unfortunately, she didn't stay there.'

It was all starting to make sense. 'Shall we see if we can catch her now?' Sam suggested. 'I can do that if you like. It shouldn't be too difficult in the yard. Should I put her in a stable, Maggie?'

'That might be best for now. Thanks. I was hoping Phoebe could scan and see if there's a microchip – you've got a scanner, haven't you, Phoebe?'

'Yes, of course.'

'I'll help catch the horse,' Frazier offered swiftly. 'If you guys want to go in and start talking weddings.'

Phoebe saw her brother and boyfriend exchange meaningful glances and knew immediately that the two men would far rather be catching errant horses than talking weddings. She didn't really blame them. There'd been a great deal of wedding talk lately.

'We're going to need some male input,' Louella objected. 'So don't be too long about it.'

'We'll be as quick as we can,' Frazier reassured. 'And we wouldn't dream of trying to get out of talking weddings, would we, Sam?'

'Nope. We're looking forward to it,' Sam said promptly.

'Actually, you can take us long as you like because we're also going to need to make some more sandwiches,' Phoebe said, remembering. 'I – er – think we may have had a cat burglar in the kitchen – well, a dog burglar, anyway.'

'Tiny?' Maggie said with a rueful shake of her head. 'Oh, Lord, I forgot to lock him out, didn't I?'

'He's left us a few of the veggie sausage rolls and all of the egg mayo sandwiches.'

James Dashwood, who was a big fan of egg mayo sandwiches, snorted with laughter and Alexa looked as though she was trying not to laugh too.

Then they were all laughing, even Maggie and Eddie.

'I'll nip into town and get us some fish and chips,' James suggested. 'Not that I'm trying to get out of the wedding talk, obviously.' His face went pink. 'I can't wait to talk about colour schemes and what music we're having at the reception and, er, all the other interesting details that we haven't already thrashed out till we're, er, blue in the face.' He cleared his throat and Louella gave him a sharp nudge with her elbow.

'We ladies will go in and have a lovely chat about it all, won't we,

Mum?' Louella looked at Maggie. 'We'll make sure we've got every i dotted and every t crossed.'

'Thanks, love.' Maggie beamed at her daughter. 'And we'll have some male input because we'll have Eddie.'

Eddie nodded sagely. He clearly didn't mind the wedding chat. Phoebe wondered if it was different when it was your own wedding. She couldn't imagine being married. Or maybe Eddie would just turn down his hearing aid again and let the whole thing wash over him.

*　*　*

James had got back with several fragrant parcels of fish and chips and Phoebe and Louella had laid the table and dished them all up before Sam and Frazier reappeared.

'You were a long time,' Maggie remarked as they came across the flagstones, looking a little ruffled. 'Did you have problems?'

'She didn't want to be caught,' Sam said, and Phoebe knew by the ultra-casual, understated tone of his voice that he was playing it down.

Her brother wasn't so subtle. 'That horse is bonkers. I'm not surprised the thieves dumped her in the forest. Assuming she was stolen, I mean.'

'What do you mean?' Maggie asked, narrowing her eyes.

'She kept standing on her hind legs,' Sam replied, frowning. 'That is pretty unusual, I have to say.'

Maggie spoke briefly to Eddie in a mix of words and sign language and he looked surprised.

'Colin said she was a handful. He didn't mention any rearing, though.'

'Are you two OK?' Alexa moved across to her husband, her face concerned. 'You didn't get kicked, did you?'

'No. We're fine. It was just unexpected. I was glad Sam was about. What makes them rear up like that, Sam?'

'They do it for all sorts of reasons. I think often the initial reason is fear and then they can develop a rearing habit. I don't think that horse was scared of us, though. She didn't look scared. It's odd.'

'But she's safely in a stable now?' Maggie questioned.

'Yes, we left her a hay net and water. And I checked her over in case we needed Phoebe's expert eye, but she looks fine.'

'Thank you.' Maggie gave them both a sweet smile. 'Eddie and I can sort her out tomorrow. Hopefully she won't be here too long. If she's microchipped, we can track down her owner. Come and sit down and we can get back to the reason we're here.'

'Fish and chips,' James quipped.

Maggie shot him a sharp look. 'Photography. I know we said we weren't going to bother too much about official photos, but I've been having second thoughts. I think I should hire a professional.'

'You don't need to hire anyone professionally,' Phoebe said. 'Not these days. Everyone has a phone camera. We can all take shots.'

'I'll sort out a plan,' Alexa offered. 'To make sure we get pics of everyone on the day.'

'Thank you.' Maggie beamed at her. 'OK then, I'll stop worrying about photography.' She tilted her head on one side, her eyes reflective. 'Do you have those soft-focus thingies on phone cameras? Daylight can be very harsh.'

'We'll make sure everyone knows to put on their soft focus,' Phoebe promised. 'And the beauty of digital photos is that they can be edited.'

'Can they really?' Maggie looked delighted. 'Does that mean I can have a peep at them before you print out the final versions?'

'Absolutely it does. Not that they'll need any editing, Maggie. You are going to look absolutely beautiful.'

This was a side Phoebe had never seen of her grandmother, who didn't usually give two hoots about her appearance. She spent most of her time slobbing about on Puddleduck Farm in old scruffs and ancient but comfortable boots which she said fitted her bunions perfectly.

Maggie's eyes shone. 'While we're on that subject, I'm planning to have my hair done at the little salon in Bridgeford. The one that's a few doors up from Hendrie's.'

'We can all go there, Mum,' Louella agreed. 'We should probably have a hair and make-up trial. That's the thing, these days, I think.' Her eyes twinkled. 'We could have our make-up done together too.'

'Or we could have a hair and make-up trial via a proper wedding company,' Alexa suggested, leaning forward and looking excited. 'That's definitely a thing.'

'Won't that cost a fortune?' Maggie looked doubtful.

Alexa shook her head. 'Frazier and I have been wondering what we could get you for a wedding present. In view of the fact that you said there's nothing you need, and you haven't got a wedding list.' Her eyes sparkled. 'This could be our present. We can pay for us all to have professional make-up and hair for the wedding. We can still use Bridgeford salon if you like them.'

By her side, Frazier was nodding enthusiastically. 'Brilliant idea.'

'Oh, good Lord.' Maggie's eyes widened. 'Do we really need to go that far?'

'It would save using the soft-focus button,' Phoebe told her happily. 'Although we can use that as well if you like. I'm definitely up for it.'

'Sorted,' Alexa said. 'Have you made a final decision on your outfit now, Maggie?'

This was another of the things that Maggie had been changing her mind about. The first outfit she'd chosen had been a maroon suit, but then she'd decided the colour made her look washed out. Then she'd picked a cream and yellow creation before deciding it wasn't very suitable for a winter wedding, and the last time they'd talked about it she had decided on emerald green, which was a colour that really suited her, but as far as Phoebe knew she hadn't chosen an actual outfit yet.

'I've seen a possible dress and jacket in Belinda's Boutique,' Maggie said. 'I was wondering if maybe we could all go and look at it together? Maybe one day next week or the week after – they're open till seven on a Wednesday, which I thought might be OK for you, Phoebe? Would that suit everyone else?'

There was a chorus of agreement, although Alexa said she might have to leave it until the Wednesday after as she had a long-standing arrangement with a girlfriend.

'Once we have your outfit sorted, we can sort ours out and the men's,' Louella said.

The men weren't listening. They'd been discussing wedding cars – Eddie had a mate who had a white Rolls-Royce he thought they could use – but they were now talking about ordinary cars and whether the government would ever get the infrastructure in for the number of electric cars they had planned.

Everyone had finished their fish and chips now and Buster had accepted a few pieces of leftover batter. Tiny had declined his. He was obviously still too full of sausage rolls and sandwiches.

Phoebe glanced at Sam across the table, chatting happily with her family. He fitted in so well, but then he'd known them all his life. As if aware of her gaze, he glanced up, caught her eye and smiled.

She smiled back. There was nothing like wedding talk to make you think about your own relationship. In the weeks when the practice wasn't so busy, she could see their future. She and Sam, sharing a life where their jobs jigsawed perfectly around each other and there was plenty of time for their relationship and all of their animals – well, Sam's animals.

Despite the fact that she was surrounded by them most of the time, Phoebe hadn't had her own pet since she was a child.

She leaned across the table and caught Maggie's attention. 'Sam and I were wondering if we could have a look at the dalmatian pups,' she began.

'Have you forgotten what they look like then, or is this a leading question?'

Phoebe felt her heart thump with excitement. 'It might be.'

'They're in the barn.' Maggie's eyes gleamed with amusement as she looked at her granddaughter. 'Same place they were yesterday.'

Phoebe knew Sam was listening with interest. He was now smiling at her too.

'We could just go and have a look, couldn't we?'

A few minutes later, Maggie, Phoebe and Sam were all in the barn, peering into a sectioned-off area where the pups were. Maggie had set up a crate at one end with bedding in and the run part was enclosed. The pups were currently asleep in the bed end of the run: four little spotty white bodies with their eyes tight shut. As they stood there, one of the pups stirred and yawned and the yawn ended in a small whine, before the pup rolled over and then woke up, looking surprised to see the visitors.

'Ahh,' breathed Phoebe and Sam in unison. 'They are so cute.'

'Aren't they?' Maggie clicked her tongue and the pup who'd woken got up and toddled across to meet them, blinking sleep out of his eyes.

He had brown ears and a sprinkling of brown spots on his head and dozens on his body.

'He's the only male,' Maggie said idly. 'So are you really thinking of getting a dog, you two?' She looked from one to the other and Phoebe saw the warmth in her eyes. 'Or did you just fancy a cuddle?' As she spoke, she leaned into the pen, scooped the puppy up, and handed him to Phoebe.

Phoebe took him gently, hugged him close to her body and breathed in the smell of young pup. 'What a little cutie. He's gorgeous. And yes, we are thinking of getting a dog, aren't we, Sam?'

'About time too,' Maggie said approvingly as Sam grinned in response. 'I wondered when you were going to realise you couldn't live without one.'

'I've always held off because of how busy I am,' Phoebe murmured, kissing the pup's head, who was trying to wriggle out of her grasp. 'But it's not as though a dog couldn't come to work with me. I've known a few practice dogs.'

'And it's easier with two people,' Maggie agreed. 'I couldn't think of a better couple to have a dog.' She glanced at Sam. 'What would your Snowball think of a canine companion?'

'Not much to begin with, I shouldn't think. But if it's a pup, at least he'd be able to show it who was boss from the off.'

Maggie nodded approvingly.

Phoebe handed the pup to Sam and he held him gently, tenderness in his eyes. 'He's gorgeous but I think he wants to get back in with his mates,' he said as the pup started to wriggle again. The other three pups were awake now too and they were all on their way to say hello, wagging their little tails so their whole bottoms wiggled in their enthusiasm to greet these unexpected playmates.

The one bringing up the rear, and also the smallest one, got side-tracked by a fly that had buzzed into the run and she fell over trying to catch it, before leaping up to try again and doing exactly the same thing.

Everyone smiled.

'If there was a definition of joy,' Maggie said, 'I think pups would be it. Are you thinking you'd like a girl or a boy? Or don't you mind?'

'We hadn't really got that far, had we, Pheebs?' Sam answered. 'Although I'm rather struck on our little flycatcher.'

'Me too.' Phoebe leaned into the run and stretched her fingers out to the smallest pup. 'She is beautiful. So pretty.'

The pup seemed to know she was the focus of their attention and she trotted across to Phoebe's outstretched hand, sniffed her fingers and then sat down and gazed up at them all.

She had a black spot above her left eye and a line of three black dots that ran diagonally across her white nose.

'She's my favourite too,' Maggie said. 'She's the most independent one. The others tend to hang around as a little gang but Madam here does her own thing. I was actually dreading letting her go.'

'Do you have homes lined up already?' Phoebe asked.

'Natasha's had more enquiries than we have pups,' Maggie said. 'Although we haven't vetted anyone yet, so nothing's arranged. As you might imagine, the vetting's pretty stringent.'

'Can they all hear OK?' Sam asked. 'That can be a problem with dalmatians, can't it?'

'Not with these. They've all got perfect hearing.' Phoebe clicked her tongue and the smallest dalmatian pricked up her ears and then gave a little whine and fixed her gaze on Phoebe, who picked her up. The pup snuggled into her neck with a little snuffle of contentment.

'She's adorable.' Phoebe felt a huge protectiveness welling up in her. 'What do you think, Sam?'

'I think we've made our decision, haven't we?'

He stepped across to her side and stood close, stroking the pup's back with the side of his index finger. After a few moments of this, Phoebe relinquished her for a cuddle and she could see Sam was just as smitten as she was.

'When are they ready to go?' she asked Maggie. 'How old are they now?'

'They're only about six weeks old. They won't have their jabs for another few weeks. You've got plenty of time to make sure it's definitely what you want.'

Phoebe nodded and kissed the top of the pup's head. 'I don't think we're going to change our minds, are we, Sam?'

'Not a chance.'

'Where's Saddam? I was a bit worried when you said the pups were in here. He wouldn't hurt them, would he?'

'No,' Maggie said. 'Funnily enough, that crazy cat's quite protective of these puppies. I was watching him the other day. He was over here sniffing about and then when one of the other farm cats came in, he arched his back and spat at her as though he was on guard. It was most odd. I thought it may be a coincidence, so I obviously kept an eye on things, but he did it more than once.'

'Maybe he's softening in his old age,' Phoebe said.

'Perhaps.' Maggie looked reflective. 'Your Marcus has been practising some of his behavioural stuff on Saddam. He said it's early days, but he thinks he's actually getting somewhere. And I think he might be right.'

'He never mentioned that to me. That he'd been practising on Saddam, I mean. Obviously I know about the behaviourist course. I'm paying for it.'

'To be honest, he told me to keep the Saddam thing under my hat. Your Marcus doesn't have much self-confidence, does he? I think he's scared he'll jinx things if he talks about it too soon, but he's a bit of an ace with animals.'

'Yes, I think you're right. Don't worry, I won't say anything.'

She knew her grandmother had a soft spot for her receptionist. It was Maggie who'd suggested Phoebe take him on in the first place. Marcus adored animals and he was good at his job, but Phoebe had noticed lately that he was far happier when he was in direct contact with animals than he was around people. She and Max had thought it would be great to have a qualified behaviourist at the practice, which was why Marcus was doing the course. He was loving every minute of it.

Being a full-time behaviourist would probably suit Marcus much better than being a full-time receptionist. They'd have him for at least a year when he was qualified because that was the agreement they had. But what about after that? Phoebe frowned.

She would have to cross that bridge when and if they came to it.

* * *

When Phoebe told her staff the next morning, before surgery began, that she and Sam were going to have one of the dalmatian pups, there was much excitement.

'I knew you wouldn't be able to resist,' Jenna said. 'I'd be having one myself if I didn't work all day.'

'Me too,' Marcus said. 'I'd have all of them.'

'What are you going to call it?' Max asked. 'Are you having a bitch or a dog?'

'A bitch.'

'Perdita then?' he suggested. 'After the one in *101 Dalmatians*.'

'No way,' Marcus objected. 'There are probably a thousand and one dalmatians already called Perdita in England. We've got at least two on our system.'

'Spot,' said Jenna with her tongue firmly in her cheek.

'Dotty?'

'Patch?'

'Penny?'

'Darcie?'

The names came thick and fast.

'Dolores,' Max suggested. 'I went out with a girl called Dolores once.'

'Was she very spotty?' Marcus teased.

'No, I just thought it would be good to have an alliterative name. Dolores the Dalmatian. Or Deidre maybe? If I had a male, I'd call him Dick. Spotted Dick,' he added, winking at Marcus.

'Candy Crush,' Marcus said. 'That's a good name.'

'Candy Crush?' Phoebe stared at him in amazement. 'It's a bit random?'

'I know.' He grinned at her. 'My old gran is hooked on online Candy Crush at the moment. She's just discovered it and my grandad can't get her off it – not even to make his tea.'

Everyone laughed.

The main door opened and Maggie came in. 'Morning, all. Sorry, did I interrupt something?'

'We're talking about names for dalmatians,' Marcus told her.

'Ah. Good. Names are very important. The quicker she has a name, the quicker she can learn what it is.' She put her elbows on the counter. 'Is it OK to borrow your scanner, love? I said I'd phone Colin first thing about that horse.'

'What horse is this?' Marcus asked, and Maggie told him while Phoebe went to get the scanner.

When she came back, they were still talking about the horse and all offering up various theories of how it had come to be wandering loose in the forest.

'What a mystery,' Jenna said.

'Well, hopefully it won't be a mystery for much longer,' Phoebe murmured. 'I've got a universal scanner – in fact, I've got two. I'll bring them both.'

'Have you got time, love?' Maggie asked. 'I'm sure I can scan an old mare.'

'No, it's fine.' She glanced at her grandmother. 'Besides, after what Sam and Frazier said last night about her behaviour, I'm a little wary. It might take more than one of us.'

'She's in a stable. She can't do very much damage in there.'

'Does she kick?' Marcus asked with interest.

'Sam said she reared a couple of times when they were trying to catch her,' Phoebe told him. 'She may have been quite het up. She'd just been galloping across a field.'

'Fair comment. But if you need a hand.'

'Thanks. We'll shout if we do.' Armed with the scanners, Phoebe followed her grandmother out into the yard.

A few minutes later, they were standing by the stable, which was really an old outbuilding that Maggie didn't use very much. It had once been a feed store and had a stable door. The mare looked peaceful enough at the moment. She was tugging on a hay net that Sam had hitched up to a hook, Phoebe observed, as her eyes adjusted to the dimmer light within, and she whinnied softly when she saw them.

'Hello, sweetie,' Phoebe said. 'It's a good job Sam thought to leave a headcollar on her. That should make life easier.'

'Would you like me to lead her out, or can you scan her in there?'

'No, it's fine. I'll go in. I'll be careful. Maybe if I bring her over to the door you could hold onto her headcollar. Just to stop her fidgeting.'

'OK, love, if you're sure. But promise me you'll come straight out if she kicks off. I'm not risking you getting hurt.'

'I promise.' Phoebe slid back the bolt and let herself into the stable, breathing in the scent of horse and trying not to show she was nervous, because she knew horses could pick up fear. She didn't have much to do with horses professionally. There was a specialist equine vet in the New Forest who picked up most of the work. But she'd ridden since she was a child and she was pretty comfortable around them.

To her relief, the mare did seem a lot calmer today. She blew on Phoebe's fingers and seemed happy enough to be led across to the stable door.

'Why did the agister bring her here anyway?' she asked Maggie. 'Was he expecting you to look after her?'

'Only as a temporary thing. He spoke to Eddie. But I think we were the nearest place and he knew I wouldn't say no. He said he'd already phoned the police to report the unauthorised grazing. It's illegal to release horses into the forest without permission, obviously, but the local station was closed. It's only manned part-time.'

Maggie's disparaging tone told Phoebe exactly what she thought of a police station that was only open part-time.

Phoebe stroked the mare's neck and then showed her the scanner and the horse blew on it, her nostrils wide, but quickly lost interest.

'OK. Here we go.' Phoebe ran the scanner up and down her neck. 'Microchips are always put in the same place. The nuchal ligament on the left side of the neck, just below the base of the mane.'

'What if she's not microchipped?'

'She should be. It's been compulsory since 2018, I think.' But despite running the scanner up and down very slowly a few times, Phoebe couldn't find anything.

Frowning, she repeated the process with the second scanner, while Maggie fed the mare some pieces of carrot she'd produced from one of her pockets.

'No joy?' Maggie asked.

'No. It's possible it may have moved. It's also possible that my scanners aren't picking it up. It depends when it was done.'

The mare whickered, almost as if she understood what was going on. Phoebe stroked her neck. She was so obviously used to being handled and seemed perfectly calm and gentle. It was odd about the rearing. If anyone but Sam had said it, she'd have assumed they were being overdramatic, but Sam wasn't a drama queen. Maybe last night, the mare had just been het up and afraid. Who knew what went on in animals' heads? Phoebe knew it was a mystery they'd probably never solve.

Neither were they going to solve the mystery of her owner any time soon either, Phoebe realised, as she took a closer look at the mare's neck.

'Can we get her out in the daylight for a moment, Maggie? I've just spotted something odd.'

A few minutes later, while Maggie held the mare's head, Phoebe confirmed that what she'd suspected in the dimness of the stable was unfortunately true.

'Take a look at this,' she told Maggie, hearing the edge of anger in her own voice. 'There's a scar. I think this mare's had her microchip surgically removed. Or dug out. It's something that I'd say would probably be done for nefarious reasons. Can you see, just here, there's a tiny little scar?'

Maggie's face darkened as she leaned in to look. 'Yes, I see it. Does that mean she's been stolen?'

'It means someone didn't want her microchip read. So yes, almost certainly. The odd thing is that this was done some time ago. Years, maybe. It's well healed, almost invisible. I'd say this is definitely a matter for the police.'

Maggie sighed. 'I'll let the agisters know. I'll let the police know too, but I'm not holding my breath. I don't think stolen horses are very high on their priority list.'

'I'll let Sam know as well. He's pretty well connected with the horse world. Someone must know something about her, surely.'

'Thank you.' Maggie stroked the mare's neck absently and fed her another piece of carrot. 'I'm guessing you might be around for a while then, my lovely.'

14

Sam was at Hendrie's, chatting to his mother. He had just flipped the sign on the door to closed for lunch. They'd been talking about holidays, which had been a hot topic in the shop that morning. It seemed every customer had just come back from one and was keen to share their experiences, and their photos.

'Are you and Pa planning anything now the kids have gone back to school?' Sam asked in his most ultra-casual voice as Jan tidied things on the counter. 'I can't remember the last time you went away on holiday.'

'We went to Pembrokeshire to see your Aunt Grace and your Aunt Judy last year,' she reminded him.

'Yes, but that was last year. Besides, I meant more of a proper break. Don't you ever fancy completely getting away from it all and lying on a sunny beach under a palm tree?'

'Abroad, you mean? Me and your pa?' She sniffed disparagingly. 'What would we want with abroad? Your pa would be bored senseless after five minutes and I'd get burnt to a frazzle. You know I'm not good in the sun.'

'Well, how about a canal trip then? Like Maggie and Eddie did at Easter. That would be good. You wouldn't get bored doing that, there's plenty to do on a canal. Drifting along on the water. Stopping for lunch at the waterside pubs.'

'Going in and out of locks every five minutes.' Jan gave a theatrical shudder. 'Sounds like hard work to me.' She shot him a look. 'We'll have a staycation like we usually do, I expect. Now stop mithering me, son, and go and put the kettle on. Or we'll have wasted our lunch break. Are you not going off to see Phoebe today?'

'She's usually too rushed to get away on Mondays,' Sam said. 'It's one of the practice's busiest days.'

He was aware he was being fobbed off on the holiday front, although he wasn't sure quite why. He decided to have a word with Pa about it when he could next get him on his own. His father worked like a trooper and Sam had often wondered if he was happy with the insular life that he and his mother shared.

Ian Hendrie certainly never complained but they rarely socialised or even went out very much. The highlight of their year socially was when his maternal grandparents came over from Spain. Jan Hendrie's mother, Eliza, was much more of an adventurer than Jan had ever been. She and Jan's father, Pat, had sold up in England and bought a villa in Benidorm years ago and they'd come back less and less in recent years – they'd pretty much grown roots in Spain. Sam had never had much to do with his paternal grandparents. He had vague memories of them being around when he was young, but Pa had lost touch with them years ago and so had Sam.

His mother sometimes said that she got most of her socialising from the shop – and Sam supposed to an extent this was true – she talked to people all day long. She certainly didn't miss much that went on in Bridgeford. The latest news on who was marrying who,

who had died, who'd started a new job, who'd retired, and who'd had a grandchild was all brought to the shop for her to digest. Hendrie's sold greetings cards, which helped. While people chose their cards, they gossiped to Jan, and because she was known as the soul of discretion – a woman who'd listen but wouldn't pass gossip on – everyone told her their secrets.

And she was good friends with Louella, Sam consoled himself. That wasn't work related.

Upstairs, Sam made coffee, while Jan made them a ham sandwich, and the subject switched to dalmatians. As Sam had expected, his mother was delighted that Sam and Phoebe were planning to get one.

'It'll be OK if I bring her in to work occasionally, won't it?' he said, and she laughed.

'Well, you brought that cat in to work for long enough when he was sick.'

Back in April, Snowball had had a run-in with a car and had come off very much worse than the car. He'd had a fractured pelvis and some internal injuries which Phoebe had fixed in her surgery. Sam had spent weeks nursing him back to health and had taken him into work every day.

Jan continued, 'Actually, I think Snowball was quite a draw. I reckon I had a 20 per cent increase in customers over those few weeks. I'm sure they came in to see Snowball, but most of them bought something while they were in.'

'Hmmm. I reckon we could up that. Dalmatian pups are incredibly cute. I could put her picture up in the window. Pet the pup while you post your letters.'

'Sam Hendrie, you know as well as I do that you'll never be that hard headed.' Jan's eyes twinkled and they both laughed.

Sam decided that he was seeing problems where none existed.

His ma did seem fine. Even if she didn't go out very much or fancy a holiday.

* * *

'We must be crazy,' Phoebe told Sam, as they stood in the pet shop in Bridgeford. They were both on their lunch break.

They'd just picked out a lightweight leather collar, a dark navy rope lead, a pack of puppy training pads and two sets of stainless-steel bowls. They were now standing at the checkout, waiting for the cashier, who was finishing up with the customer before them.

'At least we won't need to get a crate for her,' Sam said, 'I've still got the ones I bought for when Snowball needed confining. We can have one crate at yours and one at mine. They should be big enough.'

'We'll only need them for house-training. Although I was thinking that maybe that bit would be easier to do at mine because the garden access is easier. Or are you going to carry her up and downstairs every time she needs a wee?'

'Whatever it takes. I don't mind helping with house training.' Sam met her eyes steadily.

'I'm worried that we might confuse her if we keep shifting her from your place to mine. Perhaps we should do all of the house-training at mine.' Aware that the cashier was looking at them curiously, Phoebe added in an aside to her, 'We're co-parenting our puppy.'

'You're co-parenting from day one?' The cashier, who had pink hair and a nose stud, raised her eyebrows. 'Most couples only do that when they split up.'

'We live in separate places,' Sam said.

'It would be easier if you moved in together,' the cashier said, as she scanned the items through. 'Save a lot of back and forth.

Although then you wouldn't need two lots of bowls.' She hesitated. 'Are you sure you need two lots of bowls?'

'Yes,' Sam said, far too quickly for Phoebe's liking. A flush had crept over his face and he looked a little rattled at the cashier's question. 'We definitely need two lots of bowls.'

'And you're going for a lead, not a harness?' she queried. 'Lots of people use a harness these days.'

'We're starting with a lead,' Phoebe said, 'but thank you.'

When they were outside again on the street, which was busy with lunchtime office workers and tourists making the most of the Indian summer, Phoebe caught Sam's hand. 'Are you happy with me having her at mine for the initial house-training? I wouldn't have thought it would be that long?'

'I'm fine with it. And we'll need to think about how Snowball's going to react too – find out the best way to introduce them.'

Right now, Phoebe was less interested in Snowball's reaction and more interested in Sam's reaction to the cashier. He'd looked positively shocked. Was the thought of living with her so they could co-parent a puppy really that terrible a prospect?

'I didn't want you to think I'd just palm the difficult bits off on you, Pheebs.' Sam added, squeezing her fingers. 'I'm more than happy to do my share. A dog's a big commitment.'

'Great.' She decided she was being massively oversensitive.

A dog *was* a big commitment, and they'd spent quite a bit of the last week discussing it. On many levels, Phoebe knew it was crazy to add an extra responsibility to their lives, but a puppy would also be such a joy. When they'd talked about the practicalities, they'd mostly talked about the time when their pup would be big enough to go to work. They were both in a position to take a dog to work. Sam could take her riding when she was big enough, and Phoebe could take her on her rounds and she could be introduced properly to Tiny and Buster and all the other animals at Puddleduck Farm.

They'd also looked into which dog training classes they might go to – there were a couple of schools in the New Forest and they both did puppy socialisation classes. It had all been so exciting and Phoebe had felt a little like they were planning their child's future. *What school will she go to? Are we in a good enough catchment area or do we need to move?*

They hadn't talked about the nitty gritty practicalities of puppy training in two places. Until Sam had mentioned that it was a good job he had two crates, she hadn't really thought about it either. There was a part of her that had envisaged they'd do it together and in her imaginings they'd always both been at Woodcutter's because it made more sense to be there than at Sam's. But now it seemed he'd got other ideas.

She was so deep in thought that it was a shock when Sam spoke.

'Penny for them,' he said.

Phoebe realised they were back at Hendrie's Stores, she'd been walking on autopilot, and she was jolted into reality. 'I was just thinking how exciting it's going to be,' she said, which was pretty much the gist of what she'd been thinking.

She didn't want to tell him she felt disappointed they wouldn't be sharing the house-training. Of course he wouldn't want to be at Woodcutter's all the time. In the brief time she'd been seeing Sam, they'd stayed mostly at his place in Bridgeford. This was because of Snowball. It wasn't so much that the cat needed feeding, he was a very good hunter and perfectly capable of feeding himself, but understandably, Sam worried Snowball might wander too far afield again, and liked to be around as much as he could to keep an eye on him.

'How's your mum?' Phoebe asked as they stood outside Hendrie's on the busy lunchtime street. 'Has she been OK lately? No more... panic attacks?'

'None at all,' Sam said, his eyes shadowing. 'Although I must admit she hasn't been out much either.'

'Maybe we could ask her if she wants to come and see pup at Puddleduck,' Phoebe said.

'I'll ask her. Although it won't be long before we can bring pup to see her. We must think of a name,' he added. 'We can't keep calling her pup all the time.' He bent to kiss her. 'I'd better get going, Pheebs. Are we still on for a drink tomorrow night?'

'Ah, no, I can't. I'm so sorry. I'd forgotten that was the night Maggie wants to go dress shopping and it's the only Wednesday Alexa could do. You could come along with us if you like?' She kissed him back.

'Let's, er, play that one by ear,' he said in a voice which Phoebe knew meant 'not in a million years'. Sam hated shopping. Especially clothes shopping. And then he was gone, heading into the shop, and Phoebe strolled back towards where she'd parked her car in the next street.

She felt unsettled, although she wasn't quite sure why. Again, she told herself that she was being oversensitive. Maybe it wasn't all that surprising that she was ultra-aware of possible problems, though. Before she and Sam had finally begun their love affair, she'd had two pretty difficult relationships.

Both of them had been with what had turned out to be emotionally unavailable men. Hugh, her first serious boyfriend, had been so out of touch with his own emotions he'd ended up in therapy. Rufus Holt, who'd seemed so keen at first, had backed off because he couldn't cope with intimacy.

Was it any wonder that she was hyper-vigilant where Sam was concerned? Was it any wonder that she often found herself second guessing his feelings? Phoebe wondered if she should talk to him about it and then decided this would come across as her being terribly needy. Of course there was nothing wrong between them.

The chemistry was amazing. They were best friends. Her family loved him. The fact that he didn't want to jump into a full-on live-in relationship when they'd only actually been properly seeing each other for a couple of months was hardly surprising.

It was way too soon. Phoebe decided she was seeing problems where none existed.

15

On Tuesday evening, while Sam was teaching at Brook Stables, Phoebe went to see Tori and Harrison's new rental.

Tori must have seen her pull into the driveway because she had opened the front door before Phoebe had even got out of the car.

'Hey, lovely. It's so good to see you. How are you doing? What do you think of the neighbourhood? It's very handy for work, isn't it? Even closer than the flat was.'

'Yes. You can virtually walk from here, can't you?'

'Waddle, I think you mean.' Tori giggled. 'I've forgotten what it's like to just walk anywhere. I'm so big.'

'You look amazing,' Phoebe told her, and it was true. Tori's complexion glowed, her red hair shone and her green eyes sparkled. 'You're a perfect advert for motherhood.'

'I know. That's what Harrison says. Who'd have thunk it! Come in. I can't wait to show you around.' She led Phoebe along an airy hallway towards the back of the house into a large bright kitchen with a granite-lookalike breakfast island, circled by white-painted stools. There was a double drainer sink, black granite worktops and a window that overlooked the lawn.

'It's lovely,' Phoebe said. 'I do love kitchens you can sit in.' Through the window, she could see a big back garden sprinkled with apple trees and a red and green summerhouse tucked against the end fence. 'Wow, was that there already? That's handy.'

'It was, but it was a bit dilapidated. Harrison spent last weekend painting it. Doesn't it look great?' Tori was glowing with happiness. 'Come upstairs and see the nursery.'

She darted ahead. She might be a lot bigger than usual, but it definitely wasn't slowing her down, although Phoebe did notice she was puffing a bit when they reached the top of the stairs.

Tori flung open one of the three doors off the landing. 'Ta dah,' she said, and Phoebe stepped into a pretty room that had the most gorgeous wooden crib along one wall and a shelving unit and big cupboard opposite. Both were painted a vanilla colour but the crib had pink edgings too. The room smelled of wood and new paint.

'What do you think? Harrison made them. Aren't they amazing?'

'They're beautiful,' Phoebe breathed. 'I had no idea he was so talented.'

'He can turn his hand to pretty much anything to do with wood.' Tori beamed proudly and pointed towards the window. 'I made the curtains.'

The curtains were pale cream, patterned with pink roses.

'I didn't know you could make curtains either.'

'Well, technically I didn't make them from scratch, but I did turn them up and I hung them. Mum gave me a hand.'

'It all looks brilliant.'

'It's not quite finished. Harrison's making an animal mobile to hang over the crib so Vanessa Rose has something to look at. Apparently it's good for babies to look at things. It helps them focus. There's still loads of stuff to buy. But we've got time.'

Impulsively Phoebe went across and hugged her. 'I couldn't be more thrilled for you. You look so happy. I bet you can't wait until she's here.'

'We can't. Although we're not looking forward to the sleepless nights. But it's not for a while yet. Ten weeks to go.' She looked at Phoebe keenly. 'Come on, let's go downstairs and have coffee. I want to hear all about you.'

A few minutes later, they were in the diner at the opposite end from the kitchen, sitting on armchairs with a percolator and a plate of chocolate biscuits on the low table in front of them.

'How's it going with Sam?'

'It's going great! We're getting a puppy.'

'Oooh, how brilliant. Is it one of the dalmatians? Does that mean you've moved in together?'

'No.' Phoebe felt deflated all over again and Tori, whose radar was as sensitive as a policeman's speed camera, tuned in immediately.

'What's up?'

'Nothing, really. I'm being premature.'

'Well, as long as Sam isn't.' Tori clapped her hand over her mouth. 'Did I just say that out loud? Sorry, I think my tact and diplomacy filter has stopped working since I've been pregnant.'

Phoebe giggled. 'Has that filter ever worked?'

'Fair comment. I try to switch it on when I interview people, but other than that... Anyway, you already told me he was an eleven.' She grinned.

'More like a twelve now we've been practising a while,' Phoebe said, feeling better. 'No, it really is me being impatient. I love being with Sam. I love everything about our relationship, except that we've got exactly the same problem I had with Rufus. A distinct lack of time. I've got a 24/7 career, much as I love it, and Sam's got two jobs and a horse.' She sighed. 'Spending any time together is really tricky. How do you and Harrison manage? Your jobs are pretty full-on, too.'

'Well, yes, they are, but we haven't spent many nights apart since we met. Either I was at his or he was at mine, and now of course we're living here together. Also, me working from home has helped. You and Sam are stuck on that front, aren't you?'

'Yes. This is going to sound mad, but I think I assumed we'd spend a lot more nights together if we got a puppy. Without realising I'd got carried away, I had also assumed Sam would move over to Woodcutter's because the house-training will be easier there. But neither of those things can really happen. He's got Snowball. You can't really move cats around like you can a puppy.'

'No.' Tori touched her friend's arm. 'But it won't be forever. You and Sam are for keeps. Having waited for you all this time, he's hardly going to jump ship now, is he?'

'I know.' Phoebe realised that on some deep level she did at least know this.

'Then stop being so impatient. Things will work out.' Tori helped herself to another chocolate biscuit and offered the plate to Phoebe. 'Changing the subject completely,' she began, and her voice took on a conspiratorial tone, 'Harrison just told me some interesting gossip about your old friend, Emilia.'

'Archie's nanny?' Phoebe looked at her, surprised. Tori knew that Phoebe and Emilia had never seen eye to eye. Emilia had done her best to sabotage Phoebe's romance with Rufus from the moment it had begun.

'Yes.' Tori nibbled her biscuit thoughtfully. 'Rufus gave Emilia her marching orders a while back, apparently. Obviously she won't be needed when Archie goes off to boarding school. But she's never actually left.'

'Maybe she's working out her notice.'

'Harrison said she *was* working out her notice, but then when

Lord Alfred died, he thinks they changed the arrangements. He thinks Rufus asked Emilia to stay on and cook for him in more of a housekeeper capacity.'

'That sounds like a good idea. I know Emilia and I never got on, but I'm glad Rufus isn't totally alone up there. And Archie, bless him.'

'You are *so* lovely.' Tori looked at her consideringly. 'I don't even know if I should tell you this next bit.'

'You've started so you'd better finish, as they say in all the best quiz shows.'

'Harrison saw them kissing in the garden last week.'

'Blimey.' Phoebe looked at her in shock. 'I wasn't expecting that. Although it does explain a lot. I did wonder sometimes if that was why she was so antagonistic towards me. I thought she may have designs on Rufus. But I never realised he felt the same.'

'Maybe he doesn't. Or maybe he does. Harrison says he's incredibly vulnerable at the moment. After losing his father.'

'Yes, I bet he is. Poor Rufus.'

'I know, and I know it's none of our business. And I'd certainly never dream of telling anyone but you. I just thought it may explain why Rufus and you had the problems you did. It was never your fault, Phoebe, is what I'm trying to say.'

'Thank you,' Phoebe said. In some ways, it was a relief to know the new Lord Holt had some company up at the big house. Whatever else Rufus may have been, he'd never been a bad person and she wished him well. Maybe Emilia could release him from the dark ghosts of his past in a way that Phoebe had failed to do. She truly hoped so.

* * *

Wednesday morning at Puddleduck Vets began with a bang. Or more to the point, a lot of banging. It was coming from the direction of Henna's stable. Maggie had nicknamed the lost horse Henna, after the colour of her reddish bay coat, when they'd discovered they weren't likely to find out her real name any time soon.

'She's been doing that on and off since Natasha arrived at seven thirty,' Marcus told Phoebe as she put on her scrubs. 'I don't think she likes being in a stable much.'

Marcus must have got here early, Phoebe thought – she was early herself and neither Max nor Jenna had arrived yet.

'Why is she in anyway? Did Natasha say?'

'Maggie was worried about a sore patch on her tendon. I think she wants you to have a look if you've got time.'

'The sooner the better by the sound of it. I'll pop over now. I take it there's still no news of her owner?' Phoebe hadn't seen Maggie for a couple of days to talk to, but she knew if there was news, Natasha would have told Marcus.

'No. Natasha said they've drawn a complete blank. The police said no one's come forward to claim her. There are no reports of stolen horses in the area, and a horse without a microchip, while illegal, isn't really a police matter. Natasha and Maggie have been in touch with all the local riding schools, just in case. They tend to know what's happening in the horse world. It's quite a small world.'

Phoebe knew it was. 'Sam's been putting the feelers out too. I guess there's only so much you can do to find a horse's owner.'

'She'll be tricky for Maggie to rehome as well.' Marcus frowned. 'What with the rearing problem, I mean, and the fact she's difficult to keep shut up anywhere. You'd have to mention that to any prospective re-homers, wouldn't you?'

'Of course you would.'

He was hesitating and she had a feeling he wanted to say something else.

'What is it?' she prompted.

'I was wondering if you'd mind if I went and had a look at her later. I could go in my lunchtime.' He reddened. 'I know I haven't been on the behaviourist course that long but we've already done the equine section. I might be able to do something. Maybe get a handle on the rearing and the catching problem. Just in case she has to be re-homed.'

It was a self-confidence she wasn't used to seeing in Marcus, who was naturally shy. Phoebe remembered what Maggie had told her about him doing some work with Saddam and she nodded thoughtfully.

'I don't mind at all, presuming Maggie doesn't. You will be careful, won't you?'

'Course I will, boss.' Marcus sounded pleased. 'I know my way around horses. My gran used to have them. Her owner might turn up anyway. She's a very nice-looking horse.' He switched on the practice computer. 'Hopefully they won't come too soon,' he added under his breath.

'As far as I'm concerned, they can't come quick enough,' Maggie said, when Phoebe caught up with her later and they went across to Henna's stable. 'Not that there's any sign of an owner as yet,' she added. 'It's quite a mystery, to be honest. Sam was right about that horse being in tip-top condition. She's obviously been well looked after by someone – and until very recently too. Although it is odd about the microchip being removed. You said you thought that was done some time ago?'

'I do. Years, possibly. It's hard to tell once it's healed.'

Maggie shook her head in mystification. 'Very odd. But yes, it's fine for your Marcus to come and have a look at her. Do tell him to be careful, won't you?'

'I will. He said you wanted me to look at a sore patch.' She leaned into the stable and saw the bit Maggie must mean. 'She probably did that banging on the door. I'll pop some iodine spray on it.'

'Thanks, but it's her back one. I think she must have caught it when she was doing her rearing thing. Flaming horse. Could I buy some wormer too for her, love? Stick it all on my account.'

'Expensive flaming horse,' Phoebe echoed Maggie. 'Are you regretting taking her?'

'No, love. It's not her fault she was abandoned in the forest.' Maggie bent her head and rubbed Henna's cheek softly, and the mare whickered. 'Taking in abandoned animals is why I started this place.'

They smiled at each other.

'I'm really looking forward to going to Belinda's Boutique tonight,' Maggie added.

'Me too,' Phoebe said truthfully. 'I can't wait to see the latest outfit you've chosen.'

Maggie gave her a slightly anxious look. 'You will tell me if I become a bridezilla, won't you?'

'Of course I will.' Phoebe crossed her fingers behind her back.

'Oh, and while I remember, have you been over to Anni Buckland's lately?'

'Yes, I popped in about a month ago to see a duck.'

'Did she seem all right to you?'

'Yes. Why?'

'Because Eddie said there was an odd message from her on the answer machine a few days ago. Some garbled nonsense about crackheads and rehab and release dates. Unfortunately, he deleted it before I got the chance to listen. He said he thought she must have phoned us by mistake. I hope she hasn't been having problems with that wayward grandson of hers again.'

Phoebe smiled at her grandmother. 'Now that's a mystery I think I can explain.'

16

Maggie had laughed and laughed when Phoebe had explained what was going on over at Buckland Farm. She'd phoned Anni back that afternoon, and then she and Eddie had gone off to help Anni release Quackhead back into the wild.

'I'll see you at Belinda's Boutique,' was her parting shot to Phoebe.

Belinda's Boutique was an upmarket women's clothes shop in Bridgeford which had been there for as long as Phoebe could remember. It had the kind of window display where only a couple of outfits were on show, coordinated with gorgeous accessories, and there was a sign in the window that said: '*Mother of the Bride outfits our speciality. We offer a bespoke fitting and dressmaking service.*'

Phoebe had picked up her mother en route and the two of them were now standing outside, ostensibly looking in the window but in reality chatting. They hadn't gone in because it wasn't very big inside and until Maggie arrived they didn't know what they were supposed to be looking at.

They were chatting about Jan Hendrie.

'I'm still a bit worried about her to be honest, love,' Louella said, her face anxious. 'She swears she's fine and on the surface she does seem fine. It's hard to put your finger on it. She's just, I don't know, maybe more subdued than usual. And I don't think she's been out anywhere since the night of the reunion. We've arranged to meet for coffee twice, but she's cancelled both times.'

'That doesn't sound good. Did she say why?'

'One time it was because something had come up at work and the second time she said she had a cold coming on. I'm not saying she was lying but I just got this feeling, you know?'

'And she's your best friend, so you probably would know.'

Louella sighed. 'Until someone admits they have a problem, they can't really get any help, and you can't make someone admit they have a problem.'

'No.' Phoebe thought about Rufus and his PTSD and an image of him kissing Emilia popped unbidden into her head. That was gossip she certainly wouldn't tell her mother, even though she did trust her utterly.

'Hey, guys.' Alexa arrived, slightly out of breath. 'I thought I was late. No Maggie yet?'

Before they could say no, there wasn't, Maggie arrived too.

A few minutes later, they were all packed inside the small space that was Belinda's Boutique. It smelled of clothes and bergamot, which turned out to be Belinda's perfume. It was Belinda herself who served them. An elegant, smiling, forty-something woman, she introduced herself and produced the outfit that Maggie had clearly put by earlier. She also got out a dress. 'This would go very nicely with the jacket, if Madam would perhaps like to try this as another option as well?'

Madam would, it seemed. She went off to the changing room, bright-eyed.

'Do you need any assistance?' Belinda called after her.

'To get dressed? Goodness me, no. I can manage. I shall be out when I'm done.'

Phoebe, Louella and Alexa made small talk with Belinda while five minutes went slowly by, and Phoebe decided that the boutique owner must have endless patience. It seemed that Maggie had been coming in once a week or so since the end of July. Her usual routine was to pick out an outfit, say she was 99 per cent sure, but would like a second look, and then come back a week later and say she'd changed her mind again.

'She's very anxious to get it right,' Louella said, jumping to defend Maggie, not that Belinda had been complaining.

'Oh, please don't get me wrong,' Belinda said quickly. 'I don't mind at all. Choosing an outfit for your wedding is a very important decision. It's a bride's prerogative to change her mind as often as she likes. And I do feel that we may be nearly there. Particularly now Mrs Crowther's asked you all to come in and give her a second opinion.'

There was a rustling of curtains as Maggie came out of the changing room and they all turned to look.

She was wearing the skirt she'd chosen, which was made of a heavy tweed, teamed with a soft cream blouse that had pearl buttons and was, in Phoebe's opinion, the nicest part of the outfit. She'd put on the jacket too, which was very stylish but didn't quite work with the skirt.

'What do you think?' Maggie frowned uncertainly. 'I'm not so sure now. Neither are you lot, are you? I can tell by your faces.'

Belinda stepped forward and adjusted the jacket slightly. 'I think the skirt you tried on last time you were here would go better with this jacket. Or possibly we need a different jacket.'

'But I like this one,' Maggie pouted. 'This is a nice blouse too. Maybe it's the size.' She brightened. 'The skirt does feel quite loose.'

'I'll get you a different size. I think I still have both colours.'

Belinda returned with the items over her arm, Maggie disappeared, and again they all waited expectantly. This time there was a ten-minute delay and when Maggie finally reappeared, she was back in her own clothes once more.

'I need a rethink. Maybe I should try a trouser suit.'

'Have you tried the dress I found?' Belinda asked with only the slightest note of desperation in her voice. 'I do feel that would go very well with the jacket you like.'

'I don't know. I'm not really a dress person.'

'Oh, but it's worth a try, surely, Mum,' Louella said. 'Then maybe if you don't like that we can have another look around.'

'OK.' Maggie's voice was grudging as she went back into the changing room.

They all waited another ten minutes, but finally she was out again, wearing a floral green dress, and looking much happier.

'Ta dah,' she said, and gave them a twirl so the skirt of the dress she was wearing swirled out slightly. High necked, long sleeved, and nipped in at the waist before coming out into a full skirt, it was incredibly flattering.

'Wow,' said Phoebe and Alexa in unison. 'That's a beautiful dress.'

'You look fabulous, Mum,' Louella added. 'It really suits you.'

'Does it?' Maggie was suddenly shy, as she plucked at the bodice. 'I don't usually do dresses. Is it not too fitted? Do you think I need a bigger size?'

'I can get Madam a bigger size,' Belinda said quickly. 'But I don't think it's necessary. Truly, I don't.' She stepped forward, expertly smoothing and patting. 'This one really is the perfect fit. Now have you tried the jacket with it?'

'Not yet.' Maggie looked anxiously in the mirror. 'Does this dress come in another colour?'

'I believe there's something similar in rose, but I seem to

remember you thinking that the last rose-coloured outfit you tried didn't suit your complexion as well. Whereas this one really does. What do your family think?' Belinda shot them a 'please help me' look.

'It's perfect,' Phoebe said, smiling at her grandmother. 'Can we see it with the jacket?'

'I'll get it.' Belinda disappeared sharpish into the changing room and returned with it over her arm. As she helped Maggie to slip her arms into the lined sleeves of the single-breasted, beautifully cut emerald-green jacket, it was as though the whole party held their breath. As though the whole room held its breath, Phoebe thought, although they were the only ones in it.

Maggie gave another twirl and then frowned at them uncertainly. 'Are you sure I don't look like mutton dressed as lamb?'

'You look beautiful,' Phoebe told her.

'That's a stunning jacket,' Alexa added.

'Very smart,' Louella chipped in. 'And you can wear it afterwards too. So you'll get plenty of use out of it.'

'Where else would I wear an outfit like this?' Maggie scoffed. 'Maybe I should just make do with something already in my wardrobe.'

'You don't have anything in your wardrobe remotely suitable to wear at a wedding. Any wedding,' Phoebe pointed out gently, 'let alone your own.'

Maggie looked outraged and for a moment Phoebe thought she'd been too harsh. She was searching for a tactful retraction that didn't involve mentioning the fact that Maggie's wardrobe was stuffed full to the brim with boiler suits and old trousers – with possibly a few out-of-date skirts squashed in – but before she could find it, Maggie suddenly snorted with laughter.

'I'm sorry, I've been a proper bridezilla, haven't I? I don't know how you lot have put up with me. I really don't.'

'No, you haven't. You couldn't be. You're fine.' There was an over-emphatic chorus of denial.

'It's a hard decision to make,' Belinda said with infinite tact. 'But I do think this is the perfect choice. It is, of course, your decision.'

'I'll take it,' Maggie said decisively. 'I think you're right. I'm not going to get anything better.'

'Have you got shoes to go with it?' Alexa asked. 'Shoes will make or break an outfit. And you'll need a bag. A clutch bag would be perfect.'

Phoebe shot her a look and Alexa began to backtrack hastily, as if suddenly aware that Maggie might change her mind again if shoes and bags came into the mix.

'Maybe we should go shopping separately for those,' Alexa added diplomatically. 'When we don't need to rush.'

Louella looked at her watch and nodded. 'I think Belinda's probably ready to close.'

Belinda had turned the sign on the door round to the closed position about half an hour ago.

'Yes, I'll come back another time for accessories,' Maggie said. 'There are only so many clothes decisions a woman wants to make in a single day.' She glanced at Phoebe and winked. 'Or clothes peg decisions, come to that.'

Louella and Alexa exchanged mystified looks, but Phoebe winked back.

* * *

'Bless her,' Sam said, as Phoebe recounted the events of the boutique outing over a fish and chip supper on Friday. They were sitting at the breakfast bar in his kitchen and Snowball, who was in for once, was prowling around, giving a plaintive meow every now and then, to remind them he was waiting for leftover fish.

It was the first time they'd met properly this week – Phoebe had either been working late or had call-outs.

'I don't suppose Maggie goes shopping for clothes very often, does she?' Sam continued. 'Is that why she's so uncertain, do you think?'

'I think it's partly that, but it's struck me lately that despite all her brusqueness and bluster, Maggie's not very confident about her looks. Do you remember how thrilled she was when we were over there, and we mentioned soft-focus photography?'

'Yes. I do.'

'And she's never been one for dressing up. She and Farmer Pete never went anywhere that meant they had to dress up.'

'I see your point,' Sam said, frowning. 'And a wedding's high pressure, isn't it? What did she wear when she married Farmer Pete?'

'A traditional, full-length white gown. There's a framed photo on the sideboard in the front room. Or at least there was for years. I haven't noticed it lately.'

'I guess it would be tactless having your previous wedding photo on the sideboard when you're getting ready to marry someone else.' His blue eyes warmed, the skin crinkling around the edges. 'Will they both live at Puddleduck Farm when they've tied the knot?'

'Yes. It'll be a proper homecoming for Eddie too. Considering he lived at Puddleduck for about thirty years when it was a dairy farm. He used to live in that ancient old blue caravan way back when we were kids, do you remember?'

'Of course I do. And then he went upmarket and got a trailer. It was amazing that trailer, fully fitted out with cooker, microwave, loo, shower, and a permanent double bed. He was really proud of it, wasn't he? What happened to that?'

'He sold it when he went to live with his son. He got a fair bit for it. Eddie was always pretty financially astute. He lived on a pittance and spent his wages on buy-to-let flats. He had three by the time he retired.'

'I never knew that.' Sam looked amazed. 'So Maggie's not marrying a pauper then?'

'Far from it. He's pretty well heeled, Eddie May.'

'Eddie May. I didn't know that was his surname either.' Phoebe saw Sam's eyes widen as he processed this information. 'So is Maggie – er – taking on his name when they get married?'

'No. She's staying Crowther. She said she absolutely refuses to become a Rod Stewart song.'

'Yeah, I bet she does.' Sam shook his head and reached for the wine bottle, which was still half-full. 'I'm surprised Eddie hasn't already moved back in.'

'Maggie says not. He's there an awful lot, obviously, but he doesn't stay overnight. She said he's waiting until they're officially husband and wife. She's quite traditional in lots of ways. And I think he is too.'

Phoebe's eyes were suddenly reflective and Sam wondered what she was thinking. It was one of the differences between them. Phoebe had lived with Hugh for six years in London, but Sam had never lived with anyone. It might be old fashioned, but he wanted marriage, not cohabiting.

'Good for them,' Sam said, putting down his knife and fork. 'Have you finished? I've got some salted caramel ice cream in the freezer if you're up for it?'

'Have you ever known me to turn down ice cream?'

This was a rhetorical question which Sam didn't bother to answer. He cleared up their plates and then picked out some fish for Snowball, making sure there weren't any bones in it as he put it in the cat's bowl on the kitchen floor.

'It's only a couple of weeks until we have a new addition to the family,' he reminded Phoebe. 'Are you getting excited?'

'Very excited. Do you think we should have her at mine for the first few nights? So as not to confuse her too much. We could both stay there – I mean if we can work it around Snowball.'

'I'm sure we can work something out. We should decide on a name too. We can't keep calling her pup. How do you feel about Roxie? I had a favourite rabbit called Roxie when I was a kid. She was black with white spots. I loved her to bits.'

'Ahhh, I love the name Roxie, Sam. That's perfect.'

Sam washed up the plates. Phoebe seemed a bit distant, but he couldn't put his finger on why. Maybe he was imagining it.

He still had to pinch himself sometimes to remind himself that it was all real. That this beautiful, amazing woman who he'd loved for as long as he could remember actually wanted to be with him. Actually wanted to share his bed and wake up beside him.

He hadn't been surprised when she'd gone up to London and worked her way through vet school with flying colours. Nor had he been surprised when she'd chosen Hugh as her partner. High-flying Hugh with his rich father, who was a consultant and had a zillion contacts to help his son forge his way in the world.

It had been more painful for him when she'd started dating Rufus Holt, though. Much closer to home. But Sam had done his best to put his own feelings about Rufus to one side because, above everything else, he wanted Phoebe to be happy.

'Are you OK, Pheebs?' he asked her now. 'You seem a bit quiet.'

'I'm pretty tired.'

He nodded, although he was almost sure there was more to it than that. 'How about we have an early night? I could give you a massage and a foot rub.'

'All right,' she conceded without much enthusiasm, and Sam felt a twinge of foreboding. He'd heard an unsettling rumour from one of the livery owners at Brook Stables the other day that he hadn't mentioned to Phoebe.

Sam didn't like gossip and he certainly didn't intend to pass it on, but the rumour had been that Rufus had been seen out walking in the forest, holding the hand of a pretty blonde.

The livery owner had told him this with glee in her voice, but had shut up when Sam had just shrugged noncommittally.

Sam really hoped Phoebe hadn't heard the rumour. She might insist she was over Rufus, but Sam was painfully aware that the only reason she'd crashed her car into a ditch on that day back in July was because Rufus had just ended their relationship. That had been barely three months ago.

Sam had worried she was on the rebound ever since. He occasionally had nightmares where Phoebe came round one evening and told him it had all been a mistake. That she loved him still, but not in that way, and could they go back to being friends?

He didn't know what he'd have said if this had happened. But he sure as hell knew he couldn't go back to being just friends.

17

The new Lord Holt was having very similar thoughts to Sam, and it was driving him crazy.

Since his father's death nearly six weeks earlier, absolutely everything in his life had changed. When he'd woken up on the morning after his father had died, the first thing he'd been aware of was that he wasn't in bed alone. There was a woman lying next to him; he could hear her soft breathing. The second thing he was aware of was a thumping headache that hammered across his temples. His throat felt dry and parched and there was a foul taste in his mouth.

As he shifted, opening his eyes, the woman shifted too, and then she spoke.

'Hey, I think you are awake... ja?'

Rufus had jumped out of his skin. Oh my God, he was in bed with Emilia. He was in bed with Archie's nanny. How had that happened? Maybe he was having some kind of bizarre nightmare.

He closed his eyes again, swiftly. The events of the previous night crashed back into his head. Driving Archie home from summer camp and discovering his father was in hospital. The nightmarishness of the situation hit him afresh. Oh, God, his father was dead. That was real. Rufus could feel the sharp clarity of that like a knife in his chest. He groaned but was barely aware he'd done it aloud until he felt Emilia's soft touch on his forehead.

'It's OK. It's all OK.' Her fingers stroked his head rhythmically and for a second Rufus let her. He more than let her – he welcomed the touch. It was as though he was a child again. Being comforted by his mother. It was decades since he'd thought of his mother.

'Archie. Where's Archie?' he said, acutely conscious that his son couldn't find them like this – couldn't find him in bed with Emilia.

'Archie is cleaning out the mini pigs,' Emilia told him confidently. 'Don't worry. I saw him go out when I went to the bathroom. He is fine.'

'But even so. I need to get up. What time is it?' He'd reached for his phone, jumped out of bed and was aware fleetingly of Emilia's eyes on him.

For a second, he'd been tempted to get back in bed with her. To shut out the world, and the reality of what he now had to face, for a few minutes longer. But the horror of Archie finding them in bed together had stopped him.

Rufus didn't think he'd have got through those first few days without Emilia. She had stepped up to the plate in every sense of the word. As well as cooking for him and Archie, and caring for them both, which Rufus realised she'd always done without question, she had helped him prioritise the endless things that needed doing in the wake of his father's death. She had seemed to know what was important and what was not. It was almost as if she'd dealt with the death of a parent before, and when he'd asked her, she'd said that yes, she had dealt with her grandparents' deaths back in Switzerland, and the protocol hadn't been so very different.

She had listened to him when he'd been troubled, had told him endlessly that it was only possible to do one thing at a time, and that the world must wait until he could manage to do the rest, and she'd got out of his way when she'd sensed he needed to be alone.

Then there were the nights. The nights were wonderful. Having finally let down his walls, and the years of his denial when Rufus had managed to convince himself that autonomy was everything, he was defenceless. He didn't want to shut Emilia out, either from his bed or his heart, and she had made it crystal clear that she wanted to be in both. Their lovemaking was sweetly satisfying.

Especially as, after that first night, Rufus had gone to Emilia's part of the house, which was self-contained and had locks on the doors. He was still worried that Archie might happen across them in bed, and Emilia had agreed it was better this didn't happen. The boy had had enough changes in his life already.

Harrison had been great too in the aftermath of Lord Alfred's death. His best friend had been a pallbearer alongside Rufus at the funeral, and in the days after it he'd helped with a backlog of paperwork and phone calls. He'd shouldered everything that Rufus temporarily couldn't deal with and had kept all of the plates spinning at Beechbrook. He'd been a rock.

But the biggest surprise had been Archie. It was almost as if his son had grown up overnight. At the funeral, in the dusty old church, he'd sat in his smart suit, his face very serious. Rufus had given a eulogy and when he'd gone back to his hard wooden pew, Archie had slipped his hand into Rufus's and whispered, 'Grandad would have liked that.'

'I'm so proud of you,' Rufus had told him later when they were finally alone, the last few mourners who'd come to the house having finally drifted away. 'Your mum would have been really proud of you too.'

'Won't you get lonely living here by yourself, though, Dad?' Archie had asked. 'Once Emilia's gone back to Switzerland.'

'No, I won't get lonely, son. Besides, Emilia's not leaving just yet.'

'You can always ask Phoebe to come and live here,' Archie had said glibly, and Rufus had told him gently that he and Phoebe had split up.

Archie had taken the news of their split better than Rufus had expected. He'd reacted so well that Rufus had wondered whether he'd really taken it in and then he'd realised that Archie had only ever thought he and Phoebe were good friends anyway. Phoebe had said that Archie could still visit Puddleduck Farm whenever he liked. She had said she would help Archie with his animals if he needed her. Maybe for Archie, nothing much had changed.

A brighter spot had been when they went to buy a pony for Archie. Because of his terror of horses, Rufus had been dreading this too, but there was no way he was going to dip out. Thankfully he'd had plenty of support.

He'd had so much support that on the day of the visit they'd needed two cars. Jack's parents went in their capacity as equine experts. Harrison was ostensibly driving, but was really there to support Rufus in case he had to leave in a hurry, Emilia went 'to make sure this pony is safe'. And of course there were Archie and Jack.

Rufus felt as though they were going in mob-handed, and the family were a bit surprised to see so many people, but they were amenable enough. And the focus was off Rufus, which was a major bonus.

He hung back, chatting to Harrison, as the group of experts looked at the horse, a little grey mare, and Emilia folded her arms and watched from a few paces away.

'Her name's Sea Breeze, Breezy Bubs for short,' the pony's current owner, a tall youngster with pigtails told them all. 'Sadly, I've outgrown her. But she's a little darling, aren't you, Breezy Bubs?'

Breezy Bubs tossed her head in agreement while the girl petted her. Behind her back, Rufus saw Archie mouth the words, 'Breezy

Bum!' to Jack and the two boys exchanged a smirk. Rufus hid his amusement, realising it was the first time he'd felt the urge to smile since his father had died.

Minutes later, Archie was mounting the fully tacked-up pony and riding her expertly around the paddock. Rufus hadn't seen Archie ride for several months and he was amazed at how much he'd come on.

'He looks good on a horse,' Harrison murmured, echoing his thoughts.

'Fabulous,' Emilia agreed.

Rufus nodded. 'Thanks so much for coming.' He glanced gratefully at them both. 'I really do appreciate it.'

Archie's eyes were alight when he eventually rode back to them all and dismounted. 'I love her, Dad. She's brilliant. I think she's the one.'

'She's the only one you've seen,' Rufus said, feeling a surge of relief that they wouldn't need to see any more horses, mixed with anxiety in case they were rushing into things. 'Are you sure you wouldn't like to look at any others?'

'Nope, she's the one.'

Rufus glanced at Jack's father questioningly.

'You'll need to get a full vet check,' he told him 'But subject to that being OK, I think she's a great little mare. It looks like she and Archie have really hit it off.'

Rufus decided he would ask Phoebe to do the vet check, and when he'd phoned her later that day, she'd been very gracious and said she'd be delighted to help. Which she'd done very quickly. She'd gone out to the stables the day after with Harrison, given the mare a clean bill of health and had told Archie that she approved of his choice.

This had meant that Phoebe and Archie had the chance to say a proper goodbye before he left for boarding school, for which

Rufus was also grateful. Phoebe had always been wonderful with his son.

A couple of weeks later, Archie had gone happily off to school with his new pony, who'd been rechristened Enola, after Sherlock Holmes's fictional teenage sister. 'No way is she being called Breezy Bubs!' he had told his father indignantly. 'What sort of name is that to give a horse?'

Rufus had felt some of the dread that had been building at the prospect of waving goodbye to his son lift away.

After Archie had started school, Rufus and Emilia had given up pretending they weren't a couple. At least they had in Beechbrook House and its grounds. They touched each other constantly and walked around the estate hand in hand.

Emilia was a very tactile woman and Rufus was discovering the delights of being a tactile man. He'd thought it was Phoebe who had found the key to a locked door in his heart, and she had certainly opened the door a crack. But it was Emilia who had pushed it wide and strolled right on in.

Rufus suspected that this was partly because he'd known her for so long and partly because she was so direct. Phoebe had always been quite shy, but Emilia, since they'd been sleeping together, had dropped her politeness. She had never been backward in coming forward. She also made him laugh. Rufus was amazed that he could laugh so soon after such intense grief and also in such intense circumstances.

Emilia found humour in lots of situations where Rufus would have deemed it impossible. She'd helped him clear out his father's belongings, which could have been heavy and sad, and she'd even found humour in that.

'I want to keep some of his things,' he'd told her when they'd sorted through his father's wardrobe.

'Of course, but not this ridiculous hat,' she'd said, picking up the late lord's bucket hat and sticking it on her head. 'It is ridiculous, ja?'

'It is,' Rufus had agreed.

'So are these braces.' They were red striped.

'Yes,' Rufus agreed again.

'But he had very good taste in gloves.' She handed a pair of brown Hestra gloves to Rufus reverently and he took them and touched them to his face.

Fleetingly he'd caught his father's scent and he was reminded of walks around the estate in winter and holly berries and starkly bare trees. An ache of loss caught in his throat and Emilia was beside him instantly.

'It will get better,' she'd said. 'This *trauer*.'

She'd placed her hands over his, the gloves were still in his hands too, so that Rufus had felt that both Emilia and his father were very close. Holding him, lending him strength.

18

Phoebe had found it cathartic vet checking Sea Breeze aka Enola for Rufus, and it had been wonderful seeing Archie, who was very excited about the prospect of going to boarding school with his very own pony. Phoebe felt as though that chapter of her life had finally completely closed, that they were all happily moving on.

Co-parenting a puppy with Sam was very exciting too. Having made the decision over which pup they were having, Phoebe found it was impossible to stay away from the dalmatians and she'd got into the habit of going into the barn to say hello to them at every opportunity.

She wasn't the only one. The pups had a cuteness factor that was off the scale, and they had a constant stream of visitors, which included all the volunteers who helped out at the sanctuary and also any clients of Phoebe's that knew they were there. And that was before you even got to the staff of Puddleduck Vets.

All of the pups had homes now, and their prospective owners, two of whom were regular volunteers, had been home checked by either Natasha or Maggie and had been interrogated to within an inch of their lives.

'I wish I could have one,' Natasha told Phoebe, 'but Marcus and I have decided to wait until we get our own place. Also, Marcus thinks we should have a dog that no one else wants. Maybe the oldest or the ugliest one in the kennels.' She blushed. 'Not that I think any of them are ugly. They're all gorgeous to me.'

That was so typical of Marcus. He would always be on the side of the underdog, or the animal no one else wanted.

'That's a really nice thing to do, and very sensible,' Phoebe said. 'I should probably have done the same thing.'

'You do much longer hours than we do,' Natasha said loyally. 'So we've got more time to sort out behavioural problems and stuff than you have.'

Phoebe was convinced Roxie was beginning to know her name too. She certainly knew the sound of Phoebe's voice and would come toddling across every time she heard it, her little tail wagging ten to the dozen.

On this particular lunchtime, a few days before Phoebe did their first vaccinations so they could go to their new homes on Friday, she found both Marcus and Natasha had beaten her to it. Natasha was playing with the pups and Marcus was doing something with Saddam on the other side of the barn. The air smelled of dogs, cats and the sweeter smell of hay – the barn was a quarter full of stacked hay bales – and light spilled down from the skylight windows and caught dust motes swirling.

Phoebe called Roxie over, petted her and played with her for a while, then she went to see what Marcus was doing with the feral ginger cat. He was sitting on a haybale at the bottom of the stack, and Saddam was standing beside him.

To Phoebe's amazement, as she got closer she could see that Saddam was standing close to Marcus and allowing his chin to be stroked, although when he saw Phoebe approaching, his tail stiffened and he let out a warning hiss.

'Would you mind just holding on a sec, boss?' Marcus said in a very gentle, even voice.

Phoebe stopped in her tracks. 'Sorry. Shall I back off?'

'No, it's fine, he's definitely getting more tolerant of humans, but I'm taking it really steady.'

'You've done wonders with him. I've never seen him allow anyone to stroke him before. He doesn't even let Maggie that close.'

'It's just a matter of building up trust. It's a two-way thing. He's learned to trust that I'm not going to hurt him. And I've learned to trust that he's not going to sink his teeth into my thumb.' There was warmth in his voice. 'Although that last bit took a while.'

Saddam had stopped hissing now and had returned to letting Marcus tickle his chin. 'Should I come any closer?' Phoebe asked.

'No. Not today. It's amazing how long these things take. Most people try to rush it and then they find that the little progress they've made is smashed again. He's probably had enough today. I'll come to you.'

Phoebe waited for him to get up, which he did slowly and without fuss, before he crossed the dozen or so steps it took to join her. Saddam stayed where he was briefly and then melted like a ginger shadow back into the haybales.

'It looks like you're making great progress,' Phoebe said admiringly. 'How are you getting on with Henna?'

'Great, actually. She's a beautiful horse. Someone's spent a lot of time handling her and she's so sweet natured.'

'Is she still rearing?'

'She has once or twice. I haven't got to the bottom of that yet. But I will, I'm sure.' He hesitated. 'Natasha said there's no more news on her owners.'

At the mention of her name, Natasha came to join them too. 'Eddie was telling me about fly grazing. He said that if a horse is abandoned on your land and the owner doesn't reclaim it, you become legally responsible for it. Does that mean Maggie is now responsible for Henna?'

'I don't think so,' Marcus answered before Phoebe could speak, 'because Henna wasn't found here. She was found in the New Forest. The agisters brought her here. So Maggie doesn't have legal responsibility, does she, Phoebe?'

'No, I guess not. But it's not legal responsibility that matters with Maggie, it's moral.' They both nodded. Maggie would never turn away an animal in need. They all knew that.

'She could rehome her, though, couldn't she,' Marcus continued, 'if I can get to the bottom of the rearing? She might even be able to sell her. On the surface she's a valuable horse.'

'Yes, that's true.' Phoebe hadn't been thinking that far ahead but she knew Marcus was right. 'We probably shouldn't give up on her owner too soon,' she said, in an attempt to reassure them. 'It's still possible that they'll come forward. I'll speak to Sam about it again when I see him.'

* * *

Phoebe cooked Sam a chilli midweek and they'd eaten it in her kitchen at Woodcutter's and were now drinking coffee and discussing the mystery of Henna the horse.

'Could we maybe take some photos of her and put them on social media?' Phoebe suggested. 'If we got enough people to repost the photos on Facebook or Twitter or TikTok or whatever, we might get somewhere.'

'We could if I had the first clue how to do it. And since when have you had a Facebook account? Or a TikTok one, come to that?' He grinned.

'I used to have Facebook, but that was ages ago, I'm not sure it even works now. As for TikTok, no, I haven't got a clue how to do anything but watch videos. But the youngsters at work are bound to have one. Well, Natasha probably will – and Max is pretty likely to have one too. And Jenna's kids. They're young.' She paused. 'Tori does social media for the magazine. She could put something in the actual magazine too. I should have thought about that before. It could be a good story. New Forest Mystery Mare.'

'You've had other things on your mind, what with work, weddings and puppies,' Sam said, kind as always. 'And we all thought a horse like that wouldn't stay lost for long anyway. So don't start beating yourself up about what we could and couldn't have done.'

Phoebe caught his hand across the kitchen table. 'True. Thank you for rescuing me. But now I have thought about it, there's lots we could do to help. We could try circulating some photos at Brook Stables. Maybe someone there would recognise the horse.'

'If we could mock up a poster, I'm sure Marjorie would display it in the office. I wish I was more technical. I'd do it myself.'

'I'm pretty sure we've got the capacity to do posters at Puddle-duck. Eddie does something similar for the adoptions. So don't worry about that. I'll speak to him.'

'We'll get to the bottom of it, I'm sure.' Sam leant forward and kissed her and Phoebe felt a huge tenderness well up in her.

'I love you, Sam Hendrie. I don't say it often enough.'

'I love you too, Phoebe Dashwood.'

'Are you staying over tonight?'

'I am.'

'And you're still staying over on Friday and Saturday when we pick up Roxie?' Phoebe hoped she didn't sound too needy.

'Of course.'

'I've booked all of next week off so she can settle in a bit and get used to Woodcutter's before we start shuttling her around too much. Besides, she can't mix with other dogs until she has her second vaccination anyway.'

'And I've got Monday and Tuesday off next week and I'll book some more days as and when we need them,' Sam said, clearing their plates and getting up. 'I'll just wash these. You stay there. You look tired.'

And even though they weren't at Woodcutter's very often, Sam looked totally at home, standing at her sink, moving around in her little kitchen, wiping down the work surfaces, opening cupboards and drawers and putting stuff away. It was the perfect domestic scene. Phoebe decided that she'd imagined the fact that his feelings were cooling. Tori was right – she was being impatient. She needed to let things develop naturally, not try to rush them. Everything was going to work out fine.

19

Taking Roxie home to Woodcutter's was so exciting. Even though Phoebe saw the pup several times a day, it was different actually putting her lead on and knowing she was going to finally belong to her and Sam.

Roxie was also the last one to go, because the other pups' owners had picked them up in the morning, and she was overjoyed to see Phoebe and Sam when they arrived to collect her.

'Hello, little one. I'm so sorry to keep you waiting.' Phoebe leant into the run to pick her up. 'You are so gorgeous, aren't you?'

Roxie cuddled into her arms, snuffling in agreement, her warm little body snuggled against Phoebe's.

Beside them, Sam was beaming from ear to ear and Maggie, who'd come into the barn to say goodbye, was also smiling.

'You two won't be thinking that when she has you up at 4 a.m. howling her little head off because she misses her litter mates.'

'Hopefully that's not going to happen because we're going to have her in the bedroom, aren't we, Sam?'

'That's a slippery slope,' Maggie warned. 'She'll be on the bed before you know it.'

'No, she won't, she'll be in her crate. Beside the bed.'

'Mostly,' Sam added.

'Talk like that, there's no hope for you.' Maggie rolled her eyes and then spoiled her scolding tones by adding, 'I'm so pleased you're having her. She's my favourite too. It's lovely to know I can still see her.'

'Anyway, you had Buster on your bed when he was a pup, I seem to remember,' Phoebe said.

'Only because he was so little. I stopped that as soon as he was old enough to be independent.'

'That's not how I remember it.'

They all laughed and Maggie changed the subject deftly. 'Are you going to be OK for the hair and make-up trial next week? It's booked for Thursday. Or should I rebook it? We've plenty of time.'

'No, that'll be fine. It shouldn't be more than an hour or so, should it? We want her to get used to being left for short periods in her crate, right from the off, and if there's any problems Sam can step in, can't you?'

'Of course I can. That's the whole point of us dog sharing,' Sam agreed happily.

'Thanks.' Phoebe gave him a grateful smile. She was also aware that despite Maggie's assumption there was plenty of time to get the wedding plans sorted, that was only true if Maggie was happy with the first hair and make-up trial. Judging by how the rest of the planning had gone, this was not necessarily a done deal.

'Oh, and I wanted to give you this too.' Maggie produced a rolled-up piece of paper she'd been holding, and handed it to Sam. 'It's the missing horse poster to put up at Brook Stables if you don't mind, love? Eddie's done a few. Could you put one up at Hendrie's too?'

'Sure.' Sam unrolled it for a look. It showed the bay horse, face on to the camera, with her ears pricked up. Underneath were the words:

Do you recognise this horse? Please phone us if you do.

The Puddleduck Vets phone number was printed below that.

'We put your number on because it'll get answered by someone, twenty-four hours,' Maggie said. 'I hope that's OK? I should have asked you before he printed them.'

'It's absolutely fine,' Phoebe said. 'We'll put one up in reception as well, and maybe we could ask Mum if she can put one up at school. I guess we never know who's going to see it.'

'Thanks. I've also had a word with Natasha about the whole social whatsits thing. She said that there are some special designated groups where you can put in photos of horses you're trying to trace, with their names and other relevant details, so she's going to try that.' She shrugged. 'It's all double Dutch to me, to be honest, but it might help.'

'That's brilliant. Fingers crossed.' Phoebe turned her attention back to Roxie, bending her head to breathe in the sweet puppy scent of her. 'Now, little one, I think we'd better get you home.'

* * *

The next few days passed in a blur of puppy happiness. Phoebe had expected that having Roxie would be hard work and it was certainly full-on; feeding the pup four times a day, keeping the toilet area in her crate clean and playing with her, but she hadn't expected there would be so much joy.

Roxie was endlessly entertaining as she explored her world. She raced around in the garden, chasing leaves, toys, insects and anything else that crossed her path, regularly fell over when she misjudged her little legs and spent a lot of time asleep between Sam and Phoebe as they watched YouTube videos on Phoebe's phone with titles like *Puppy's First Week* and *Bringing Your New Pup Home*.

Apart from the first night when she cried briefly, Roxie was pretty good at sleeping through the nights too, and she slept happily in the crate which they'd put on Phoebe's side of the bed.

They'd decided it was more sensible if the pup stayed at Wood-cutter's until she was house-trained and fully vaccinated.

'I don't know what we were thinking,' Phoebe had told Sam. 'It's much fairer on Roxie if she just has to get used to one routine. And it's so much easier in a house with easy access to the garden than a flat.'

'And she can get to know us a bit more before we introduce her to Snowball,' he'd agreed and Phoebe had found herself thinking about what Natasha had so sensibly said.

'Marcus and I have decided to wait until we get our own place together before getting a dog.'

Still, it was done now, and they were muddling through fine.

The hair and make-up trial was booked for five thirty in Bridgeford and Sam, who was back at work, had offered to come over and sit with Roxie while Phoebe went.

'I'm sure she'll be perfectly fine. But thanks. That'll be brilliant.'

'It's like being new parents, isn't it?' Sam had said when she left him at Woodcutter's.

'Although we'd probably live in the same house if we were new parents,' Phoebe replied, a little bit more sharply than she'd intended.

'Er, yes.' He laughed uncertainly and Phoebe left him to it. As she drove the Lexus over to collect Maggie, who she was picking up en route, she found herself wondering if they would ever be parents. Bizarrely they had never discussed it. She had always assumed she'd have her own children one day. She had always assumed that Sam would have a family too when he got married, but they had never actually discussed it with each other. Subjects like that had seemed too heavy for those first early blissful days of their new romance when all they'd done had been to stay in bed.

To Phoebe's surprise, Maggie seemed a lot more amenable to the hairdresser and make-up artist's suggestions than she had been to Belinda's suggestions about wedding outfits.

They had the shop to themselves and the two women, both smiley and in their mid-twenties, Phoebe guessed, fussed around them with brushes and colour charts and pictures of brides.

'Just don't make me look like mutton dressed as lamb,' Maggie told them.

'We certainly won't do that,' they had both assured her.

It was actually quite fun having such a girly time with Maggie, Louella and Alexa, Phoebe thought. None of them usually did anything like this, although Alexa confided she used to go on pamper days at Champneys with girlfriends way back in the days when she and Frazier had been fancy free with no responsibilities.

'Frazier used to get me spa vouchers for birthdays and Christmases. It was his stock present. He hasn't done it since the twins were born.'

'He probably thinks you haven't got time to go,' Louella remarked. 'But you do know that we could always babysit, don't you? You deserve a pamper day.'

'I can always babysit too,' Phoebe offered.

'Thank you.' Alexa glowed with that inner serenity she always seemed to exude. 'I might take you up on that. Although I'm guessing you'll be pretty busy yourself for a while, Phoebe, being a puppa mumma.'

For a while the talk was on puppies and in between having their make-up and hair done, everyone cooed over the dozens of pictures Phoebe had taken of Roxie.

* * *

At Woodcutter's, Sam had fallen asleep on Phoebe's sofa with Roxie on him, also asleep. They were both snoring a little, when the jangling of Sam's phone jolted him from a great dream involving him driving a top-of-the-range Mercedes sports car.

He reached for it groggily, realised his arm had gone numb where Roxie had been lying on it – she might be little, but she was getting heavier by the day – dropped it on the carpet and then saw that whoever had been calling him had got cut off.

Bleary eyed, Sam stared at the missed call on the screen. An unknown number. Thinking it might be a student he didn't have in his contacts list, he sat up and dialled them back.

'Hi, you just called me.'

'Oh, is that Sam Hendrie? Thanks for ringing back, it's Becky Arnold.' A vaguely familiar voice filled his ear. 'My daughter, Poppy, had some lessons with you, two or three years back.'

'Oh, yes. I remember.' Sam glanced at Roxie, who'd gone straight back to sleep, and turned his attention back to the call. He had a vague memory of teaching a very keen, but not terribly talented teenager who wanted to improve her riding for the show ring.

'How is Poppy?' he asked politely.

'Poppy is fine, thank you for asking. She's more interested in boys than ponies, these days. She's got to that age. She's sixteen. You know how they are.'

'Right, er, yes,' Sam said, wondering where this was going. 'And how's the pony?' He racked his brains to remember a name and found it. 'Candy Girl, wasn't it?'

'Gosh, you have got a good memory.' Her laugh tinkled out. 'We haven't got her now. Once Poppy lost interest, we sold her on. A nice home, we made sure of that. But anyway, I expect you're wondering why I'm phoning.'

It was a rhetorical question which Sam didn't answer and there was barely a gap before she carried on, her voice more business-like now. 'Poppy saw the poster up in Hendrie's Stores. The one about the mystery mare. And she thinks she recognises her. She insisted I phone you and tell you personally.'

'Really?' Sam sat up straighter, suddenly wide awake. 'That's great. We've been trying to track down her owner.'

'She recognises the horse because she had a very similar name to her pony, and she used to turn up quite regularly at the shows Poppy went to – they were often in the same classes. I think the rider used to beat Poppy too. That's one of the reasons she started lessons with you so she could up her game.' Again her laugh tinkled out. 'You know how competitive youngsters are.'

Was she ever going to get to the point? 'So what was the name of the horse?' Sam prompted gently.

'Casey's Girl. See what I mean about the similarity?'

'Casey's Girl. Wow, yes, I certainly do. What was the name of the rider? Does Poppy remember that?'

'I'm afraid she doesn't. I'm so sorry. To be honest, I was reluctant to phone you as it's probably not that much help. But Poppy insisted I spoke to you.'

'Thank you. I'm glad you did.' Sam felt a wash of disappointment. 'Does she remember anything else? Any other detail that might help?'

'Poppy was pretty sure the girl was local. To the forest, I mean. We're over at Lyndhurst. Also that Casey's Girl and her rider were regularly placed. I think the girl was a couple of years older than Poppy, so she'd be eighteen or nineteen now. She stopped competing before Poppy did, anyway.'

'I see. Well, that might be very useful. Thanks again. And please pass on my thanks and good wishes to Poppy.'

'I will. And you're welcome. I hope you manage to find the owners.'

After she'd disconnected, Sam took Roxie outside – she'd just woken up and he knew she might need a wee. As she wandered around the dusky garden looking for the best patch of grass, he thought about what Becky Arnold had just told him.

It wasn't a lot to go on, but it was better than nothing. And if Henna's owner had once been local, then surely it was only a matter of time before they tracked her down. He couldn't wait to tell Phoebe.

20

Phoebe agreed with Sam that knowing Henna's real name was Casey's Girl was a great start, but it would have been a lot more helpful if Poppy had remembered her owner's name too.

When Phoebe got into work on Monday morning, she discovered that Maggie, who she'd told at the weekend, and the rest of her staff were of the same opinion.

'We can't exactly go knocking on every horse owner's door in the New Forest,' Maggie said. 'And that's assuming this Poppy was right and that the owners of Casey's Girl were actually local.'

'How would we know who the horse owners even were?' Max asked of no one in particular. They were standing in reception, prior to opening up for the first customers of the week.

'They'd have a paddock or a field,' Marcus said. 'Dur!'

'OK, but we can't go knocking on five-bar gates, can we?' Max shot him a look. 'Besides, the New Forest is full of fields and paddocks.'

'And stables tucked away out of sight,' Jenna pointed out, obviously on Max's side. 'It would be like looking for a needle in a haystack. There's a horsey joke there somewhere,' she grinned.

'We could put up posters on lampposts,' Marcus said stubbornly. 'We could target Lyndhurst and Burley and anywhere else that might be relevant.'

'Oh, great idea.' Max's voice was laced with sarcasm. 'Let's not forget trees. We'll have hundreds of options.'

'Max,' Phoebe said sharply. 'Are you OK?' Her lovely vet was usually so positive and charming.

'Sorry.' He caught her gaze. 'I've got a bit of a headache. Tough weekend. I had to put a horse to sleep yesterday. RTA in the forest. I wish people would slow down. Bloody inconsiderate drivers.'

The mood in reception changed instantly as they all sympathised with him. Everyone knew how heartbreaking that would have been.

'Anyway,' Jenna said when there was a gap in the conversation. 'To get back to nicer subjects, where's Roxie? I thought you were bringing her into work.'

'Sam's taken her to Hendrie's. We want her to get used to both of our workplaces, especially as I've got her at home with me until she's house-trained, which will be a little while. Sam's going to take her to work with him until she's had all her jabs.'

'Ah, yes,' Jenna said. 'This is the last place she needs to be before she's fully vaccinated. Good call.'

They moved on to work and Maggie left them to it, and as the day sped by Phoebe felt like she'd never been away.

When she caught up with Maggie after work up at Puddleduck Farmhouse, her grandmother said idly, 'I did have one more thought about Casey's Girl. I know it probably wouldn't work adding her name to the posters and sticking them on lampposts, but we could put her name in *New Forest Views*, couldn't we? On that story that Tori is doing about her, I mean. Would it be too late? Has she already gone to press with it? If the headline had her name in it, that might well jog someone's memory.'

'I'll check,' Phoebe said. 'I'll do it right now.' She grabbed her mobile and called Tori while Maggie waited expectantly, leaning with both hands on the kitchen table.

'I'm so sorry, Phoebe. The magazine was printed yesterday. How annoying. I'll put it in the next one. I'll also ask Laura to add something to the digital version. Someone might see that. Sorry, I've got to go. I'm late for an interview. Catch up soon, yes? I want to come and see Roxie.'

'Yes. Definitely. Thanks again.' Phoebe disconnected and told Maggie, who'd been listening and had already guessed from Phoebe's disappointed tone. 'It's a bit of progress, though,' Phoebe said. 'I'm sure we'll get there in the end. There are no mysteries that can't be solved, given enough time.'

'That's one of the things I love about you,' Maggie said in an uncharacteristic declaration of emotion. 'You're so unfailingly positive. Do you know that? I would never have ended up with Puddleduck Pets if it hadn't been for you.'

'Yes, you would. You were bursting at the seams with animals when I got back from London.'

'If I remember correctly, and I'm not yet decrepit enough not to, I was actually sinking fast. I was on the verge of rehoming all the animals and selling up. This place just wasn't sustainable.'

'Ah but—'

'No, let me finish...' Maggie put a hand on her arm. 'It was down to you that it became sustainable – you and Sam and Tori – helping me to get a proper adoption system going, persuading me to employ Natasha full time. Making sure that animals actually got rehomed.'

She gestured to a scattering of adoption posters that were on the vast kitchen table. 'Not to mention paying me rent for your unit. That helps a lot.'

'It helps me a lot too. I wouldn't have my own vet practice if it wasn't for you.'

'You might not have it here,' Maggie acquiesced. 'But you'd definitely have had it somewhere. It's been your destiny since you've been a little girl.' Her hazel eyes held Phoebe's in a look of such tenderness that Phoebe felt herself welling up.

Maggie never said things like 'your destiny' but she could feel the truth of it, deep in her heart.

'I'm really happy that it is here, Gran. And I'm really happy that you're happy too. And that you're marrying Eddie, enjoying retirement and taking a little bit of a back seat at running this place.'

Maggie's face lit up as she nodded fervently in agreement. For once, she didn't even tell Phoebe off for calling her Gran.

The two women hugged, and, over by the Aga, Tiny raised his head for long enough to wag his tail while Buster gave a little whine in his sleep. Phoebe felt as though the room was full of love. But then Puddleduck Farmhouse had always felt like that. A place full of animals and a place full of love.

* * *

Rufus was finally coming round to the idea that he had fallen in love with Emilia. It had crept up on him these past few weeks. The feelings that had started out as a tender and gentle comfort, before growing incrementally into a rather lovely reliance, had now become a raging need. At least Rufus thought it was love. But what if it was obsession?

There was a part of him that hoped it was obsession. That would have been easier to resolve, because with time, with stubbornness, with a stiff upper lip, maybe even with therapy, it was possible to move on from obsession. Rufus wasn't sure it was possible to move on from love though, and with that knowledge came a terrible conflict.

While Rufus knew on an intellectual level that times had changed, even royalty married divorcees these days, he couldn't ignore a lifetime of programming drummed into him by his father.

'Rufus, don't be so ridiculous. There is no future in a relationship with your son's nanny.' He could hear his father's voice as clearly as if he were standing in the room with him.

He'd grown up knowing he was part of the ancient feudal system with a title whose history went back hundreds of years. He'd known he would one day inherit that title, and although the obligation to sit in the House of Lords had been removed in Tony Blair's day, Rufus still felt the weight of duty and responsibility.

'One must set a good example, and that means courting the right type of girl.'

The last Lord Holt might be physically in his grave, but his opinions had been etched into Rufus's subconscious. Despite the clear-out, there was evidence of his presence in every single room in Beechbrook House. It was there in the dark antiques, the thick carpets, the ancestral portraits, the fact that no one was ever allowed to open a window because Alfred had always hated the cold. Half the windows had seized shut with disuse and were now impossible to open anyway.

His father might just as well still live here. Rufus was so glad he didn't. And he was suffused with guilt that he felt this way. On the night his father had died, he would have given anything to have had him back for a few more weeks, days, even hours, so they could talk – say things they'd never had the chance to say. There was so much unfinished business.

But Rufus didn't need to speak to his father to know what he would have said about Emilia.

'Sleep with her if you must, Rufus, but get it out of your system quickly. It can't go any further. You can't have a relationship with the nanny.'

He would have wrinkled up his nose on the word 'nanny' in that fastidious way he did when a plate of food at a function displeased him. On those occasions he would have pushed away the plate, and smiled at the hostess. 'It looks delicious, but I'm really not that hungry.' Lies... hypocrisy... they were part of his social make-up.

When Rufus's mother had died, Alfred had never married again. He'd never dated anyone again, dismissing all possible women that came onto his radar as unsuitable – *can't hold a candle to your mother* – instead he'd thrown himself into Beechbrook, into making money, being on committees and boards, and, in his later years, into playing golf.

In some ways, Rufus had admired him for that; his devotion to duty and responsibility and to keeping a stiff upper lip and carrying on, no matter what. When history had repeated itself and he'd lost his own beautiful wife to that terrible riding accident, Rufus had, to a large extent, followed in his father's footsteps and done the same thing.

But he hadn't been as committed to the path as his father had been. He'd succumbed to the attractions of Phoebe. In his father's eyes, Phoebe had probably been even worse than Emilia, Rufus thought a little ruefully.

He stood up from his office chair, where he'd been sitting for a long time, mulling things over, stretched his arms above his head before rubbing distractedly at his aching shoulders.

Phoebe had been effectively a Crowther, and therefore also an impossible match for a Holt. The Holts and the Crowthers, thanks to that long-ago poker game, were sworn enemies. They weren't quite in the realms of the Capulets and the Montagues, but they weren't that far off.

Deep down, Rufus knew it wasn't just the past that had sabotaged his relationship with Phoebe. Their present lifestyles had been incompatible. The fact they'd never once made love had made it easier to step away from Phoebe, but Emilia had ducked under his carefully erected barriers.

He'd always relied on Emilia. He'd had virtually no defence on that awful night his father had died. She'd found the door in his vulnerability and slipped inside, and having allowed himself to be seduced once, Rufus now couldn't get enough of her. He wanted to be with her. Like a prisoner who has been in solitary confinement and has been denied human contact, he *needed* to be with her, and she was more than happy to be with him.

Rufus had also now relaxed about being seen in intimate situations with her outside the house. One gorgeous Sunday afternoon, they'd gone for a walk through a plantation, not far from Beechbrook, and when Emilia had slipped her hand into his, Rufus had let it stay there.

Hand in hand, they'd walked along a cinder track, through the summer green foliage, past dog walkers, families and other couples and even a woman on a horse, exchanging, 'Good afternoons,' and he'd felt exhilarated, free. He'd felt as though for once in his life he'd come out from beneath his father's shadow. He'd felt so safe with Emilia that even the horse hadn't set off his PTSD.

But there was a world of difference between walking through a forest, where he'd be unlucky to be recognised, and going public. He hadn't even told Harrison what was going on. Fortunately, Harrison had been too distracted lately with the prospect of finding a place to live with Tori and forthcoming fatherhood. They'd not talked much, although his old friend had said a number of times lately, 'I'm only at the end of a phone if you need me. You do know that, don't you?'

Rufus did know it, but talking about it would have made it more real. He also knew that he couldn't keep Emilia a secret forever. Sooner or later, they would either have to go public, or he would have to stop the relationship. But right now, he couldn't bring himself to do either.

21

Then one Saturday evening in early October, the situation was taken out of his hands. Rufus was at a charity dinner in Salisbury, organised by the board of governors of a school in Bridgeford. His father had been on the board and Rufus had been invited to go to the dinner in his place. He'd wanted to turn the invitation down because he knew he was going to be asked to step into his father's shoes and join the board – something that Rufus had no intention of doing. But he'd been asked by Geoffrey Bartley-Smythe, a friend of his father's, and had procrastinated so long about whether or not to go that in the end it would have seemed churlish to refuse. At least if he went, he could explain his reasons for refusing the position, face to face.

It was the first public engagement he'd done since his father had died and several people had already offered their condolences.

'So sorry to hear of your father's passing, Lord Holt.'

'Jolly bad news about Lord Alfred.'

'If there's anything we can do, you only have to say the word, Lord Holt.'

These platitudes had been offered with a selection of back slaps and arm pats. Rufus didn't think he'd ever get used to being addressed as Lord Holt. He told anyone who said it that Rufus would be fine.

Even Alfred hadn't been overly keen on the strict use of the title, except on the odd occasion when he'd wanted to impress or to bring weight to some negotiation.

The event was being held in a private room on the first floor of the Royal Plaza Hotel. It had red curtains, chandeliers and wooden floors and there were four or five round white-clothed tables, each laid up for six. Most people seemed to be with their partners.

Dinner – a dry roast chicken, accompanied by a paltry amount of peas and carrots, but plenty of potatoes – had already been served and eaten. A few minutes ago, the servers had brought out little terracotta dishes of apple crumble, accompanied by jugs of bright yellow custard – Rufus had eaten about a quarter of his – it had tasted better than it looked, but he was no longer hungry. He had decided to leave straight after the coffee. He'd already explained to Elizabeth Featherstone, chair of the board, who was seated on his left, that flattered as he was to receive the invitation to take his father's place on the board, he was regretfully going to have to turn it down.

To his relief, Elizabeth, a jovial woman in her mid-fifties, had accepted this with good grace.

'We thought you might have too many other commitments, Lord Holt,' she'd said. 'Please don't worry, and thank you for coming tonight. I'm sure you must be completely overloaded with work up at Beechbrook.'

'I am a little. Thank you for being so understanding.'

Sitting on his right was Geoffrey, the reason he'd felt obliged to come at all. Geoffrey was in his late seventies and had been drinking wine steadily since he'd arrived. He was now quite drunk.

To Rufus's relief, for most of the dinner, Geoffrey's attention had been focused on a pretty dark-haired woman in her mid-thirties who was sitting on his other side, but she'd just excused herself and had got up from the table. With no one else to talk to, Geoffrey now turned and fixed his slightly unfocused gaze on Rufus.

'I do feel for you, Rufie,' he said. 'Rattling around in that old place all on your ownsome.' Leaning in, he lowered his voice to a stage whisper, which must have come out louder than he thought, or maybe it was just unfortunate there was a gap in the hubbub of general conversation at that moment. 'But it hasn't been all bad, has it...' He gave a leery wink. 'Bedding the staff, eh, old boy?'

His words hung in the little silence. But Geoffrey carried on, oblivious.

'I don't blame you, Rufie. Fine-looking filly. If I were thirty years younger, I'd have taken her for a canter around the paddock myself.' He guffawed.

The table went quiet for a good four seconds. Or at least, to Rufus's horror and mortification, that's how it seemed. They were all too polite to stare for long, but he could feel several curious gazes before they quickly averted their eyes and the murmur of polite chatter resumed.

Geoffrey nudged his arm. 'Whatever gets you through, eh, Rufie. Ah, sorry, Lord Holt?'

He hiccupped loudly and almost fell off his chair.

Rufus put down his fork and spoon, folded his napkin neatly by his plate and stood up. His heart was hammering so loudly it was all he could now hear, but he forced out some polite words.

'Always good to talk to you, Geoffrey, but I really should be going. Thanks for the invite.'

He left with as much dignity as he could muster. His table was one of the furthest from the door and it seemed like a long walk of shame across the hard wooden floor. His face was burning, and he could feel sweat trickling down the back of his neck, but he kept his back straight and looked neither right nor left as he exited the room.

Outside on the stairs, he felt a surge of relief that he'd driven himself and there was no need to wait for a taxi, or for Harrison, who'd offered to drive him.

A few minutes later, he was in the municipal car park, sitting in his Mercedes, his hands clammy on the steering wheel, feeling his heart still thundering in his ears, and taking deep breaths to try to calm himself.

Had they all known about him and Emilia? Or had it just been Geoffrey? They all knew now, that was for sure. Rufus had never felt so ashamed and so guilty in his life. He disliked social occasions at the best of times but after Geoffrey's revelations tonight, which had made him the sole focus of attention, he doubted he'd ever attend one again.

The shame and the mortification of Geoffrey's casually uttered words burnt in him. He felt as though that awful phrase, 'bedding the staff', was now branded on his heart. A permanent reminder of the fact that he'd failed in his duty, he'd betrayed his family, all of the moral upstanding men that had gone before him. He had shown himself to be not a suitable guardian of Beechbrook House. He had shown himself to be the utter failure he'd always suspected that he was.

The only thing that made him feel marginally better was that at least his father was dead and hadn't been witness to his errant son's misdemeanours. Rufus rested his head on the cool leather of the steering wheel. Even that was only a small consolation. He knew that, if such a thing were possible, the late Lord Alfred would at this moment be turning in his grave.

* * *

On the same Saturday that Rufus's world had been turned upside down by Geoffrey Bartley-Smythe's casually brutal, insensitive words, Sam had spent the afternoon teaching at Brook Stables. His last lesson had been tutoring Georgia, a teenager who was polishing up her skills to enter a working hunter class the following weekend, and now they were standing in the yard, chatting about shows in general.

Georgia had just dismounted while Sam held her pony, and she was now running up her nearside stirrup and unbuckling Tiger Lily's girth. She was chattering happily.

'I was reading *Farmer's Life* last week and they had a write-up on the Oakley Riding Club's latest show. Lucinda Fox did pretty well by the sound of it. Have you met her? She's only twelve, but she's done really well with her pony Peter Pan. They were pretty good last year but they're sweeping the board this year.'

'I don't think I have met her,' Sam said, trying to recall, 'although the name rings a bell.'

'So then I started looking at some other old *Farmer's Life* mags in the office,' Georgia nodded towards the open door of Brook's office, 'and I saw how well she did last year. She had the same pony too. Do you think that's the secret, Sam, just persevering with the same pony and getting a little bit better each year? Mummy has suggested that I move up a gear and we buy a better pony, but I'm not sure I agree. I think Tiger Lily's got so much potential. And I love her.' She dropped a kiss on Tiger Lily's sweaty chestnut neck.

'Sticking with the same pony can't hurt, especially if you've got a good one,' Sam said thoughtfully. But his mind was leaping ahead. Of course. Why hadn't he thought of it before? 'Are there a lot of *Farmer's Life* magazines in the office?' he asked Georgia.

'Piles and piles. There are loads of *Horse and Hounds* too. I don't think Marjorie ever chucks anything out. She really should. It's quite difficult to get to the notice board. And it's probably a fire hazard.'

But Sam had stopped listening. 'Good luck at the show next week. Let me know how you get on.'

'I will,' she promised, and Sam excused himself and headed for the office. There was no one else there – Marjorie must be out somewhere in the yard.

But as Georgia had said, there was a huge tottering pile of *Farmer's Life* magazines on the floor beneath the notice board, and as he began to riffle through them, he could see they were pretty much in date order, and they went back years. It was a simple matter to find the ones from three years ago. He went back a further year just in case Becky Arnold's memory was at fault and then he laid them out on the table in between the show schedules, the appointments book – Marjorie still kept a paper book – and a scattering of empty coffee mugs.

Sam began to flick through them methodically. He soon found some show write-ups and, as Georgia had said, the names of the placed contestants, along with their pony's names, had all been carefully listed.

There couldn't be that many horses called Casey's Girl – luckily it was an unusual name.

Ruby Milton and Sasha were on top form, taking the win, in the working hunter and...

Sam's heart missed a beat. Bingo. There it was.

...just behind them in second place was Cassandra Hastings on Casey's Girl.

He blew out a breath he hadn't realised he'd been holding.

Cassandra Hastings on Casey's Girl. He should have guessed there would be a connection between the names, there often was, but it didn't matter. It was there in black and white. They finally had the name of the horse's owner – or at least they had the name of her rider. Sam was pretty sure they would be the same person.

He read a few more results, just to be sure, but as Poppy had said, Casey's Girl and Cassandra Hastings had been regularly placed. Feeling his heart speed up again with a mix of excitement and relief, Sam gathered the relevant magazines and rolled them up.

They could probably have found out the same result if they'd checked online, he thought, except that no one had thought to look at old show results online.

And now they wouldn't need to. Thank goodness Marjorie Taylor was a hoarder.

22

'Cassandra Hastings, well, I never.' Maggie shook her head, as she looked at Phoebe and Sam. It was now Sunday morning and they had called round to Puddleduck Farm to tell her the good news in person.

'I think Casey is short for Cassandra,' Phoebe added. 'We should have guessed, shouldn't we, that her owner's name would have been something like that.'

'It's easy with hindsight,' Maggie said. 'Besides, I'm not sure that guessing her owner's first name would have helped us that much. I don't suppose you've got an address, have you?'

'Not yet,' Phoebe said, 'but I have looked online. There are quite a few websites where you can search for addresses linked to names, so that's a start. According to the one I was on last night, there are a hundred people called Hastings in Hampshire. Fewer in the New Forest but none of them were called Cassandra. I tried narrowing it down by post codes in the actual New Forest,' she gave a sigh of frustration, 'but it didn't help much.'

'That's because she probably lives – or lived – with her parents,' Sam said. 'We'd be better looking on social media, I reckon.'

'I had a quick look on Facebook on my phone.' Phoebe had done that late last night when he was asleep. 'But they said I had the wrong password. Then they wouldn't let me reset it and when I finally managed to do that, I discovered there were dozens of people called Cassandra Hastings. So I gave up. Temporarily.'

'Let's go and ask Natasha,' Maggie suggested. 'She's a hotshot on all things techie. Actually, I think she's with Marcus. They said something about doing some work with Saddam.'

A few moments later, they were walking across the yard to the barn, accompanied by Tiny and Buster, the two dogs having roused themselves from Sunday-morning sleepiness. It was a beautiful October morning. The sky was a crystal blue and the scents of ploughed fields and harvesting were in the air. The first signs of autumn, Phoebe always thought.

'I think you guys had better stay out here,' Maggie told the dogs, as she pushed open the barn door. 'Is it OK if we come in?' she called into the gloom.

'Of course, Mrs Crowther.' Marcus was at the other end of the barn with Natasha. 'But could you come slowly, please?'

As Phoebe and Sam went in slowly too, Phoebe thought for a second that she was imagining things – or that her eyes hadn't properly adjusted to the light, which was dim compared to the brightness of the day.

Marcus was sitting down, but he had a cat-shaped ginger adornment laid across his lap. Surely that couldn't be Saddam. Phoebe gasped.

So did Maggie, who'd now stopped dead in her tracks. 'My, my, my... I never thought I'd see the day. That is that half-feral, dog-mugging fiend of a feline you've got draped across your lap, I'm guessing. Or do I need new glasses?'

Marcus laughed quietly. 'You don't need new glasses. Yes, it is, but I'm not sure how long he's going to stay here now.' Even as he spoke, there was a swish of ginger tail and Saddam got up and stalked haughtily across the barn until he was a few hay bales away from Marcus. He leapt nimbly across a few more, heading upwards with each one, until he was about a quarter of the way up the stack and sat there. Amber eyes glared at them crossly and he swished his tail again for good measure.

Natasha, who was sitting a few bales away from Marcus, stood up to greet them. 'Isn't it fantastic? He's done amazing stuff with him, hasn't he? I wouldn't have believed it was possible either. There are some animals that you just assume will never be OK.' She linked her hand into Marcus's. 'The man's a genius.'

'I'm not,' Marcus said, looking a little flustered beneath this onslaught of praise. 'I'm just patient.'

'He might one day be able to go to a new home,' Phoebe breathed, glancing towards the sectioned-off part of the barn where the puppies had been, and hoping Roxie was OK. They'd left her asleep in her crate. There were still another couple of weeks before she could go out for walks.

'It will be a while yet,' Marcus said quickly. 'And it would need to be the right home. It can't just be anyone.'

'I will leave the rehoming of Saddam to you and Natasha,' Maggie said. 'So don't you worry about that.' She cleared he throat. 'We've got some more good news, but we need your help.'

A few minutes later, they were sitting on haybales, gathered around the screen of Natasha's phone, which fortunately was big enough for them all to see, while Natasha scrolled expertly through pages on Facebook.

Even Phoebe was impressed at the speed with which she found a picture of a girl called Cassie Hastings on a horse that looked suspiciously like Casey's Girl.

'How did you find it so fast?' Phoebe said, leaning forward. 'Is that her profile photo?'

'No.' Natasha flicked back a screen. 'But this is.'

The profile was of a horse in profile jumping a small fence.

'Bingo,' said Marcus, as Natasha navigated back to the main page and started flicking through photos of a blonde girl on a horse.

'These are just the public photos we're looking at,' she explained to anyone who needed it explaining. 'There will be loads more, I'm sure, but I'll have to send her a message and a friend request to get a look at those. This is definitely the right person, though, isn't it?' She had stopped the screen on a picture of Casey's Girl and her rider, head on to the camera. 'It's not just a similar-looking horse with a white blaze?'

'We probably need to go and have a good look at Henna,' Sam said. 'It would be bad to make a mistake. Is she in the field or the stable?'

'The field,' Natasha confirmed. 'She's settled down a lot since she's been here. I'm putting that down to Marcus too. She hasn't jumped out of her field once lately, has she, babe?'

'I don't think so.' He flicked her a gaze. 'Although I haven't got to the bottom of some of her other issues. She still rears.' He looked at Sam. 'But it takes time to reverse bad habits, I'm guessing.'

Sam nodded. 'Judging by what you've done with Saddam, I'm sure you'll get there given enough time,' he said, as they all trooped out of the barn.

Buster was still waiting patiently outside. Tiny had disappeared. As they strolled past the kennel block, they saw that the wolfhound was being petted by a volunteer, who called across to Maggie. 'I wish he was up for rehoming. He is so gorgeous. My grandma used to have one of these. Do they come in to rescue very often?'

'Thankfully not. But I will certainly keep you in mind if we ever get another one.' Maggie's eyes sparkled.

Phoebe found herself smiling too. Maggie adored Tiny and would never let him go, but she was in her element, rehoming animals, helping them to be rehabilitated, tracking down lost owners. It was so good to see.

* * *

At the neddies' field, Maggie rested her elbows on the five-bar gate. Henna was at the far corner, grazing.

'Does anyone know a quick way of getting her over here?' she asked as they stood in the lunchtime sunshine.

The three donkeys were already trotting across to them. They all knew that Maggie was the giver of treats, but the bay horse showed no signs of following.

'Cover your ears, guys,' Marcus said, and put his fingers to his lips. He let out two piercingly sharp whistles and, to Phoebe's amazement, the bay horse lifted her head, pricked her ears and trotted down the field towards the gate.

'I think you could go into business as a horse whisperer,' Sam said, looking at him in admiration. 'I've seen a lot that will come to the bucket, but not many horses that'll do that.'

'The thing is, I didn't actually teach her to do it,' Marcus said. 'I just found out that she did it.'

'How?' Sam asked, but his question was drowned out by a thundering of hooves and a cacophony of squealing as three donkeys and a horse all tried to get to the five-bar gate at the same time. There was some jostling as they worked out their pecking order.

Maggie fed the donkeys some of the carrot slices she seemed to carry everywhere, while Marcus stroked Henna's neck. Phoebe, Natasha and Sam compared her markings to the picture on Natasha's phone. Each of them pointed out things in turn.

'Three white socks.'

'Yep.'

'One offside fore black.'

'Yep.'

'White blaze that goes across right-hand side of nose.'

'Yep.'

'Bit of black on nearside hock.'

'Yep. I think that's pretty categoric,' Natasha said. 'Our Henna's definitely Casey's Girl. We'd better rechristen her.' She straightened her shoulders and looked back at her phone. 'I'll send Cassie Hastings a friend request and see what happens. I'll also send her a message, which she may or may not see, depending on how she's got her Facebook set up. But hopefully she'll be interested that we've found her horse. Is that OK with you, Maggie?'

Maggie hesitated, her face screwed up in consternation.

'My only reservation is that she might not be the original owner. What do you think, Phoebe?'

'Are you asking me how long ago her microchip was removed?' Phoebe had been thinking the same thing herself.

'Could you give it your best guess?'

'At least a couple of years, maybe three. It's so hard to tell.'

'And those two were entering competitions longer ago than three years. So it does seem likely that Cassie is her proper owner.'

'But don't you need a microchip and passport to enter shows?' Natasha asked Sam.

'Technically yes, and they're quite hot on it now, but a few years back they were more interested in vaccination certificates than anything else. And a lot depends on the competition organisers.'

'I think the only way we're going to find out is to message her,' he added, and everyone nodded in agreement.

Once more, Natasha typed on her screen, at a speed which made Phoebe feel old, before finally saying, 'All done. Now we just have to wait and see.'

Phoebe half expected the mysterious Cassandra to reply instantly, and clearly she wasn't the only one because for a few seconds they all stood there expectantly while the donkeys and horse hung about, tossing their heads and swishing their tails, hoping for more carrot.

Nothing happened. There was no answering ping to tell them a message had come flying back.

'She might not be glued to her phone like I am,' Natasha said, correctly interpreting their expressions. 'She might not even see it until later.'

Phoebe looked at Sam. 'We'd better get back to Roxie, hadn't we? You will let us know what happens, won't you, Natasha?'

'Of course I will.'

* * *

'That all felt like a bit of an anticlimax,' Phoebe said to Sam as she drove them back to Woodcutter's in the Lexus. 'What do you think?'

'I'm just really pleased we finally tracked down someone who can help solve the mystery,' he replied peaceably. 'Let's hope she sees the message quickly.'

Phoebe knew he was right.

It was wonderfully warm for October. Late blackberries still clung to brambles in the hedgerows, and it was still T-shirt weather. They spent the rest of Sunday in the enclosed garden at Woodcutter's playing with Roxie, who to Phoebe's delight could now sit and lie down on command and, to a limited extent, wait on command too. The latter wasn't so easy because she couldn't keep her bottom still, so keen was she to move about.

'The world is far too exciting,' Phoebe said, picking up the puppy and cuddling her. 'I'm so glad we went ahead and got her, Sam.'

'Me too. Our own little family.'

It was the perfect time to ask him about children. They were both half sitting, half lying on the grass outside, on an old tartan picnic blanket Phoebe had found in a cupboard. They'd had a cheese and biscuits lunch outside too, which had been fun because Roxie, who'd already shown herself to be a foodie, had assumed everything was for her and had kept darting in to sniff plates. In the end, they'd had to move the picnic to the table on the decking where the puppy couldn't reach everything, although Phoebe had still slipped her a few morsels of cheese.

Now Phoebe put Roxie down gently and the puppy ambled off across the grass to explore. Phoebe rolled onto her front on the blanket. She said softly, 'Do you want your own children one day, Sam?'

He'd been lying on his side, on his elbow, with his head supported in one hand and now he leaned to pluck a blade of grass from the lawn and looked at her. 'Yeah, of course I do. You know I do.'

'I meant with me,' she murmured, suddenly realising how massively important his answer was to her. Her throat hurt with the enormity of it.

'You're not pregnant, are you?' Sam looked slightly startled.

'No, I'm not pregnant. Why? Would it matter if I was?'

There was a tiny pause before he said, 'No. Not at all, although I'm relieved you're not. It feels like we only just started dating.'

'True, but we've known each other for ever.'

'Yes, we have.' He put the piece of grass in his mouth and chewed one end of it. His gaze held hers. His eyes were as blue as the endless sky above them.

'What?' Phoebe prompted. 'What are you thinking, Sam?'

But whatever it was, she wasn't destined to find out because a little yelp distracted them and when they looked up, they saw Roxie pawing at her nose.

Phoebe rushed to her side and saw a bee fluttering around on the grass. 'Oh, no, sweetie, you didn't try and eat that, did you?' She examined her quickly. 'I think she might have been stung, Sam. Bees are so dozy at this time of year. I'll pop her inside and stick something on it.'

'I'll come and help.' He jumped to his feet and they headed for the house with the puppy. Phoebe knew the moment for talking had passed.

23

It was almost another week before Cassie Hastings finally returned Natasha's message.

Phoebe had just finished Saturday appointments when Natasha came hurtling into Puddleduck Pets, waving her phone.

'She finally got back to me,' she called to Marcus, who was in the process of closing down the computers for the day. 'She's coming over.'

'Who is?' Jenna asked, turning curiously from a prescription she'd just made up.

'You took the words right out of my mouth.' Phoebe went to meet Natasha, who was beaming.

'Cassie Hastings. It's her horse. Casey's Girl is her horse. I'm just on my way to tell Maggie.'

'Is she coming to collect her? Where does she live?' Both of these questions were from Marcus.

'I don't know. She didn't say. She said she'd explain everything when she got here.' Natasha dashed out again.

Marcus looked at Phoebe and gave a slight shake of his head. 'I'm as mystified as you are.'

'But I guess now you will at least get some answers,' Jenna said. 'I'd like to stay and hear them but I've got a school concert, so I'd better go. I'll drop this prescription off on the way. See you Monday, guys.'

Max had already gone on a call-out so it was just Phoebe and Marcus who were still in reception when Natasha and Maggie came back again.

'I said we'd meet her outside Puddleduck Pets,' Natasha said. 'I thought you guys might be interested to hear what she's got to say.'

'Oh, definitely.' Phoebe took a last look around to check that she'd switched everything off before going outside. It was a nice evening, although the nights were drawing in fast now. In another fortnight the clocks went back but it was still warm in the day. It was still possible to pretend that summer hadn't quite left them.

They didn't have long to wait. Barely ten minutes had passed before they heard the side gate clang and a blonde, petite young woman wearing black jeans, a hoodie and pink Converse high-tops hurried into their view.

'Hi, I'm Cassie.' She looked taken aback to see such a big reception committee. But she smiled at each of them in turn. 'I understand you've found my horse.'

'Have you only just noticed she's gone?' Maggie asked, straight to the point as usual. 'She's been here several weeks.'

'I've been away. I've actually been away since August. I was travelling across Europe. Doing my gap year.' She glanced at Natasha, who was probably the person closest to her age. 'You know how it is?'

Natasha, who'd never been to university, let alone had a gap year, shrugged. 'Not really. But anyway, I guess you had someone looking after her for you? What happened there?'

Cassie shook her head. 'No one was looking after her specifically. Apart from my family, I mean. She was at home in her field, as usual. At least I thought she was. Daddy didn't tell me she'd gone missing. He said he didn't want to worry me while I was away. And the rest of my family have been abroad too.' Her face crumpled a little. 'Oh, poor Casey. Is she OK?'

'She's absolutely fine,' Marcus told her quickly. 'She was out in the forest for a while but luckily a couple of agisters managed to catch her and they brought her here.'

'I'm really grateful that they did. And I'll pay for whatever we owe you for her keep obviously.'

Phoebe glanced at her and then at Maggie's face. Her grandmother looked tired and Phoebe guessed she would say there was no need, so she stepped in. 'We will need to do you a bill, yes.'

'A donation will be fine,' Maggie contradicted her. 'I'm just glad you've turned up, frankly. Better late than never.' She sighed. 'Did your father tell you what had happened?'

'He said he thought a bit of fence had been knocked down by people using the footpath. There's a footpath that goes across her field. It's happened before. Or that someone may have left the gate open. I'm really not sure.' She blushed a deep shade of red.

She definitely wasn't telling them everything, Phoebe thought.

'Can I see her?' Cassie asked and for a moment she looked so vulnerable that Phoebe felt herself soften.

She might be lying through her teeth about what had happened, but it was clear that she really cared about the horse. Phoebe reminded herself that Casey's Girl, or Henna, as they'd nicknamed her back then, had been in tip-top condition when she'd first arrived. She hadn't been neglected.

'Of course you can see her.' Maggie glanced at Cassie's footwear. 'I take it you're not picking her up today.'

'No, it's too far to ride her back. We're over towards Lyndhurst.

Daddy will have to bring the box over. I was hoping we could collect her tomorrow – that's if you don't mind having her for one more night.'

'That's fine.'

They walked across the yard and on to the five-bar gate to the field.

Phoebe was half expecting Casey's Girl to come cantering across to meet her owner, like she had to meet Marcus the previous week, but she didn't. Neither did Cassie whistle nor make any attempt to call her horse.

'She's always been difficult to catch,' she murmured. 'I usually rattle pony nuts in a bucket. I don't suppose we could get a bucket.'

'I can fetch one,' Maggie offered, but Marcus shook his head.

'No need for that.' He put two fingers to his lips and whistled.

Phoebe had a strong sense of déjà vu as the horse lifted her head, pricked up her ears and came in a fast trot across the field towards them, just as she had the previous week.

Cassie looked at him, wide-eyed. 'Wow. How did you teach her that?'

He shook his head. He was clearly about to say he hadn't when Natasha put her hand on his arm. 'Marcus is our resident behaviourist,' she told Cassie. 'He's an absolute whizz at training.'

'Well, I'm very impressed.' Cassie grinned in delight as the horse wheeled to a halt by the gate. Before anyone else could react, she had climbed nimbly over and she threw her arms around her horse's neck. For a few moments, they all witnessed the joyful reunion of horse and rider. Casey's Girl tossed her head and whickered on her young owner's fingers and Cassie had tears in her eyes as she stroked her neck over and over. 'I'm so glad you're OK,' she was saying. 'My gorgeous, gorgeous girl.'

The donkeys, who'd been further away from the gate than the

horse, were also on their way over but there were a few moments before that when Phoebe, Maggie, Marcus and Natasha all witnessed the love that horse and owner shared. There was no doubt the two knew each other. No doubt at all.

* * *

'Although there's definitely something odd about this whole situation,' Maggie said when Cassie had finally left, having promised to return the next day with the horse box. 'For a start I didn't buy her story that her father hadn't told her because he didn't want to worry her.'

'Neither did I.' Natasha's face was serious. 'Even if he hadn't wanted to worry her, surely he'd still have tried to find the horse. He'd have reported her missing to the police. She's obviously quite valuable.' She looked at Marcus, who was frowning.

'I'm more curious about the whole whistle business,' he said. 'I was amazed when Cassie said she didn't teach her that. Thanks for stopping me saying anything. That was a good call. But obviously someone has taught her and if wasn't Cassie, then who was it?'

'Her previous owners,' Phoebe suggested. They all stared at each other. 'It's odd that she's not microchipped now. All horses have to be microchipped legally, and have a passport, although to be honest there are still quite a few who just have a passport and no microchip. There's definitely more to this situation than meets the eye. Hmmm. If Casey's Girl was stolen, it couldn't have been recently. The show schedules Sam found were all from around three years ago.'

'I hate to say it, but I think you might be on to something there, love.' Maggie narrowed her eyes thoughtfully. 'I'm not very comfortable about any of this. It's very odd and it puts us in rather a difficult situation. If that mare is stolen, I can't in all conscience let the people who may have stolen her just rock up and collect her tomorrow, can I?'

'No.' Natasha shifted from foot to foot. 'We really do need to go back to the police again.'

'I'm still waiting for a follow-up call from the last time,' Maggie said disparagingly. 'They clearly have other priorities.'

Marcus cleared his throat. 'Putting the stolen theory aside for a minute, I have another spanner to throw into the works,' he said. 'I realised something else this week. It's about the rearing.'

They all turned to look at him, and he blushed a little. Marcus never liked being the centre of attention.

'It might be easier if I show you. We'll need to bring her into the yard. Or at least away from the neddies.'

'OK. I'll distract them with bread, while you bring her out,' Maggie said.

The donkeys were thrilled to be distracted with bread and a few moments later, Marcus had clipped a lead rope onto Casey's Girl's headcollar and had led her into the yard, where her unshod hooves thudded dully across the concrete.

'I think that the same person who taught her to come to a whistle also taught her some other things,' he said. 'Including to rear on command.' He led the mare a little distance away. 'I need you to all stand well clear while I do an experiment.'

They did as Marcus said, giving him and the horse a good ten feet of clearance. Then Marcus stood a few feet in front of the mare, lifted a hand, and said something very softly to her.

Instantly she rose up on her hind legs, her forelegs pawing the air before coming down again in front of him.

'Good girl,' Marcus praised. 'And again.'

The mare reared again.

'Good girl. One more time.' This time he didn't make any kind of signal with his hand, but again Casey's Girl stood on her hind legs and pawed the air.

'Yay. Super girl,' Marcus said, as she hit the ground again in front of him. He led her back towards his audience. She was tossing her head up and down, clearly very pleased with herself.

'Someone taught her to rear. I think she's responding to both visual and verbal commands. But for obvious reasons I'll put her back in her field, before I tell you what they are.'

* * *

In the end, it was Eddie who'd come up with a way Maggie could keep Casey's Girl at Puddleduck Pets while they tried to get to the truth of the situation.

'You just tell them they have to prove ownership before you can sign her over,' he told Maggie and Phoebe. 'I doubt the Hastings family have got a passport.' His shrewd old eyes narrowed speculatively. 'Not a real one, anyway. Passports have to be linked to microchips.'

Phoebe's head was whirring. 'We surely don't think Cassie's family stole her, though.'

'If they did, Cassie doesn't know anything about it,' Maggie said with authority. 'I'd put money on that. This is all just conjecture, though, isn't it? Let me have another word with the police. But I think Eddie's right. I'll stall the Hastings family for now. I'll blame red tape and bureaucracy.'

* * *

'It was amazing watching Marcus getting Casey's Girl to rear on command,' Phoebe told Sam later that evening when they were both settled at his flat with Roxie.

Roxie had recently got acquainted with both the stairs, and Snowball, the latter whom she now treated with the utmost respect, after an early warning tap on the nose.

'I don't think I'd have believed it if I hadn't seen him actually demonstrate it. I didn't even know you could teach horses to rear.'

'You can teach horses loads of things, they're highly intelligent,' Sam said. 'How did Marcus work out the voice commands?'

'Trial and error, I think. And you know how observant and patient he is when it comes to animals. He'd started to notice that her rearing wasn't as random as it seemed. Then he just put his theory into practice. He thinks she's been taught to rear both on hand signals, quite subtle ones, but also on certain words and phrases. He's narrowed it down to a few so far, but he thinks there are probably others.'

'Go on.' Sam looked fascinated.

'She rears if you say, "and again", also if you say, "one more time" and – get this,' she paused for dramatic effect, 'she also rears if you say the word, "secret".'

'Bloody hell. Why on earth would anyone go to the trouble of teaching her to do that?'

'Why indeed?' Phoebe looked at him speculatively. 'And it also begs the question, what were you and my brother talking about when you were trying to catch her that time and she was rearing? Did either of you mention secrets?'

'No, I'm sure we didn't. I don't remember what we were talking about. Blimey, it was ages ago. Who knows! We must have said one of the other phrases, I honestly can't remember.'

Phoebe had been half teasing, but Sam's ultra-defensive reaction surprised her. He seemed quite flustered. And his neck had gone red. How very odd.

'I'm sure we'll get to the bottom of it sooner or later,' she said quietly.

'We will.' Sam's eyes were gentle, and some instinct told her not to push him.

Then he bent to pet Roxie, and neither of them said any more about suspected stolen horses or secrets.

24

Rufus had just spent what had turned out to be one of the worst weeks of his life.

When he'd got back from the board of governors' dinner, the first person he'd seen had been Emilia, but he'd barely been able to bring himself to look at her.

She'd tuned in instantly to his mood. 'Rufus, what's happened? You look terrible. Are you ill?' She'd fussed around him, picking up his jacket where he'd missed the hook by the door so it had landed on the floor, and then brushing it off before she hung it back up again.

'No, I'm not ill.'

He'd gone past her into the kitchen and she'd followed him.

'Then what is it?'

'It's nothing.' He'd made to move past her again but this time she'd blocked his way.

'Rufus, you must tell me, please? This is not nothing.'

How could he find the words to explain? Rufus knew he could never find the words, either in his language or in hers, but Emilia was not going to be deflected.

She moved closer, and put her hands on his shoulders, leaning in so all he could smell was her scent. That intoxicating scent that lately had sent his head spinning. She must have had a bath and waited for him to get back. But right now, he didn't feel intoxicated. He just felt sick.

Feeling like the cornered rat that he knew he was going to be, Rufus said, 'OK, I'll tell you. I can't go on like this. I've made a decision. You need to leave.'

'What?' Her voice was high with shock. 'What do you mean?'

'I mean that I want you to go. Move out. Leave Beechbrook.'

'No, you don't.' She leaned forward, her face soft. 'You have feelings for me, and I have feelings for you. I know this is true.'

'It's not true.' Rufus held her shoulders, gently but firmly, keeping her at arm's length from him. 'It's not true. I don't have feelings for you. I've used you for sex, Emilia. That's all. But it's over. I want you to pack your bags and get out of my house.'

The expression on her face was something that Rufus knew he would never forget. He had thought she might shout or rage or threaten him, but she didn't. Her face crumpled, just closed in on itself, and she gave a small sob, before stepping away from him. Across the other side of the kitchen, he saw her bend over the sink and her shoulders heaved for a few silent seconds before she somehow managed to regain some self-control. Then she straightened her shoulders, pulled her back ramrod straight and left the room without looking at him and without saying another word.

He let out a breath. Every instinct he had screamed at him to go after her. To say that he hadn't meant it. But he couldn't go after her. He mustn't. He had clenched his fists into balls by his sides. This was the only way. The kindest way. At least in the long run. It was much better this way than letting this fantasy run on any longer. It would only get harder. It would only get harder for both of them if he didn't end it now.

He didn't see her again that night. He holed up in his office until he could no longer hear her moving around. He consoled himself with whisky, just as he'd done on the night that his father had died, but this time he drank alone. Sometime around 2 a.m., he had stumbled up to bed and had fallen into a drunken oblivion.

In the morning, when he woke up in the harsh glare of the autumn sunlight, he discovered that Emilia and all traces of her had gone. He had no idea if she'd gone last night or whether she'd left this morning – or even how she'd got to the train station, or wherever she had gone. He realised that he had absolutely no idea where she would go or even if she had anywhere to go, and the guilt bit deep.

It wasn't until later that day when he'd seen Harrison outside that he'd found out the details.

'I saw her go off in a taxi this morning,' Harrison said, 'complete with her bags. What happened? I thought you two were getting on OK? More than OK.'

His oldest friend's eyes were knowing, and Rufus wondered bleakly if everyone had known what was going on between him and Emilia. The relationship he'd thought he'd hidden so well had clearly not been hidden at all.

'It's been obvious to me,' Harrison said when Rufus asked him, as they strolled across the Beechbrook lawns and past a pile of auburn leaves raked into a pile by the gardener. 'You haven't exactly been subtle, have you?'

'We hadn't really been out anywhere in public,' Rufus said wearily, rubbing at his throbbing temples. No amount of painkillers and pints of water had softened the terrible hangover. 'Apart from the occasional walk in the forest.'

'That would probably be enough, mate. One wagging tongue's all it takes. I wouldn't worry too much. She'll be back.'

'You don't understand,' Rufus said quietly. 'I asked her to go. I ended it.'

'But why?' Alerted by the pain in his voice, Harrison paused to look at Rufus properly. 'Judging by the state of you, you don't seem very happy about it.'

They had stopped by the rose bower that Rufus had built for Rowena. A few white roses, enjoying the Indian summer, still bloomed, scenting the air. Harrison gestured that they sit on the bench and Rufus had slumped beside him.

Rufus had told him everything from the beginning. He told him about the night his father had died, how Emilia had seduced him, but how he'd welcomed it, how his feelings had grown into something more than just physical attraction, and then right up until the dinner the night before when Geoffrey Bartley-Smythe had made those crassly insensitive remarks.

'So you asked her to go, because you're worried about what other people think?' Harrison said flatly. 'That is the craziest thing I've ever heard. Even for you, Rufus.'

'What do you mean, even for me?'

Harrison shook his head. 'For as long as I've known you, you've done what your family want. You've kowtowed to that autocratic father of yours all your life. You've scurried around doing his bidding, no matter what it was you actually wanted yourself.'

'That's bollocks. I married Rowena. I moved out of Beechbrook House.'

'Yeah, but you soon moved back in again, didn't you, and brought the boy, gave Lord Alfred his own little ready-made family.' Harrison waved a hand. 'Besides, he was happy for you to marry Rowena. "Right class, my boy, right class. People like us." More old Etonians than you can shake a stick at in Rowena's family, weren't there!'

Rufus punched him, which was difficult as they were sitting

down and he also had a raging hangover, but it was enough of a whack to make Harrison wince and cup his nose, and stand up hastily.

'What was *that* for?' Harrison raised both hands in front of him, palms outwards. 'I'm telling you how it is, Rufus. And trust me, it's long overdue, but if you don't want to hear it...'

'I don't want to hear it. You're right.'

For a second, the two men stared at each other, both breathing heavily. Then Rufus put his head in his hands, knuckled his eyeballs and glanced back up at Harrison. He hadn't felt this ill for years.

'I'm sorry. I shouldn't have hit you.'

'And I shouldn't have laid into you about your father when he's barely cold in his grave.' Harrison bit his lip. 'I know I need to get tact and diplomacy lessons. Tori tells me often enough.'

'It's OK. The truth is that it probably riles so much because I know you're right. I *have* always tried to do what my father wants. I've done it since I lost my mother. I think I was trying to make up for the fact that we no longer had her.'

'Christ,' Harrison said. 'No wonder you're so messed up. You do know that you could never have done that, don't you?'

'Yes. Of course I do. I haven't done years of therapy sessions with Bartholomew flaming Timms without learning a few... *things*. But I'm not like you, Harrison. I could never have just walked out on my family and cut all ties.'

'Yes, well, to be honest, it was easier for me. Especially after Serena died.'

Harrison's eyes darkened and Rufus stood up and put a hand on his arm. Harrison rarely mentioned his younger sister, who had committed suicide when she was just eighteen.

'It's fight or flight, isn't it?' Harrison continued. 'We either fight back or we run away.' Harrison stared briefly across the garden, before meeting Rufus's eyes once more. 'Taking your own life is the ultimate running away. Poor Serena. She couldn't handle the pressure of being in a family where nothing was ever good enough. I just left home. But really, I guess I just ran away too.'

By tacit agreement, they'd begun to walk across the grass towards the silver birch woodlands at the back of the house, the woodlands that were full of bluebells in spring, but were now littered with fallen leaves as the trees began to drop their summer foliage. The air was full of the scents of autumn, although it wasn't yet that cold and there hadn't yet been a frost.

The path that led through the woods also orbited the estate and for a little while neither of them spoke. From somewhere far away came the faint sounds of rutting deer. Adding insult to injury, Rufus thought. It still seemed surreal, his relationship with Emilia and its abrupt ending.

It was Harrison who broke the silence first, pointing out a row of broken fencing that he'd just arranged to get repaired.

'If it's broken, it encourages the fly tippers, despite the cameras.'

Rufus nodded and for a while they talked about safer subjects – fence repairs, the lavender production, the plans for next year's crops. Rufus was grateful. The fresh air and exercise were working. His head was starting to clear.

'Is Archie coming back for half term?' Harrison asked him when they were almost back at the house.

'No, he's not. I can't drag him away from school. I'll be going up there to see him.' He shook his head. 'He's not like we were. We couldn't wait to get away from school.'

'Archie's got a horse, though, hasn't he? A horse trumps his old man any day of the week if I know Archie.'

'You're right. I don't know whether to feel rejected or pleased that he's so independent.'

'I think you should probably be proud.' Harrison's eyes warmed.

'That he's turned out to be so well balanced, given the fact that he lost his mum so young. You've obviously done something right. Whatever else you are or aren't, you're a great dad, Rufus.'

Rufus inclined his head in acknowledgement. 'Not long now before you're a father yourself.'

'A fact that bloody terrifies me. I don't mind admitting that either, although I feel better than I did when Tori first told me it was happening. I wanted to run away then.'

'But you didn't. That's the main thing.'

'Yeah, we get there in the end, don't we?' Harrison blew out through his teeth. 'It's not easy. People are the hardest things in the bloody world. I think I prefer trees.'

'I think I prefer trees too,' Rufus said, thinking of his tree house in the woods. He and Emilia had once made love up there. The memory was like a punch in the gut.

He blinked and stumbled and Harrison looked at him in concern. He put out a steadying hand. 'You OK?'

'Yes. No.' Rufus shook his head and felt sick again.

Harrison studied his face and Rufus knew it was senseless lying to his oldest friend.

'I was so sure that telling her to go was the right thing to do.'

'But now you're not.'

'No.' He forced out the word through gritted teeth.

'If you love her, Rufus, then get in touch with her and tell her. It doesn't matter a stuff what other people think. It doesn't matter that you're a lord and she's a nanny. Love trumps everything else. That's the last thing I'm going to say about it.'

Rufus had nodded, and for the last week he'd thought of not much else. He'd gone round and round, backwards and forwards. He'd rehearsed the conversation he'd have with Emilia a dozen or more times. He'd even picked up his phone and studied her contact details – as though they weren't already burned on his brain.

But he'd never actually made the call. He'd thought of the conversation he'd had with Harrison about fight or flight too. And he'd come to the conclusion that much as he hated himself for doing it, he was a coward through and through, and he was still running away.

25

Fortunately, when Maggie had told Cassie she couldn't collect Casey's Girl on Sunday morning, as planned, neither she nor her father had made a fuss.

'Cassie seemed disappointed,' Maggie told Phoebe when she updated her. 'But when I told her it was down to red tape and out of my hands, she understood. She also said she was sure her father must have the passport and she'd ask him, but they haven't got back to me yet. In fact, they've gone very quiet. Which makes me even more convinced there's something odd going on.'

'I take it the police haven't got back to you yet either?'

'No.' Maggie sounded resigned. 'I'm not as surprised about that, to be honest. I guess we'll get to the bottom of it eventually.'

'That does seem suspicious, I agree,' Sam said when Phoebe passed all this on to him. 'I've been talking to Marjorie about microchipping and passports. It used to be a lot more complicated because passports got issued by lots of different places, and tying them up with a microchip was harder, but there's only one central register these days, and all horses legally have to be on it. If the Hastings family had a passport, they'd have produced it. I think it's worth us doing a bit more digging even if the police don't want to get involved. I'll have another word with Marjorie if you like. See if she can remember anything about any unsolved horse thefts going back a few years. It's a long shot, but the horse world is a small one.'

'Thanks, Sam, I'd really appreciate that. And I know Maggie would too.'

* * *

Thanks to the Indian summer, autumn had come slowly to the New Forest, but by the last fortnight of October, the landscape had been transformed. The heather seemed to have changed overnight from a lush vibrant green to a colour somewhere between rust and antique gold. The trees wore glamorous outfits of scarlet and gold and the hot breath of summer had been replaced by the cooler temperatures of the approaching November.

Phoebe and Sam had both been really busy at work, not to mention shuttling Roxie back and forth between them. But on the bright side she'd now had all her vaccinations, as had the other pups, all of whom had been registered with Puddleduck Vets. The new owners had set up a WhatsApp group where they could exchange pictures of puppy milestones – Phoebe had shared a great video of Snowball and Roxie's first meeting – the big cat had made it clear he was in charge – and all the owners had promised to keep in touch and have puppy parties.

But on this particular Sunday afternoon, two days before Halloween, Phoebe and Sam were walking in the forest close to Woodcutter's Cottage with just Roxie. They were discussing when would be a good time to take her to Brook Stables.

'Why don't we go across now?' Sam glanced at the puppy running ahead of them along a path littered with fallen leaves. To either side of them, the forest floor had become a mulch of red and gold. The trees were beginning to look bare and skeletal. It wouldn't be long before the nip of winter stole the remainder of their leaves.

Today, though, the sky was blue and a pale sun warmed the air. Roxie was clearly enjoying herself, beetling along with her nose to the ground and occasionally checking back to make sure they were still following.

'It's best to take her when I'm not actually working,' Sam added. 'She'll be tired now she's stretched her legs. Marjorie keeps asking me when I'm going to bring her in for a cuddle. She loves dogs.'

Half an hour later, they arrived at the stables just in time to see the 3 p.m. hack go out. There was a Halloween theme going on. Two of the riders were dressed as witches, with spider web make-up, black star-spangled cloaks and pointy hats over their riding hats. Outside reception, an orange hollowed-out pumpkin, also wearing a witch's hat, leered at them. Someone had strung a frieze made up of bats and black spiders over the entrance.

'I love Halloween.' Phoebe gave a delighted shudder. 'Are we dressing Roxie up?'

'No, we are not.'

'She'd look so cute in a black pointy hat,' Phoebe teased. 'It'd go well with the spots.'

Sam was about to reply when she touched his arm. 'Just kidding. I think there's enough for her to take in here. She's not at all scared, is she?' she added, as Roxie strained on her lead, to stare wide-eyed at the horses, who were jostling impatiently, their tack jingling, eager to get going.

They were standing a safe distance away; you couldn't be too careful around horses, although most of the yard horses were well used to dogs because a couple of the livery owners had them.

'She's not scared of much,' Sam said proudly, bending to pet the puppy's head. 'We've come at the right time to get maximum attention,' he murmured as several people looked across. A few moments later, they were surrounded by a circle of admirers including a young zombie wizard wearing garish face paint. There was lots of oohing and aahing over Roxie.

'She's absolutely gorgeous. You don't see many dalmatians, these days,' said one woman. 'My gran used to have them.'

'Didn't dalmatians used to be carriage dogs?' someone else asked.

'Yeah, they did,' Sam answered. 'They were used to protect the occupants from bandits. That's why they're so fearless.'

'I assume you're going to introduce her to Ninja?' This was from Marjorie, who'd just emerged from reception and was heading their way. 'Hello, Sam, hello, Phoebe... and you must be Roxie?' She joined the circle of admirers. 'My, what a cutie.'

Roxie was in her element, wriggling and fawning and loving every moment of being the centre of attention. The zombie wizard was crouched beside her, tickling her chin.

'There was something I was going to tell you,' Marjorie said to Sam. 'But for the life of me I can't think what it was.'

'Was it about a lesson?'

'Don't think so.' Marjorie shook her head in frustration. 'It's my age. It'll come back to me as soon as you've gone.'

When Roxie's crowd of admirers had thinned out, they took the pup down to the field where Ninja was turned out.

The big Thoroughbred cross ambled over when he saw Sam, then leaned in and sniffed the pup curiously.

From the safety of Phoebe's arms, Roxie in turn sniffed him back and the two touched noses for a second, before Ninja snorted and tossed his head up and down, making the puppy jump.

'That's probably enough of an introduction for now,' Sam said. 'But it's definitely good to get her into the idea of horses. All the new sights and smells of a yard. We'll do a bit at a time, then when she's bigger and more used to horses she can come riding with us.'

'She'll love that.'

'Me too,' Sam said. 'I've always fancied riding out with my own dog – our own dog,' he amended, his eyes soft. 'I can't wait.'

They'd left Ninja and were walking back across the yard when Marjorie called out to them from the reception doorway. 'Sam, I've just remembered what I was going to tell you. Can you come in a sec?'

They followed her into the room that smelled of leather and horse and Marjorie shuffled through some papers on her desk. 'It's here somewhere, I'm sure it is.'

As they waited patiently, Phoebe looked around the space that was so much Sam's domain. There were saddles and bridles on racks, reception obviously doubled up as a tack room, and a row of black riding hats hung from hooks on another wall. The smell of horses was strong, and Roxie tugged at her lead to get to corners. The sniffs must be amazing for a puppy.

'Ah, there it is.' Marjorie pounced triumphantly and then brandished a piece of paper. 'Remember you were asking me about stolen horses, well, I thought this might be of interest.' She held out the paper to Sam and Phoebe saw when she came closer that it was an old news item torn from a magazine.

It showed a horse's head looking over a stable, and the headline read 'Stolen Stallions Shocker'.

'Could that have any bearing on your mystery mare?'

Phoebe leaned in so she could read over Sam's shoulder.

Thieves used bolt cutters to steal two valuable stallions and a mare from a paddock in Pembrokeshire in the early hours of Saturday morning. Stephen Fitzpatrick, their owner, is putting out a nationwide appeal, asking for their safe return, and police have asked horse owners to be wary if approached by anyone trying to sell a stallion.

The stolen horses are part of a troupe of animals that are trained to perform on film sets and could be very dangerous in the wrong hands.

'Jeez,' Phoebe said. 'That's a coincidence, especially in view of what we know about Casey's Girl rearing on command. Are there any more photos?'

'No. I looked online, but I couldn't find any follow-up. Just that one little article, which was in an old *Horse and Hound*. I was thinning them out,' Marjorie said, shooting a guilty glance at Sam. 'I've been getting comments about them being a fire hazard.'

'Well, I'm really glad you kept this one.' Sam scanned the page for a date. 'When was this?'

'Six or seven years ago. I've chucked everything older than that. I just glanced through it because there was a headline on the front page about the increase in horse thefts. There's a phone number too. I think it's one of those hotlines the police use so members of the public can call with information. It may not still work, but it's worth a try.'

Sam looked back at the feature. 'Is it OK if we take it?'

'Of course. I only kept it for you.' Her face grew serious. 'It could just be a coincidence, so I shouldn't get your hopes up too much.'

* * *

They'd tried phoning the number as soon as they got back, but as Marjorie had suspected, it no longer worked.

'So where do we go from here?' Phoebe asked Sam. They'd driven back to Woodcutter's via his place to feed Snowball, which was a routine they'd fallen into on Sunday nights and meant that Sam could stay over at Woodcutter's if he wanted to. Snowball spent most of his nights out hunting so wouldn't miss him for the occasional night.

'It's a pity the news story didn't mention the name of the film training school,' Phoebe added.

'True, but we can have a hunt on Google. There can't be that many animal training schools in Pembrokeshire. It's pretty specialist stuff.'

There were in fact only a handful of companies that trained animals for film work in the UK, but none of them were in Wales.

'I could scream with frustration,' Phoebe said. 'Surely someone must know.'

'Maybe the place doesn't exist any more. Why don't we sleep on it? I know it doesn't feel like it, but we must be getting closer. This has got to have something to do with Casey's Girl. I don't believe in coincidences.'

* * *

Once again, it was Marcus who cracked the mystery – or at least came up with another jigsaw piece for the puzzle. On Monday morning, when Phoebe got into work for their usual 'week ahead' meeting, she discovered he was in a state of high excitement.

'I had another thought about Casey's Girl,' he told Phoebe. 'Last night Natasha and I did some research on animal training schools. All of the ones in this country anyway. We totally binged it.'

Great minds think alike, thought Phoebe.

'Most couples your age binge-watch TV series,' Jenna said, glancing at him across the desk with bemused affection.

Marcus reddened. 'OK. Hands up – we're not a normal couple, and we did get a bit obsessed, but it paid off. Guess what we found?'

'What did you find?' Max was involved in the conversation now and he, Phoebe and Jenna all stared at Marcus expectantly.

'We found this...' Marcus swung the laptop he was tapping into round so it faced everyone in reception.

On the screen was a picture of a rearing horse on a mountain, silhouetted against an orange sunset. The word 'Fitzpatrick Film Animals' was written in black at the foot of the picture.

Phoebe felt her heart skip a beat. 'Oh my God,' she breathed. 'I think you're on to something.'

'I definitely am.' Marcus grinned. 'That's her, isn't it? Casey's Girl. Or whatever her real name is. Fitzpatrick Film Animals was owned by a guy called Stephen Fitzpatrick, but they went bust about four and a half years ago.'

Both Max and Jenna now wore expressions of growing puzzlement, but Phoebe realised they weren't party to all of the information. She was the only one who now had the whole picture. Not wanting to steal Marcus's thunder, she kept quiet and listened while he expounded on his theory.

'I think – and so does Natasha,' Marcus said, 'that Fitzpatrick Film Animals did actually own Casey's Girl once. Maybe they sold her on. Or maybe she was stolen.'

'She was stolen,' Phoebe said, rummaging in her bag for the news story, which she'd brought in to show them. 'Listen to this.' She read it aloud and Jenna clapped her hands.

'Holy kamole, I think you're right.'

'Maybe it was some kind of insurance scam,' Marcus said. 'In view of the fact that they went bust. Maybe the horses weren't really stolen at all. Which is why they never found them.'

Max picked up on this idea too. 'That's very plausible.' He drummed his fingers on the reception top. 'Let's imagine your company's getting into financial difficulties, maybe your work's dried up for whatever reason, so you report some valuable animals as being dead and hey presto, you get an instant cash injection. That would work, wouldn't it?'

'Then you sell the horses on, because you can't have them on the premises when the insurance assessor comes to call,' Jenna finished. 'Brilliant.' She looked at Phoebe. 'Having first removed the microchips.'

'Not that it did them much good,' Marcus said, 'seeing as they went bust anyway. I wonder what happened to the others. I hope they ended up in good homes.'

Phoebe had been hoping that too. 'The main thing is that we do seem to have cracked it between us. Well done, Marcus. Thank you for being obsessive.'

'Yeah. Great work, mate,' Max said.

Marcus was now blushing to the roots of his crew cut.

'You're wasted as a receptionist,' Jenna told him. 'You should be a PD. Private detective,' she added, in response to his questioning glance.

Marcus shook his head and stared at a poster on the wall that warned people about keeping their pets safe on Firework Night.

'I love working here,' he said firmly, before glancing around at them all. 'I'm not planning on leaving. *Ever*. Getting to know you lot, training as a behaviourist. Meeting Natasha.' His voice went a little husky. 'This is the best job I've ever had.'

26

As soon as Phoebe had finished morning surgery, she went to see Maggie and Eddie, who were having their lunch in the farmhouse kitchen, and told them everything they'd managed to discover.

Her grandmother's face grew more and more serious and when she reached the end of the story, Eddie nodded sagely.

'Well, well,' Maggie said, stroking Buster distractedly, who had come to see what the fuss was about. 'What do you think, Eddie? Who are the bad guys here?'

He considered her question. 'I'd go along with the *Horse and Hound* feature. If valuable Thoroughbred stallions were taken, they probably *were* stolen to order. It's harder to shift stallions otherwise. They could have been shipped abroad to be used at stud. They've probably been renamed, given new passports and been servicing mares ever since. Odd about the mare, though. I remember a story once about a racehorse taken from a stable in Ireland. It turned up years later on a stud farm in Australia. It was easier when there were no microchips and all the other red tape.' He scratched his nose. 'I don't think the Hastings family are the bad guys. If you steal a horse, you're gonna keep it under wraps. You wouldn't be taking it to shows and such like where people might recognise it.'

'I agree,' Maggie said. 'Cassie Hastings doesn't know that horse is stolen. Although her father might have an inkling. No wonder he didn't report her missing when she escaped from her field. He was probably hoping he'd never see her again.'

It turned out that Maggie and Eddie's theories were right. Or at least most of them were, although it was another fortnight, almost the middle of November, before the whole story finally came out.

A pleasant DI had phoned Maggie and put her in the picture. He'd said that as far as he could gather, the thieves who'd stolen the horses originally, seven years earlier, hadn't been aware they were taking trained film horses until it was too late. The stallions, both stunning Thoroughbreds, had been sold on to waiting buyers, just as Eddie had predicted.

They'd turned up again eighteen months ago when police had called at a smallholding to seize assets after a fraud case. The horses had been scanned by a police vet, been found to have scars where their microchips had been removed and were currently in a horse sanctuary in Wales, pending police investigation.

Casey's Girl, or Star of Peniarth, as she'd been called back then, had passed through several people's hands, all of whom had decided she was too hot to handle, not to mention being difficult, thanks to the rearing. She'd finally ended up in the New Forest with a chancer called Jake Smith who'd sold her to Cassie's father, Dick Hastings, after they met in a pub.

Dick, who'd just gone through an expensive divorce, hadn't queried the mare's provenance too much. He'd been desperate to make his daughter's dream of having her own horse come true and Jake Smith had provided a way it could happen. He'd, quite literally, decided not to look a gift horse in the mouth.

Dick had had no experience of horses, and didn't know the mare reared, or that this might be a troublesome trait. Jake Smith certainly hadn't mentioned it, and neither had Cassie when she'd discovered it because by then she'd fallen in love with her horse and knew her father might not keep her if he suspected she was dangerous.

Instead, Cassie had thrown herself into competing. Cassie was a good rider, and she was fearless, and she'd known her horse wasn't malicious, just flawed. No one would have been any the wiser if Casey's Girl hadn't ended up in the New Forest.

'That's the whole story,' Phoebe told Sam when they were discussing it one night curled up on his sofa. 'Or at least that's what Maggie's ascertained from the bits the DI told her. No one's really sure whether Dick Hastings let the horse out while Cassie was away, or whether she really did escape, but he certainly didn't report her missing, so the police think he must have suspected she was stolen. Which would explain why he didn't get her microchipped. He didn't know it was compulsory. He seemed to know very little about the legalities of horse keeping, apparently.' She sighed. 'Maggie did find out one thing that was really interesting, though. The mare was in some kiddies' film called *The Secret Life of Animals*, and the cast needed her to rear every time someone said the word "secret". So that's why it's one of her cue words.'

'Wow.' Sam sat up straight and looked at her. 'That is interesting.'

Fleetingly she thought he would expound on the subject of secrets – there was a loaded little pause – or maybe that was her imagination because when Sam did eventually speak, he changed the subject.

'It's a shame she has to go back to Pembrokeshire. I'm guessing she's surplus to requirements now the animal training company's gone. Couldn't Stephen Fitzpatrick legally sell her to Cassie Hastings now it's all out in the open?'

'Well, yes, but I don't think she wants her. She's obviously fond of her, but she's pretty much done with riding now. She's got a job lined up in a ski resort in Banff in Canada for the season. She was only briefly home to see her parents. The last time I talked to her, she said that once she'd got over the shock of it all, she was relieved her horse had a good home to go to.'

Phoebe sighed and Sam hugged her. 'Maybe she'll be sold on to another film company or some other horse-mad teenager who'll love her. Now they know she's rearing on command it should be a lot easier to stop it happening. She could go to a more normal home. I guess it's up to Stephen to decide.'

'Yes, I know you're right,' Phoebe said, stroking Roxie, who had come over for a hug when she'd seen hugs were in the offing. 'It's certainly out of our hands, and I know Maggie's relieved. She's not really set up to take horses. Stephen's bringing down a box to collect her next week. He seemed a nice enough chap, Maggie said, when she spoke to him to arrange it.'

'I wonder if he has to give the insurance money back now he's found all his horses?' Sam said thoughtfully.

'The police say their investigation is ongoing.'

There was a loud, rather pointed meow and Phoebe glanced up. Snowball had just strolled in the door and was now waiting by his empty bowl. He swished his tail and looked plaintive. It was clear he was more interested in dinner than hugs and after a second's hesitation, Roxie jumped off the sofa and went to stand beside her empty bowl too.

'Well, that's us told,' Sam said. 'Looks like they're ganging up on us, doesn't it? I guess we'd better get dinner.'

Phoebe jumped up. 'You get theirs and I'll get ours. I got us salad,' she said, as she opened the fridge in Sam's kitchen and pulled out a bag of leaves and a pepper.

'Salad. But it's November.' Sam looked at her askance and gave a mock shiver. 'I thought Sundays meant pizza night. Are we on a health kick or something?'

'Well, no, but I've put on a few pounds lately.'

'I hadn't noticed,' Sam said loyally.

'Thanks, but I have. And Alexa and I are going for our final dress fittings next week. I know we're not getting togged up in long dresses for Maggie's wedding, but I still want to look good in the photos.'

'You always look good. But OK, salad it is.'

Phoebe smiled at him. Solidarity salad. Sam never put on an ounce. Which wasn't surprising, what with working all day in the shop, racing around after Ninja and now with them both walking Roxie.

'We can have it with huge jacket potatoes and those yummy salmon fillets you like,' she said, 'if that takes the sting out of it. And you can pile your potato high with butter and cheese.' She tried not to sound too envious. 'And I – er – won't.'

* * *

Dress fitting was overstating it, really. Phoebe and Alexa had both had beautiful three-quarter-length dresses made for them by a woman who taught maths at the same school as Louella and did dressmaking as a sideline.

The bridesmaids' dresses were made of silk and on the green spectrum to complement Maggie's emerald outfit, but slightly different from each other both in design and shade. Phoebe's was sage green and slinky and had spaghetti straps and Alexa's was olive and had a bodice and fuller skirt. Phoebe's had a simple ribbon that went around her neck and Alexa's had a waist sash.

The maths teacher, Sylvia Daniels, lived in a semi-detached on the outskirts of Bridgeford and she'd had the integral garage on the side of her house converted into a dressmaking room. To Phoebe's relief, it was well insulated and there was a fan heater warming the space very nicely by the time they arrived.

Sylvia was a nice motherly lady and she fussed around while Alexa and Phoebe tried on their dresses and then circled them, patting and smoothing the material and asking them both if they were happy with the fit.

Having bespoke dresses had been Maggie's idea – 'It won't cost much more if we get Sylvia to do them and then you can wear them afterwards. So they won't be wasted.'

Maggie, who had come along to the dress fitting, nodded approvingly as Sylvia darted about.

'You do look beautiful, girls. Are you happy with your outfits?'

'They're gorgeous,' Alexa said, and Phoebe nodded in agreement. The colouring was just right for both of them; the sage suited Phoebe's brown hair and slightly olive skin, the olive looked great with Alexa's paler skin and mid-brown hair. To Phoebe's relief, her dress wasn't as snug as she remembered from the last fitting, so maybe she wouldn't have to forego too many treats between now and 2 December.

She couldn't imagine wearing this dress anywhere else though, she thought, picking a white hair off the skirt – one of Roxie's, they got everywhere. She didn't really go to any dressy occasions, but she supposed you never knew what the future held.

Half an hour later, they were back out on the street once more.

'Let's go and have a coffee,' Maggie said, standing between them and linking both their arms through hers. 'It's not often I get you two girls all to myself.'

They headed towards the Crown, one of Bridgeford's four pubs, which was at what Maggie called the posh end and wasn't far from Hendrie's. As they strolled towards Hendrie's, Phoebe saw Jan was outside, packing away a display easel that advertised the news headlines and the fact they were a Post Office as well as a stores.

'Hi, Jan,' she called, and Sam's mother looked startled to be descended upon by three smiling women.

To Phoebe's relief, she didn't look so tired as she had last time they'd met.

Maggie explained what they'd been doing and Jan nodded enthusiastically. 'That's so special. Are you getting excited, Maggie? Not long till the big day now.'

'I don't really do excitement,' Maggie said swiftly, and then gave the game away by giggling. 'OK, maybe I've got a few butterflies. I never thought I'd get married again at my age.'

'I think it's fantastic. Ian and I are very much looking forward to it.' Jan smiled at Phoebe. 'As is our Sam, of course.'

'We're going to the Crown for a coffee,' Maggie told her. 'Why don't you join us? It's on me. I might even throw in a cream bun.'

'Do they do cream buns in the Crown?' Alexa asked, surprised.

'They're bound to do something cakey.' Maggie shrugged noncommittally, but Jan was already shaking her head.

'I'm so sorry, I can't. I promised a friend I'd meet her.' She looked at her watch. 'I'd better get going if I don't want to be late. You three go and have a lovely time.'

Then she was gone, scuttling back into the shop, closing the door and making a point of waving at them through the glass.

'That's odd.' Alexa looked at the display easel, which was now flat on the ground. 'She didn't take that. I thought she had come out for it.'

'We probably put her off her stride,' Maggie said. 'I expect she'll fetch it later.'

Phoebe wasn't so sure. Jan had been fine until Maggie had invited her for coffee. Then she'd disappeared like lightning. There was definitely more going on than met the eye. She must remember to mention it to Sam.

27

'I think Ma's OK.' Sam didn't seem unduly worried. 'She's seemed happy enough lately, although I never managed to talk her and Pa into having a holiday. She insisted a staycation was all they wanted. Still, I know she's really looking forward to Maggie's wedding. I can't believe it's only a week on Saturday.'

'Neither can I, it's crept up quickly, hasn't it? I definitely took my eye off the wedding ball, what with work and Roxie and all the kerfuffle about Casey's Girl.'

'It's all organised, though, isn't it? The cake and the venue and what have you!' He spread his hands and gave her a look that implied 'What else was there?' and Phoebe smiled at him with affection.

'It's organised to the nth degree, and then some. I'm not sure what Maggie's going to do with herself once she and Eddie are hitched. She's been wedding this and wedding that for weeks.'

'I bet you'll be glad when it's all over too, won't you, Pheebs?'

'Um, kind of.' She felt slightly taken aback at his assumption she'd be glad when it was over. 'Although I haven't minded the build-up. Some of it's been really fun. It's been exciting helping

Maggie choose everything, even if she has changed her mind more times than an English summer.'

'Rather you than me.' Sam rolled his eyes. 'I'm not a big fan of weddings. I'm only going to this one because I know I can't get away with not going.'

Phoebe looked at him quickly and saw he was grinning.

'I am joking, Pheebs. Don't look so worried.' He blew her a kiss. 'I'll be there. And after the wedding, I guess Maggie will get back to her other passion: Puddleduck Pets. What did happen with Casey's Girl or whatever her name was? Did the Fitzpatrick bloke come and get her in the end?'

'No, he's rescheduled it twice. Apparently they had a problem at the livery stables where he was planning to keep her and the last time I spoke to Maggie, she said she had the feeling he didn't really want her back. Keep your fingers crossed he picks her up before the wedding or we'll have a dancing horse on the guestlist as well as the neddies.'

'They're not really coming to the reception, are they?'

'Of course they are. Thankfully Maggie's not into dressing up animals, so they won't be having to wear straw hats or anything, but I did hear Natasha say something about getting wedding carnations to go in their headcollars. The dogs have them too, I think. But we drew the line at the ducks. Natasha said they'd just eat them.'

Sam shook his head in mock disapproval but the warmth in his eyes gave him away.

* * *

Maggie wasn't having a big hen do, she proclaimed herself too old for hectic late nights. But on the evening before her wedding, she had invited Phoebe, Alexa, Louella, Natasha, Jenna, Jan, Tori and

Anni Buckland to join her at Puddleduck for a glass of Prosecco and nibbles.

They were to arrive prompt at six thirty, she said, and they wouldn't be late as she wanted to be fresh as a daisy for the next day. There would be no silly games, just a few quiet drinks and the whole thing would be done and dusted by nine.

Eddie had been banished for the evening – he still didn't sleep over at Puddleduck – and was having a stag night at The Brace of Pheasants with his son, Jonathan, and his mate Dusty Miller, who was also his best man, and a selection of his other mates like the agister, Colin Baker, who'd caught Casey's Girl.

He'd also invited Sam, Max, Marcus, Ian Hendrie, and James and Frazier Dashwood. He hadn't asked Tori's partner, Harrison, Tori had told Phoebe, or Anni's partner Nick, which was fair enough as he didn't know them. But Phoebe imagined Eddie's stag night would be a much more raucous affair than Maggie's hen night.

Although so far the ladies were having a rather lovely evening at Puddleduck, accompanied by Tiny, Buster and Roxie, who were all hanging around in the kitchen expectantly in the hope of getting titbits. They hadn't got past the kitchen yet, although Maggie said she had vacuumed and air freshened the front room and Eddie had lit the wood burner in preparation. There was a giant seven-foot Christmas tree in the front room that Eddie and Maggie had put up earlier in the day. It glittered with tinsel and swung with brightly coloured baubles of red, silver and gold, but no chocolate decorations as Maggie said last time she'd had them, Tiny had eaten the lot and had tipped the tree over in his eagerness to get to the topmost branches.

Maggie's nibbles consisted of a finger buffet, which Phoebe and Louella had collected from Waitrose earlier. There were cocktail sausages, mini pork pies, a selection of cold meats, cheese and biscuits, smoked salmon, mini quiches, olives and various little pots of salad. Prosecco too, of course, and sparkly elderflower for anyone who wasn't drinking. They'd spent the time chatting nineteen to the dozen and Phoebe had managed to catch up properly with Tori, who now looked enormous.

'I'm beginning to wish Maggie had kept to her original wedding date,' Tori announced in between sips of elderflower. Tori's due date of 21 December was one of the reasons Maggie had brought the date forward. 'I'm sure this baby isn't going to hold on for another three weeks.'

'You'd better not give birth at my wedding,' Maggie told her sternly. 'Although if you do at least there'll be plenty of medical assistance available.'

'You mean there'll be two vets,' Tori said, outraged. 'I'm not having a vet as a midwife.'

'Why not?' Phoebe quipped. 'I've delivered dozens of mammals; it can't be that different. I'm joking,' she added quickly when she saw her friend's face. 'Of course you're not going to give birth tomorrow. You're not really worried, are you? You're not having any contractions or anything?'

'No, I'm not,' Tori said, adding in a voice only Phoebe could hear, 'I wouldn't mind if you did have to deliver her, although it would probably be better if we were in a maternity unit.' She cupped her bump protectively. 'And it would definitely be better if we weren't at Maggie's wedding. First babies are more likely to be late, apparently, than early.'

'Is Harrison looking forward to being your birth partner?' Phoebe had been very relieved that Tori hadn't asked her to do that because weirdly, although she was an expert at bringing baby animals into the world, she wouldn't have relished being in on the delivery of a human baby. What if something went wrong? What if she had to watch her best friend howling in agony? The thought of both terrified her.

'Funnily enough, Harrison said something similar to what you did, when I asked him. He said he'd be able to get scrubbed up and step in. Apparently he helped deliver a New Forest foal once. He was out in the Land Rover and he saw she was struggling so he stopped and helped. He said it was one of the most rewarding experiences of his life. I know you don't believe it, but he has a really sensitive side.'

'I could imagine he does,' Phoebe said diplomatically, because actually it was very hard to imagine Harrison being sensitive. 'How's Rufus doing?' she asked, more out of politeness than because she really wanted to know.

There were several other conversations going on in the kitchen and no one else was listening, but Tori leaned in again conspiratorially.

'The last thing Harrison told me was that Rufus had thrown Emilia out on her ear, so that relationship was short lived.'

'I'm sorry to hear that,' Phoebe said, realising that she was.

'Yeah, it is a bit sad. Harrison thinks Rufus is his own worst enemy and I think he's right.'

'Because he asked Emilia to leave when things didn't work out?' Phoebe queried.

'No, because Harrison seemed to think that Rufus did actually have feelings for her – but he couldn't square it with his ancestry. The fact that he's a lord who comes from a long line of stiff upper-lipped, up themselves, starchy punctilious nobs and she was a nanny with no pedigree got in the way when it came down to it. At least that's what Harrison said, and he knows Rufus better than anyone.'

Phoebe touched her arm. 'You sound angry.'

'I am angry still; about the way he mucked you about. I don't have strong feelings about him banishing Emilia from the big house, that's for sure. She was pretty horrible to you, wasn't she?'

'Yes, but that's all in the past. And I don't think she made that much difference in the big scheme of things. Rufus and I were never going to work out. There were too many problems.' She smiled at Tori. 'I'm really glad as it's turned out. Because if things had worked out, I wouldn't have realised Sam was the one.'

'And Sam does make you happy, doesn't he? Which is brilliant.'

'Earth calling Phoebe and Tori.' Louella's voice broke into their conversation and they both glanced up to see she was holding up a glass. 'Have you two got full glasses? We're about to have a toast.'

She waited for them to get refills and then she cleared her throat.

'I'd like to propose a toast to my amazing mum, who is getting married again tomorrow, so please join me in wishing her all the luck in the world.'

'To Maggie,' she added, and they all joined in. 'To Maggie.'

Then Louella leaned in and, although Phoebe didn't hear what she said, she could guess by the sparkle in both their eyes.

She would be saying she knew Farmer Pete would have approved of Maggie's choice of husband. And that somewhere up there, he'd be raising a glass too.

* * *

Over at The Brace, the stag night was rather more raucous.

By 9 p.m., the only three people who weren't fairly drunk were Eddie, who'd been taking it very steady and had actually tipped away a couple of doubles he'd been bought when no one was looking, and Sam and his father, Ian. Sam was driving and Ian didn't really drink that much.

At that moment, most of the guys were distracted by a curvy

red-haired WPC who'd marched into the bar seconds earlier and was now in conversation with the landlord, who was pointing in Eddie's direction. Sam watched, fascinated, as she nodded and then came across to them. She paused before producing a notepad.

'Which one of you gentlemen is Eddie May?' Her face was stern.

Eddie stared up at her, wide-eyed. He was clearly about to flee, giving every impression of a man with a very guilty conscience, when her face cracked into a wicked grin and she put the notepad down and begun to unbutton her jacket, to reveal a very saucy-looking black and scarlet basque beneath.

If anything, Eddie looked even more terrified at the turn events were taking and his eyes were so wide you could have fitted side plates into the sockets. He shrank back in his chair, his face as scarlet as the stripogram's basque, obviously terrified she was going to make him do something he didn't want to do.

Dusty Miller, who had clearly organised the whole thing, was laughing so hard he was doubled up and the rest of the stag party had settled back to enjoy the entertainment.

Sam exchanged glances with his father. 'I think Dusty's enjoying that a lot more than Eddie.'

'I think that's probably the idea,' Ian agreed with a wry smile.

They were sitting on the edge of the group and Sam could see that Eddie had got over his initial shock and was now playing along with the stripogram's gentle teasing, whilst also threating to take dire revenge on whatever bugger had organised her. But it was all very good natured.

Sam turned his attention back to his father. They'd been talking about Jan.

'She did seem a bit tense earlier,' Ian said, and Sam nodded. If his stoic and eternally laid-back pa had spotted tension in his ma, then it must be pretty obvious.

'But hopefully going to Maggie's hen night will have cheered her up, Dad.'

'Yeah, I wonder what tricks they'll be playing on the bride to be. Nothing like this, I wouldn't have thought.'

Sam took a swig of his orange and lemonade. 'I doubt it, she'd throttle them, but you're right, Ma being with her friends will do her the world of good.'

'I'm probably worrying too much. She went off fine in the taxi. She didn't want me to drop her there or anything. I'm sure they're all having a whale of a time. And she said she's really looking forward to the wedding tomorrow.'

'I'll WhatsApp Phoebe, just to check all's OK, Pa. That'll put our minds at rest, won't it?'

But when Sam checked back a few moments later, he saw Phoebe hadn't read her WhatsApp message. 'They're probably too busy chatting to check their phones,' Sam told his father. 'I'm sure we'll find out later.'

* * *

The hen night had started to wind down. Natasha had already gone home, which fortunately wasn't far – she had an early start. Just because there was a wedding tomorrow, it didn't mean work stopped. She still had to be up at the crack of dawn to clean out and feed the animals.

Jenna had gone too and Tori was yawning. 'It takes it out of you, being this pregnant,' she said. 'I'm going to have to head back and get my beauty sleep.'

Alexa made her excuses too and headed off to pick up Frazier. 'He WhatsApped to tell me he was ready to leave the stag night. Which is just as well because our babysitter will need to get off home.'

Then only Phoebe and Louella were left and they insisted Maggie sit and relax while they cleared the plates from the table, repackaged the remaining food into containers and transferred it into the fridge. They never had made it into the front room, at least not for long, but that would be put to good use tomorrow.

Phoebe pulled out her phone to see if there were any messages from Sam and discovered he'd sent one asking about his mother.

She glanced at Louella. 'It's a shame Jan couldn't be here. Sam seems to think she set off to come too.'

'I don't think she did.' Louella frowned. 'She phoned me earlier and said she had one of her heads coming on and had decided to give it a miss. She didn't want to be feeling groggy for tomorrow.'

'Oh, that's odd.' Phoebe exchanged glances with her mother and grandmother. 'Fingers crossed she's OK for tomorrow.'

'I'll message her first thing,' Louella said. 'And talking of tomorrow. We're back here at eight thirty sharp for the hair and make-up. Is that right, Maggie?'

'It is,' Maggie beamed. 'I can't believe it's almost here. In twenty-four hours, I'll no longer be a Crowther. Well, I will technically, because I'm not about to become a Rod Stewart song, but you know what I mean. I'll be married. I do hope Farmer Pete would be happy for me. Do you two really think he'd be pleased?'

Her eyes were unusually vulnerable.

'Of course he would,' they chorused.

'He thought Eddie was a great guy,' Phoebe said, and her mother nodded and added, 'He'd be pleased as punch that the woman he adored was happy again. Now off you go to spend your last night as a single woman.'

28

The day of the wedding dawned frosty and clear. A white sky arched over Puddleduck Farm with just a hint of sunshine breaking through. Phoebe's weather app said there was a 20 per cent chance of rain at midday when Maggie and Eddie were actually getting married, but there was no sign of it at the moment. It was too cold for rain.

Phoebe had arrived early for the hair and beauty session. The Aga warmth of the kitchen felt wonderful. The great old oven, the heart of the house, came into its own in the winter months. She'd brought Roxie, who was now chasing Tiny's tail and the giant wolfhound was being very good natured and gentlemanly with the rowdy pup, who occasionally skidded over on the flagstones during her attempts to catch hold of his swishing tail in her teeth.

Alexa had been about ten minutes behind her and was now making coffee for everyone. And Louella was with Maggie in a bedroom upstairs. There was a hairdresser and a make-up artist and they had already got started with Louella.

'How are you feeling?' Alexa asked Phoebe as she handed her a steaming mug of coffee. 'This is a bit different from your usual Saturday activities.'

'Yes, I'd mostly be examining small fluffy animals not a million miles from here. I love that we're all getting ready together. I can't believe you managed to persuade Frazier to get the twins ready for the wedding.'

'Your brother is surprisingly hands on. He's a great dad.'

'I know he is. And you're a great mum.'

'I love being a mum.' Alexa touched her stomach. There was something in her eyes and Phoebe gasped.

'Are you pregnant?'

'Oh, God, is it that obvious?' Alexa blushed to the roots of her hair. 'Yes, I am, but only a few weeks. Please don't tell anyone else. Not today, we don't want to steal Maggie and Eddie's thunder.'

'No, of course I won't.' Phoebe went and hugged her sister-in-law, who smelled of soap and her signature Loulou perfume. She was glowing. 'But I'm so pleased for you. I take it you did plan it.'

'We didn't exactly plan it, but, well, put it this way, we weren't being very careful. Frazier always wanted a big family. I must admit, I'm feeling a little daunted about the prospect of having three kids under five but on the other hand, as I said, he is a hands-on dad.' She tucked a strand of brown hair behind her ear. 'It'll be your turn next... are you and Sam planning kids?'

'Um, yes, I think so. One day.' Phoebe sighed. She was three years older than Alexa and she wasn't even married. Not that being married was everything but currently she and Sam were living in separate places and co-parenting a puppy and their lives were so busy that she couldn't see that changing any time soon.

'You have a massively successful business to run, though, don't you?' Alexa went on hastily. 'You guys are in a different position than we were. You have different priorities.'

That was so true. Frazier and Alexa had a much more traditional relationship. He earned enough as a solicitor to keep them both, which meant that Alexa didn't need to go out to work, although she had done freelance bookkeeping before they'd had the twins. Alexa was a whizz with spreadsheets and very au fait with online systems.

'We are living the dream,' Phoebe said, putting on her brightest voice, and wondering why a tiny flicker of doubt had just crept into her mind. Thirty-seven wasn't exactly old to start a family these days, but even so – she'd heard the stories of women leaving it too late. Thinking they had all time in the world and then realising they couldn't just get pregnant at the drop of a hat. Phoebe had never actually tried to get pregnant. She was on the pill. But that was the point, wasn't it? You didn't know if you could do something until you tried it.

Louella appeared at the door. 'That's me done. Who's next for hair and make-up?'

'You look great, Mum,' Phoebe said.

'Amazing,' echoed Alexa. 'Do you want to go next, Phoebe?'

'Sure.' Phoebe headed for the kitchen doorway. Weddings were always hotbeds of emotion and with the news of new pregnancies thrown into the mix too, no wonder her emotions were swirling.

Fleetingly, as she went upstairs, she wondered if Alexa's pregnancy could have been the secret that Sam and Frazier had been discussing when they'd been trying to catch Casey's Girl. She dismissed this almost immediately. That day must be at least three months ago, and Alexa had just said she was only a few weeks pregnant.

* * *

By the time the bridal party, with the exception of Maggie, was ready, Phoebe was feeling much better, and she'd decided her earlier mixed emotions were just a result of stress.

Now she, Louella and Alexa were all standing in the hallway of Puddleduck Farmhouse, dolled up to the nines, with the dogs firmly shut in the kitchen, waiting for Maggie to come downstairs.

It had been a chaotic morning. The caterers had been and had laid out the food on tables made ready for it in the front room. Fortunately, it was cool enough for the fridge not to be needed. The cake was in there too and the door was firmly shut to stop Tiny from getting any ideas. The flowers – both the wedding flowers they'd ordered, and several bouquets from well-wishers – had been arriving all morning and were dotted in vases everywhere and smelling glorious. Maggie knew a lot of people and they all wanted to congratulate her on her special day.

The transport, a white Rolls-Royce owned by a mate of Eddie's, was arriving to pick up the bridal party at eleven thirty sharp. It was eleven twenty-seven when Maggie finally came downstairs, looking absolutely stunning in the floral dress and emerald jacket. Her hair was piled on her head in an elegant chignon, and the make-up artist, who Phoebe knew had spent at least an hour, had managed to make her look as if she wore the minimum of make-up.

Pinned to her jacket was a gorgeous dragonfly brooch. Its tail was made up of emeralds, its wings were studded diamonds, and its head and body were linked sapphires. Louella had lent it to her, so it fulfilled the age-old bridal traditions of both something borrowed and something blue.

Maggie glowed with a quiet inner beauty. Her hazel eyes sparkled and she was smiling.

'Will I do, ladies?'

'You look amazing, Mum,' Louella said.

'Stunning,' Alexa added and Phoebe just nodded, because her

throat ached too much to speak. When her grandmother hesitated on the bottom stair, she stepped forward and touched her arm.

'You've never looked more beautiful.'

'I'm sure that's not true,' Maggie replied. But she was clearly thrilled. 'Right then, you lot. I think it's time we got this show on the road.'

* * *

Sam had arranged to collect his parents from Hendrie's and drive them to the ceremony and then afterwards on to Puddleduck Farm for the reception. Jan had got cover so the shop could remain open. Saturday was their busiest day, but Sam was surprised when he arrived and found she wasn't ready but was in fact serving a customer at the counter.

Aware that she hadn't yet spotted him, Sam waited until she'd finished and the customer had gone and then headed across, tapping his watch. 'Ma, what's going on? Why aren't you ready? We've got a wedding to get to.'

She jumped when she saw him and her whole demeanour changed. In an instant, she went from happy, smiling shopkeeper to a straight-faced and slightly slumped person rubbing her head.

'Oh, Sam, love. I've got the most terrible head. I'm so sorry. I'm really not feeling up to it.'

'I don't believe you.' The words were out of his mouth before he could edit them. 'You were fine a couple of seconds ago.'

'I wasn't. I was faking it. I was serving.'

'But why were you serving? If you're ill, you should be upstairs. And where's Hannah?' He glanced around. Their temp was nowhere to be seen. Neither was the other woman he'd asked the temp agency to send.

'I... I...' Jan stuttered and shrugged and lowered her eyes. She looked as though she'd been totally caught out. Sam didn't have a clue what was going on, but clearly something was. He strode to the shop door, flipped the sign to closed and locked it.

'What are you doing?' Jan yelped. 'We can't close on a Saturday.'

'I'm not opening again until you tell me what's going on.' He went back towards her and saw to his alarm that her eyes were full of tears. His mother never cried. Seriously worried now, he took her arm and led her into the back of the shop and she went with him without protest.

'Please, Ma, please talk to me. Dad's worried sick too. It's not just me. You need to tell us what's going on.'

The white Rolls-Royce, decked out in emerald and cream ribbons, had just pulled up for the third time outside St James', the tiny twelfth-century church where the wedding was taking place.

They had already been around the block twice because Dusty, Eddie's best man, who'd been supposed to text and tell them the groom was safely in situ, hadn't done this. Neither had he replied to Louella's two increasingly anxious messages or phone calls.

Phoebe wasn't surprised he hadn't answered his phone. He was too deaf to talk on phones, but she was worried he hadn't been looking at his texts. They'd fixed on this plan two days earlier and they'd practised texting and Dusty had been fine with it all then.

'Maybe the signal's bad at the church,' Alexa hissed to Phoebe. 'Did anyone think to check that?'

'Maybe Dusty got held up,' Louella added.

These whispered confabs took place in the Rolls, with Maggie in the front doggedly pretending not to hear what they were talking about. But in the end, she had leaned into the back and said, 'For goodness' sake, don't go relying on Dusty to communicate. It's never been his strong point. Eddie will be there, don't worry. Dusty's probably lost his phone or forgotten to charge it or dropped it down a drain or something.'

'Dropped it down a *drain*?' Phoebe queried.

'Yes, that's what he did at the New Forest Show that time when we were trying to coordinate our protest march. Dusty's never been good with phones. He gets through them at a rate of knots.'

'Right,' Louella said. 'OK then, if you're sure you're happy.'

'I'm happy,' Maggie had assured them, so they'd all just got out at the lychgate of the grey stone church. Sunshine lit up the mossy path that wound beneath the higgledy-piggledy headstones and jackdaws chack-chacked from the trees. There were red berries on all the nearby bushes. It was gloriously peaceful. Everyone must already be inside. Then Phoebe saw Dusty signalling frantically from the church doorway.

'Wait here a sec. I'll just check everything's OK.' She hurried towards him, and he smiled broadly.

'Is everything OK? Where's your phone?'

'Beg your pardon?'

'Your phone.' She mimed holding a phone at her ear and Dusty caught on and started patting his pockets before finally widening his eyes and giving an exaggerated shrug.

'OK, never mind the phone. Is Eddie in there?'

Dusty shrugged again, shook his head and said, 'Not everyone.'

'But Eddie is, yes?' Oh, heck, what was the sign for Eddie? Phoebe wished she'd spent more time learning British Sign Language. She knew for a fact Eddie and Maggie were fluent. Maybe Dusty was too. Aware of movement behind her, she turned and saw Maggie bustling towards her.

Maggie made a series of hand signals and Dusty beamed and nodded.

'It's fine, Eddie's here,' Maggie said. 'Shall we crack on?'

Dusty put up a hand, which clearly meant 'wait'. Then he stepped into the vestibule, leaned forward and gave two piercing whistles.

It wasn't the most orthodox of signals to let the vicar know the bride had arrived, but it clearly worked because the organist immediately launched into the wedding march.

Dusty scurried into the church, followed swiftly by Louella and James, who it turned out had been waiting just inside the door. Then there was a very short gap before Maggie swept into the church, closely followed by her two bridesmaids, and they paused just inside the vestibule. Maggie had already decided she didn't need giving away – 'I'm not a possession' – and she smiled at Phoebe and Alexa, mouthed the word, 'Ready,' at them and gathered herself.

Despite her diminutive size – Maggie was the only one in the family who'd missed out on the height gene – she looked every bit the majestic head of the family that she was, Phoebe thought, as her grandmother held her gorgeous bouquet of winter white roses, poinsettia, red berries and evergreens, demurely in front of her, before she set off slowly down the aisle.

Phoebe was aware of lots of faces turning to look in their direction. She scanned the ones at the front, hoping to see Sam, but there was no sign of him. There was no sign of his mum or dad either. She must be looking in the wrong place. Of course Sam was here. No way would he miss Maggie's wedding.

29

Sam had finally persuaded his mother to go upstairs into the flat where Ian was waiting for them, po-faced, in the kitchen. He was dressed in his best suit, and his face was flushed. Sam couldn't remember ever seeing his father look so agitated.

'I hope you can get some sense out of her because I'm damned if I can,' he remarked as they went past the kitchen doorway.

Sam understood why his father was so upset but he knew that this was not what his mother needed. She might not be ill physically, but she looked terrible. Her eyes were haunted and for a few moments downstairs Sam had been put in mind of Rufus Holt when he was suffering a PTSD attack.

'Please can you put the kettle on, Pa,' he asked, as he led Jan into the lounge and gestured she should sit down on the sofa.

'We've got no time for a bloody cup of tea,' Ian began, but he did as he was bid anyway.

Sam pulled up a square fabric-covered footstool so that it was opposite his mother and sat on it. She had her head in her hands. Her eyes were covered by her palms and her shoulders were shaking and Sam had never felt so helpless in his life. He had no blueprint for this, no experience, but his instincts told him that he should let her cry. That she needed to get the pain out of her body before she was in any fit state to tell him anything.

So that's exactly what he did. He just waited patiently without speaking until she finally cried herself to a halt and started blowing her nose.

His pa had come in with a tray of tea which he'd set down on the coffee table and he was now sitting straight-backed in his armchair on the other side of the room. He was drum rolling his fingers on the arm of the chair.

Jan finally looked up into her son's eyes.

'I can't go out,' she said in an oddly calm voice. 'That's what's wrong. Every time I try going further than the pavement outside the shop, my heart starts pounding. My hands go clammy and I can't breathe. I'm terrified to go any further.'

'Is that why you didn't go to the hen party last night?'

She nodded. 'I thought it would be OK, but as soon as the taxi got out of sight of the house, I couldn't breathe. I had to ask him to come back. I was terrified.'

'That's daft,' Ian said. 'There's nothing to be terrified of.'

'I know it's daft,' she said sharply. 'I'm aware that it's pathetic and absurd and that I'm a fool. Why do you think I haven't told you?' She gave a tiny little moan and Sam shot his father a furious glance and then turned back to his mother and took her hand.

'It's not daft. I think it's a recognised medical condition.'

'What's a recognised medical condition?' Ian said, his voice softer this time.

'It sounds like agoraphobia to me.' Sam squeezed his mother's fingers. 'Is it the same feeling that you got when you were on your way to the school reunion?'

Jan nodded silently.

'Didn't you have postnatal depression after I was born?' It was the last thing he wanted to bring up, but Sam knew he was going to have to mention it sooner or later.

Jan looked shocked. 'How did you know about that?'

'Aunt Grace mentioned it once when she was tipsy. But I know it can come back again.'

'That was over thirty-five years ago,' Ian said. 'Surely it can't come back after all this time. Besides, you didn't have problems going out then, did you, love? You were just a bit low. The baby blues. I thought all women got that.'

'I was more than a bit low, Ian.' She looked across at him briefly before staring back at the carpet. 'But I just got on with it. You had to in those days. There was no help.'

'We didn't know so much about it back then,' Sam said. 'But there's a lot more that can be done now. For a start, there's talking therapy – maybe even medication. But the first step is admitting you've got a problem.'

'How do you know all this, son?'

Sam was still holding her hand. He didn't think he'd held her hand like this since he was a little boy, and back then it had been for his reassurance, not hers, but he could see that for the first time since they'd started speaking there was a glimmer of hope in her watery blue eyes.

'I learned a bit about mental health issues when I went on the course Brook sent me on – Riding for Wellbeing. That's not quite the same, that was all about using riding to connect with people, and the value of being in nature. But it's not all that different, really.'

He had learned quite a lot more about PND since then too, because he'd started reading around the subject when Louella had mentioned his mother might be heading for a relapse, but he didn't want to mention what Louella had said just yet. And besides, he hadn't fully cottoned on to what was happening until now.

'We're going to have to go out in a minute,' Ian said cautiously. 'We're going to miss the wedding if we don't leave now.'

Sam knew he wasn't being unkind. His pa just didn't get it. He felt the tremble of his ma's hands in his.

'I think this is more important, Pa,' he said gently, trying not to think about how disappointed Phoebe was going to be if they all missed her grandmother's big day. 'It's OK, Ma,' he soothed, realising that she had started to sob quietly again. 'We don't have to go anywhere. We can all stay right here.'

* * *

Sam definitely wasn't in the church. As the ceremony had got underway, Phoebe had sneaked several surreptitious glances along the rows of pews. Eddie's son Jonathan and his wife and their children were on the groom's side, and a few other people who Phoebe didn't recognise, all of whom were dressed up in their winter finery. Fake furs and costume jewellery, at least she assumed they were fakes. Eddie's family and friends were clearly into bling. There was no sign of Sam or any of his family. Which must mean something awful had happened. She was trying not to panic. She was also wishing fervently that she hadn't left her mobile in her bag, which she'd given over to the care of her mother just before they'd walked down the aisle.

No way could she retrieve it without being super conspicuous. She'd have to wait until the end of the ceremony. She'd be able to find out what had happened then. Sam must have left a message. He was picking up Ian and Jan. It was the last thing he'd said to her when they'd left each other this morning.

What if they'd broken down, or worse, they'd had an accident and were all lying in a ditch somewhere? Phoebe tried to block out these black thoughts and focus on the beautiful age-old words of the wedding service.

Maggie and Eddie had gone for a fairly traditional set of vows. The white-cloaked vicar had just read out Maggie's vows and she'd repeated each line after him, her voice steady and sure.

'I now pronounce you husband and wife,' the vicar said. 'You may kiss the bride.'

Eddie leaned in for a chaste peck, and Maggie grabbed him and kissed him firmly on the lips and everyone clapped. Phoebe felt a surge of relief. She would be able to find out what had happened soon. The cloying sweetness of the lilies at the end of the pew where she sat were beginning to make her head spin. Or was that just the worry about Sam?

There was a flurry of movement as the bride and groom turned from the altar and were ushered away to sign the register. Phoebe saw Frazier get up to go and take the 'signing the register photos' as they'd planned. Her nephew and niece had been very well behaved throughout the service. They'd been tucked between their dad and their grandad, and they looked adorable. Bertie was wearing a grey suit and Flo a pretty cream dress, edged with green satin. But as soon as their father got up, Flo tried to follow him.

'You just stay here a minute.' James grabbed her before she could go, which started her yelling in protest, and Louella got up to help.

Phoebe caught Tori's eye, who was sitting behind her, and knew she was thinking that it would be her turn next, as her friend gave her a rueful eyebrow raise.

Then finally, Maggie and Eddie emerged once more from the signing of the register and Phoebe and Alexa exchanged glances. Alexa was smiling. She was clearly totally caught up in it all. Phoebe decided she must be the only one who'd noticed the absence of the Hendries but as she got up from the front pew to follow the bride and groom, her mother leaned across to her.

'Where's Sam, darling?'

Phoebe shrugged. There wasn't time to say any more. She and Alexa followed the bride and groom back down the aisle, and seconds later they were outside again in the bright winter air.

It was a perfect day for a wedding. The sun had come out fully now and it lit up the white sky. There was even a touch of warmth in its rays. That was good. Phoebe knew Maggie had been worried about everyone getting cold. There was no chance of that happening. People milled about in the beautiful old churchyard. Confetti was thrown, the type that was edible for birds, impromptu photos were taken, and Phoebe finally got the chance to look at her phone.

There was no message from Sam. Phoebe spoke to her mother. 'I don't know what's happened to the Hendries. You haven't heard from Jan, have you?'

Louella shook her head. 'No, darling, but I did call her late last night when I got back from the hen night to check if she was all right. She insisted she was fine but there's more to this than meets the eye, I'm worried about her too.'

Phoebe found a corner of the churchyard where there was a signal and dialled Sam's number and it rang a few times before going to voicemail. She left a message asking him to call and let her know he was OK.

Other than leaving the wedding party and going across to Hendrie's, which would be difficult with no car, not to mention pretty inconsiderate to her grandmother, there wasn't much more she could do.

She finally got a WhatsApp from Sam just as they were about to leave the church.

Phoebe, I'm so sorry. Problems with Ma. She's OK. We're on our way.

It had been sent an hour ago, but thanks to a signal that varied between one bar and zero, it had only just arrived. And it didn't reassure Phoebe one little bit. Sam knew how important this day was to her. If his mother was OK, why on earth hadn't he made it to the wedding?

She remembered the conversation they'd had a few days ago when Sam had confessed he was only going to Maggie's wedding because he couldn't get away with not going. Had that really just been a throwaway line, or had he meant it, deep down? Had he not made the effort because he hadn't really wanted to go in the first place? That was crazy – surely?

The gnawing worry she'd been feeling ever since she'd realised the Hendries were missing morphed into hurt and by the time they were back at Puddleduck Farm and she discovered there was no sign of any of the Hendries there either, it had escalated into irritation.

What on earth was going on? Sam had better have a bloody good reason for not making it to the church. She took several deep breaths and tried to regain some of the lovely excitement she'd felt earlier. This was her beloved grandmother's big day and she was not going to let anything spoil it.

30

Natasha and Marcus had sneaked back early to get things ready at Puddleduck Farm. A handful of volunteers had helped to deck out the front of the farmhouse with strings of fairy lights and a big banner over the front door, which said 'Welcome Home Mr and Mrs Crowther-May' – there had been a fair amount of dispute over what name to put, but Crowther-May had won. The wooden front door was adorned with an evergreen wedding wreath threaded through with white roses, poinsettia and a sprig of mistletoe to match Maggie's bouquet.

The holly bushes to the left of the farmhouse needed no extra embellishments. They were bright with scarlet berries. Even the five-bar gate between parking and the road was wrapped around with green and red tinsel to echo the wedding theme colours.

The little gate that led around to the back of the farm was also sparkly with tinsel and there was a glittering red arrow below a sign that said 'This way to the reception', just in case there was any doubt where wedding guests should go.

While the white Rolls-Royce disgorged its passengers at the front of Puddleduck Farmhouse and there were more photos and cheers and shouted congratulations, and edible confetti for the birds, Natasha and Marcus were readying the fur and feathered welcoming party around the back.

As soon as Maggie and Eddie, closely followed by the rest of the wedding party, stepped through the little side gate and on into the yard, they were greeted by three donkeys and three dogs, all of whom had a white carnation attached to them somewhere, although Natasha later confided that Diablo had already eaten two of the carnations she'd put in the other donkeys' headcollars before she'd cottoned on to what was happening. There was also a selection of puddle ducks and a triumphant-looking Saddam, who had escaped from the barn and was stalking about on the feed room roof, swishing his tail.

Maggie and Eddie had considered opening up Saddam's barn in case the weather turned rainy, but in the end they'd decided against this and had erected a marquee in the donkey field closest to the farmhouse, the donkeys having been brought in for the day.

The marquee was set up with a trestle table on which sat a cauldron of mulled wine that had been warmed on the Aga and brought out from the kitchen, and the food had been laid out too, all of it still covered and under guard from marauding animals by a selection of volunteers.

Roxie broke free from Natasha's grasp the second she saw Phoebe and she hurtled across the yard and jumped up joyfully to greet her. Phoebe was cuddling her before she realised that she had muddy paws and a very brown snout, she looked like she'd been digging.

'Sorry,' Natasha mouthed as Phoebe tried to brush off some of the mud. Luckily it was mostly dry.

A cheer went up from the small party of waiting guests when they saw Maggie and Eddie. These guests, mostly volunteers from Puddleduck Pets, had been helping Natasha and Marcus to get the animal guests ready and Phoebe had half expected to see Sam and his family amongst them, but there was no sign of them here either.

She felt like bursting into tears. But she couldn't. This was Maggie and Eddie's day and they were clearly enjoying themselves. Every so often, they turned to each other and exchanged a few quick hand signals, laughing and smiling.

The guests from the church began to mingle with those who had been waiting at Puddleduck Farm, their breath puffing out in the afternoon air, and Phoebe knew she'd have to put Sam out of her mind and make the best of it.

She went to speak to Tori, who'd been sitting on a chair close to the glass doors of the surgery with a coat around her shoulders, while they waited for the bridal party. Harrison was standing beside her, his hand resting protectively on her shoulder, and he nodded politely at Phoebe as she approached.

Phoebe nodded back, and bent to Tori's level. 'How are you doing, lovely? You're not too cold, are you? No sign of any contractions yet?'

'I'm fine and no, not even Braxton Hicks, so don't tempt fate. That was a lovely wedding, wasn't it? You all looked gorgeous. That dress is stunning on you. Hey, maybe we could switch to a green colour theme, then you could wear it to ours too. What do you think, Harrison?' She glanced up at her partner and he tilted his head and looked at her so lovingly that Phoebe decided she might have to revise her opinion of him being a miserable so and so.

'I'm quite keen on the summer blue theme we've looked at.' He glanced back at Phoebe consideringly. 'Not sure green's gonna hack it with that.'

At least he was taking an interest in things, Phoebe thought. Which was more than Sam was doing!

As if she'd read her mind, Tori asked, 'Where's your Sam?' and Phoebe shook her head.

'He's not here,' she said tightly. 'He didn't manage to make it to the wedding.'

'Oh, my gosh.' Tori clapped her hand to her mouth. 'That's not like him. Is he OK? Has he messaged?'

'Yes. I'll tell you later.' She did not want to talk about Sam, or she knew she'd get cross again. Besides, she was aware that someone else had just tapped her arm.

'Um, is that donkey supposed to be in there?' When Phoebe looked, she saw Diablo's rear end sticking out from the feed room. Someone must have left the door open. She hurried across to haul him out, which was harder than it looked because he'd managed to get the lid off the feed bin and Diablo, who was a total foodie, was not about to relinquish his prize without a lot of persuasion.

By the time Phoebe had hauled up his head and got him to back out of the feed room, she had a trail of donkey slobber down her front to join the muddy pawprints. Hopefully that wouldn't show in the remaining photos. She looked around for Natasha, who was stroking Roxie's nose, but caught her eye and came across smiling. Natasha looked beautifully elegant in a pale cream dress – why wasn't she covered in muddy pawprints and donkey slobber? Berating herself for such uncharitable thoughts, Phoebe suggested that maybe if the donkey photos were all finished, they should put them all back in their stables.

Casey's Girl, who never had been collected – Stephen Fitzpatrick had finally admitted he didn't really want her back and had asked Maggie to rehome her – whickered when she saw her donkey companions and kicked the stable door. At least Stephen had made a substantial donation to keep her in feed and hay for the winter, Phoebe thought. Casey's father had made a significant donation too. Guilt money probably. But it was a happy ending of sorts.

When Phoebe and Natasha got back, there were even more guests milling about, although most had gone into the marquee.

The people outside had red noses and pink ears, despite the mulled wine that everyone was drinking, and there were noises about migrating into the house. But there was still no sign of Sam. Maggie and Eddie were posing for a photo with Buster, Tiny and Roxie. Maggie beckoned her over and Phoebe took a deep, calming breath and went to join them.

* * *

Rufus Holt had just been to a meeting with one of his tenants in Bridgeford and he was on his way back to Beechbrook House when he saw two men in suits walking along the grass verge.

As Rufus automatically slowed the Land Rover to give them a wide berth, the man who was walking at the rear turned slightly and held out his thumb to indicate he was hitching a lift. Rufus realised two things simultaneously. The first was that the men both wore carnations, he surmised they were on their way to a wedding, and the second was that the man who'd turned and held out his thumb looked vaguely familiar.

On impulse, Rufus pulled into the kerb just ahead of them. They must have broken down. He'd passed a green Subaru at the side of the road a mile or so back. It wouldn't hurt him to stop and see where they were going. It was a cold day and if he'd broken down on his way to a wedding, he liked to think someone would have stopped for him.

Rufus watched in his rear-view mirror as they hurried to catch up, but it was only when they actually reached him and the younger of the two guys came to the driver's window that he recognised Archie's old riding instructor.

The chap clearly recognised him at the same time because he almost did a double take. 'Thanks for stopping...' There was a slight pause before he added the words, 'Lord Holt.'

'No problem,' Rufus said, remembering that Sam had once tried to punch him. He'd apologised for that long ago, but it felt good to be in a position where Sam had to be polite to him, so he didn't add that using the title was unnecessary. Instead, he asked where they were heading.

The older man looked at his watch. 'Er – Puddleduck Farm if it's not too much trouble. Thank you, sir. Shall I give you directions?'

'He doesn't need directions,' Sam said. 'He lives next door.'

'Ah. Right. OK. That's handy then.'

There was an awkward little silence as the two men got into the back and sat down on the bench seats and Rufus pulled away.

'We were on our way to a wedding,' the older guy continued. 'But unfortunately, we had a few hold-ups and the wedding itself will be done and dusted by now. The reception's at Puddleduck Farm.'

Rufus felt his hands tense around the steering wheel. He was aware that Maggie Crowther was getting married. Harrison had the day off for it, but it hadn't registered that it was today.

'I'll drop you at the gate,' he murmured.

* * *

Could today get any worse? Sam wondered, as Rufus hurtled along roads he obviously knew well with scant regard for his passengers' comfort. The Land Rover's suspension was all to cock and he and Pa were being bounced around all over the place. Of all the people that could have picked them up, why did it have to be Lord Nob?

He'd never have flagged down the Land Rover if he'd realised Rufus was driving. He was usually in a Mercedes with darkened windows. Sam wondered what had happened to that. He'd almost rather have walked than have turned up at the wedding in a vehicle being driven by Phoebe's ex.

The one saving grace was that at least his ma was safely at home. His father had tried to persuade her to come. He'd been convinced that once she was in the car and they were on their way to the wedding, she'd feel better. She had almost capitulated – it was clear she felt terrible about letting everyone down – but Sam had said no, that she should probably take baby steps when it came to getting out and about and mixing with people. Going to a wedding and then a reception was hardly baby steps.

Thank goodness she'd listened. God only knows what sort of a state she'd have ended up in if she'd been with them when the car had broken down and then had to walk miles along a country road. That would have been stressful enough for someone who wasn't terrified of new situations, which was to a large degree, Jan had explained, how she felt.

'It's not just going out, it's being in crowds, it's unpredictable situations, it's feeling totally out of control.'

She had finally confessed that she'd suffered from an extended period of agoraphobia once before. Ian hadn't been aware of it and Sam had been too young, but apparently it had happened in the early days of her PND.

'I didn't go out for weeks on end,' she'd said falteringly. 'If anyone queried it, I just told them I was too tired or that the baby was ill. Or I gave them one of a hundred other excuses I had at the time. No one ever called me out on it.'

'I do vaguely remember a time you didn't go out much for a few weeks,' Ian Hendrie had said. 'But I just put it down to tiredness. I didn't realise that you didn't go out at all.'

'You probably assumed I went out in the daytime when you were at work. But I didn't need to, because my sister Grace was here, if you remember, and if we needed anything she went and got it. Not to mention the fact that we own a store,' she'd added ruefully.

'I honestly don't remember what came first – whether it was

that after a while I just got used to staying in and going out got harder, or whether it was that I was scared of going out so I simply didn't go. All I can really remember is that the effect was the same. I ended up staying at home most of the time.'

'So what happened? Did it get better on its own?' Ian had asked her, more gently now he knew what was going on.

'School happened,' Jan had told him wearily. 'Sam started school and I had to take him. In the days leading up to it, I made myself go a little further down the road each day. Thank God it was only two blocks away.' She shuddered at the memory. 'It didn't get better for a long time, Ian, if I'm totally honest. It just got bearable.'

Sam had never heard his mother talk so much about how she felt. It was as though once she'd started, the floodgates opened and she couldn't stop. He had never seen his father listen so much either.

Sam had no doubt that this outpouring would be the beginning of the healing process for her – or at least the first step to getting some help for dealing with it. She'd finally agreed she would seek professional help, and Ian, now he knew what was going on, was happy to be a part of that process.

Now, Sam wished they'd all stayed at home. But that was with the benefit of hindsight. It had been his mother who'd insisted they go to the wedding. When they'd left, there'd been a slight chance they'd make it in time to sneak in and sit at the back of the church.

But the possibility of that happening had been smashed when midway along a forest road, his Subaru had lost power before drifting to a halt and conking out completely by the grass verge. The recovery company had given them an ETA of at least three hours, so walking had seemed the best option.

They'd been walking half an hour before the Land Rover, which was the first vehicle that had gone past, had stopped. Sam's heart had leapt with gratitude. Until he'd seen the driver. God definitely had a sense of humour.

Sam was roused from his reverie as Rufus drew up alongside the entrance to Puddleduck Farm. There were too many cars for him to actually pull right in.

'Thank you, much appreciated, Lord Holt,' Ian said, as they climbed out.

'Yep. Cheers.' Sam couldn't bring himself to say Lord Holt again.

'You're welcome.' Rufus sped away without looking back.

31

In another life, Rufus mused, he'd have been at Maggie Crowther's wedding. As Phoebe's guest. It would have been fun too, a December wedding, the season of goodwill, the run-up to Christmas, everyone drinking mulled wine no doubt, and the laughter and the dancing. Although that was another scenario he knew would have made his father turn in his grave. The Holts and the Crowthers mixing socially. 'For pity's sake, Rufus. Seriously!'

Would there ever be a day when he didn't hear his father's voice, berating and criticising, so clearly in his head? He was terribly afraid there wouldn't.

The last time he'd talked properly to Harrison, his friend had said that as long as Rufus was prepared to listen, then there definitely wouldn't.

'Tell him to piss off, mate,' Harrison had advised. 'The Holt/Crowther feud was donkey's years ago. Let it go. Move on. You can live your life on your own terms now, not his.'

Except that he couldn't. And he wasn't.

Rufus pulled beneath the life-size stag that stood astride the entrance gates of Beechbrook House, flashed past the gatehouse cottage that looked empty and sad now Harrison no longer lived in it, and drove at speed up his quarter-mile drive. There was a problem with the suspension on the Land Rover. Something else to sort out. He cursed as he screeched to a halt, spitting gravel, outside the house.

He felt so alone. Even Archie didn't want to come home any more. School finished in a few days and Archie would have to be dragged back to Beechbrook House. Rufus had promised he could bring Enola, which had sealed the deal, but the prospect of having Archie's horse stabled anywhere near the house was dreadful.

He missed Emilia more than he'd ever imagined possible. Everything had seemed less overwhelming when she'd been here. But he hadn't heard a whisper from her. And he wasn't surprised. He'd managed to drive her away pretty damn successfully too. He'd managed to drive everyone away. He was doing exactly what his father had done all his life. Which had been to put everyone he really cared about at arm's length, if not alienate them completely. For the first time, Rufus could see it all clearly.

He had become a carbon copy of his father. The man who he'd both respected and despised, loved and disliked, almost in equal measure. He'd become cold and locked down, unreachable and arrogant, and he could see no way of turning this around.

Yet despite the way he'd been brought up, the aloofness of his childhood, Rufus missed his father desperately too. Lord Alfred may have been straight-backed and stiff upper-lipped but at least he'd been constant, as predictable and reliable as the seasons. Rufus still couldn't believe he was gone.

Now, sitting in his Land Rover, feeling too shrouded by grief and self-pity to even bother with the effort of getting out, he leaned over the steering wheel and he began to sob for the complete and utter mess he had made of his life.

* * *

Sam saw Phoebe as soon as he entered the marquee, she was chatting to Natasha and Marcus with a faithful Roxie at her heels. She looked so beautiful, she was three quarters in profile – the green silk dress accentuated every curve – and she was smiling. For a few seconds, he luxuriated in the vision of a smiling Phoebe and then, as if she'd just become aware of his gaze, she turned towards him, and her expression changed completely. She looked cross.

Shit, he had some making up to do. Composing his face into what he hoped was a suitably apologetic expression, he hurried across.

Phoebe waited, stiff backed, for him to reach her, and Roxie whined and wagged her tail in adoration when she saw Sam.

'I'm so sorry,' he said, bending to pet the puppy, who was wriggling her little body in ecstasy. 'I'm so very, very sorry.'

'Me too. You know how important today was to me, Sam. Could you really not have managed to even make a call?'

Natasha and Marcus exchanged glances and then melted away. Sam touched Phoebe's arm. His fingers were tingling from the cold.

'I'm so sorry,' he said again.

'Yes, so you said. But it's Maggie you should really be apologising to.'

'And I will. Of course I will. Can I just explain?'

'It better be good.' Her voice was harder than he'd ever heard it. 'And it better be based on something more than the fact that you don't really like weddings very much.'

Crap, he *had* said that to her, hadn't he? But he was shocked that she'd taken him seriously. He took a deep breath.

* * *

Phoebe was shocked at her anger, but she was even more shocked at the intensity of her feelings. A couple of nearby guests were glancing over curiously. She must have spoken louder than she'd intended.

Sam looked so mortified, and she hadn't even given him the chance to explain. She'd just launched into attack mode. It was so unlike her.

'Phoebe, Mum had another panic attack. I couldn't leave her and I couldn't just phone you. It was all so last minute.'

'Is she OK?' she asked, feeling a sharp stab of guilt. She looked around the crowded marquee. 'Is she here?'

'No. She's at home.' He had moved a person-space back from her and she didn't blame him.

'Oh, hell, I'm sorry, Sam. I've been so worried. Then, when I got your message, I convinced myself you weren't that bothered. Which I know in my heart isn't true. It's not true, is it?'

'Of course not. For what it's worth, we left in time to get to the wedding. But then we broke down. The Subaru's stuck in the forest. We hitched a lift.'

Phoebe stepped closer to him. 'Shall we go and talk about this somewhere more private?'

He nodded and, a few seconds later, she had led him out of the marquee, unlocked the front doors of her surgery and they'd slipped inside, with Roxie their shadow, slipping in with them.

They headed for the back consulting room, out of sight in case any guests happened to go past and peer inside.

As Sam explained about his mother's agoraphobia, Phoebe felt all of her anger and stress slipping away.

'I'm so sorry I snapped at you.'

'I'd have done the same in your shoes.'

'No, you wouldn't, Sam. You're too lovely. And I'm covered in mud and I feel like a mess.'

'You look beautiful.'

They locked gazes across the examining table, and he took a step towards her and gently untied the bow of the green ribbon around her neck. He bent his head to kiss the skin he'd revealed. 'You always look beautiful.'

It was fifteen minutes before they emerged again into reception, both looking breathless and slightly more dishevelled than when they'd gone in. It was amazing what you could do on a vet's examining table!

'I think that was our first real row,' Phoebe said, sneaking a glance at Sam, as she smoothed down her dress, and he straightened his tie.

'We should have them more often if the making up's going to be that good.'

'But maybe not in such public places.' She was trying not to laugh. 'Oh, Sam, I'm sorry I was ready to think the worst of you. It's not you. It's me.'

'Go on.' His eyes sobered.

'I've been feeling insecure lately. Partly because of our hectic lives and the pressure that puts on us spending time together. But mostly because I feel like I'm rubbish at relationships. I've mucked up every one I've had and I don't want to muck this one up.'

'You haven't mucked them up. I think you've just chosen men who are emotionally unavailable. I'm not like that, Phoebe. I'm not the same as they were.' Sam's gaze held hers and she felt the truth of his words as if they'd been delivered on an arrow straight to her heart.

'I love you so much, Sam.' She could hear the huskiness of her own voice.

'I love you too. And we probably need to talk more.' He waved a hand. 'I mean about what's important to us.'

'I want us to have babies,' Phoebe blurted. 'Not right this minute. I don't mean that. But I don't want us to leave it too late.'

'Neither do I. We will have babies. And we won't leave anything too late.' He hesitated and for a moment she thought he was going to say something else, but he didn't. He put his hands in his pockets. 'But right now, I think we should probably get back and enjoy the rest of Maggie's wedding.'

Roxie, who'd thankfully been asleep for most of the last half hour, whined in agreement.

When they got back into the marquee, it was to the sound of music and the buzz of chatter. A mixture of Christmas classics and eighties disco songs were blasting from an old-fashioned CD player set up on one of the trestle tables. Two of the first people she saw were Anni Buckland and her husband Nick. They were both dressed in their finery and looked smarter than Phoebe had ever seen them.

Anni was wearing a bright floral dress with tones of burgundy and she had a white silk rose fascinator pinned into her dark ringleted hair. She was sipping a glass of Prosecco and she raised it in Phoebe and Sam's direction and then came hurrying across.

'Hello, Phoebe. What a lovely wedding. And is this your young man?' She looked keenly at Sam, who blushed under such intense scrutiny, as Phoebe introduced them.

Anni held out her hand to shake Sam's. 'Utterly charmed,' she said, when she let go again.

'I'm – er – just going to apologise to Maggie for arriving so late.' He strode off across the marquee and Anni leaned forward to speak to Phoebe.

'Now then. Do you want to hear my predictions about couples and their futures?'

Phoebe had forgotten all about that.

'Why not?' she said, seeing Anni's coal-black eyes dance with amusement and hoping she hadn't witnessed the semi-public row between herself and Sam earlier.

Anni inclined her head in the direction of Natasha and Marcus. 'Those two are made for each other. Just look at that body language. They have a very strong future.'

Her gaze panned round and rested on another couple who were in the midst of a group and standing close together. 'Whereas those two have no chance. They're pretending to like each other because they came here together, but he's not that keen and she's looking over his shoulder to see if there is anyone more interesting to talk to.'

'Yes,' Phoebe said, because she could see exactly what Anni meant. The couple in question were volunteers. She only knew them vaguely, but Anni's observations looked to be spot on.

'Now those two are interesting.' Anni's gaze alighted on Tori and Harrison. 'Their relationship is much more complex.'

'You don't think they're getting married for the sake of the baby then?' Phoebe said quietly.

'Definitely not, no. He adores her. I'd hazard a guess that she and that baby are the closest thing he's had to a family for a very long time. In fact, I'd go as far as to say that he's probably fallen out with his own family, but he'd lay down his life for his woman and unborn child.'

'Blimey,' Phoebe said, gasping a little because actually when it came to the family observation, she knew that Anni was spot on: Harrison *had* fallen out with his family, and she wouldn't have been surprised about the rest of it too. She swallowed a lump in her throat. She would tell Tori that one day. Although, actually, she probably knew already.

'It's my turn,' Phoebe said, turning her gaze towards Maggie and Eddie, who were currently conversing in sign language with Dusty. All three of them looked animated.

'I predict that they're going to spend the rest of their lives being very happy together.'

'Of course they are, that goes without saying. But you haven't asked me about the relationship that's most important to you. Don't you want to know about you and Sam?'

'Yes. No.' Phoebe gulped. 'I don't know.'

'I used to be indecisive but now I'm not so sure,' Anni teased gently. 'Don't look so worried. You two are rock solid. Communication is at the heart of all good relationships. And you can do that, can't you? Even when you fall out about something important.'

'You saw us earlier.'

'I did. And I saw you emerging from your making-up session. Don't panic,' she added swiftly, taking in Phoebe's shocked expression. 'I only saw you because I'm a people watcher. I doubt if anyone else noticed.'

'Phew!'

'I'd better go and rescue Nick from that drunk woman who's just latched on to him.' Anni winked at Phoebe. 'The other thing that's important in a good relationship is knowing when to butt in and knowing when to stay right out of it.'

She bustled away and Phoebe decided it was about time she circulated a bit more herself. She'd just caught her mother's gaze across the heads of a few people. She wanted to catch up with Maggie and Eddie too. And she wanted to give her niece and nephew another kiss, and hug her brother and say hello to Ian. And most of all she wanted to hug Sam. It was amazing how the whole world had looked brighter and shinier since she and Sam had properly talked. It was amazing how much an honest conversation could transform absolutely everything.

Her mood had lifted from sad and disappointed to being bright and shiny and full of hope for the future.

32

When Rufus had finally climbed out of the Land Rover, he'd felt physically exhausted. Or perhaps it was emotional exhaustion – he so seldom acknowledged his emotions that he really had no idea. All he knew was that crouching over a steering wheel and sobbing was incredibly hard work.

As he walked up to the front door of his house, he heard the sounds of music and laughter drifting up across the fields from his next-door neighbours. The wedding reception must be in full swing at Puddleduck Farm and the sounds of people enjoying themselves only served to increase his isolation.

Fleetingly Rufus considered going into his office and downing several whiskies to numb out the pain.

But he knew that wasn't going to help for long. He'd just end up with a raging headache. He had to get a grip. It was time to stop wallowing in this morass of self-pity.

An image of Archie flicked into his head. Archie, his beautiful son, who would one day inherit all of this: the house, the title, the privileged lifestyle, every last belt and buckle of it all. Rufus knew there were many people in the world who'd have killed for a legacy like that, and here he was, so intent on his own self-inflicted misery that he felt not a smidgen of gratitude. What the hell was he thinking? He should be embracing his life, focusing on making it a legacy worth passing on to his son and heir, not drowning in self-pity.

He had a sudden intense urge to hear his son's voice. He dialled his number and to his surprise, Archie picked up almost straight away.

'Hiya, Dad.'

'Hi, son.' He paused, having not thought any further ahead than this.

'Were you calling to tell me what time you're picking me up next week?'

'Yes, yes, that's right. What time's good?'

They made the arrangements and then Archie thew in casually, 'I've got a Christmas present for Emilia. I ordered it online, but I'm not sure what address to put on the delivery slip. Have you got one?'

'Not to hand but I could probably find you one. OK if I call you back later?'

'Sure thing, Dad. Bye.' Archie hung up.

Rufus felt much better now he had something to focus on. He would track down Emilia's address. He would phone her and if she didn't pick up, he would keep trying, and he would keep on trying until he had an answer for Archie.

This idea was scuppered at the first hurdle when his attempt to phone Emilia was met by an electronic voice saying, 'The number you have dialled has not been recognised. Please check and try again.'

She must have changed her number. No wonder Archie hadn't been able to get hold of her. Rufus racked his brains. Emilia had more than one phone – an English one and a Swiss one. She'd probably dispensed with the English one as soon as she'd got back to her own country. But with luck he'd still have the number in his contacts somewhere.

He searched through the filing cabinet in his office where he kept employment records and contracts and found Emilia's original application form for the job of nanny. Thank God he never threw anything away. There were two numbers listed, one of which looked as though it could have been a landline, complete with a Swiss STD code, so he phoned that.

After several rings, it was answered by a female voice he didn't recognise. 'Guten tag.'

'Guten tag. Is this the right number for Emilia Gubler?'

'Who is this calling, please?' She switched effortlessly to English.

'It's Rufus Holt.' He wondered if he should add, I'm her employer, although technically he wasn't any more. But before he could say anything else, the line went dead. That was odd. He tried again, just in case it was a bad signal, but this time it rang eight or nine times before being disconnected.

Maybe Emilia didn't want to speak to him and the person on the end of the phone knew that. Or maybe there was some other perfectly rational explanation he hadn't thought of. He decided to try again later.

The other number was a mobile, which was eventually picked up by a voicemail service speaking rapidly in Swiss German. He assumed it was saying he should leave a message, so he waited for the tone and said, 'Emilia, this is Rufus. I'm so...' He was cut off by another tone before he could say anything else. Either it wasn't possible to leave a very long message or the voicemail was full.

He phoned again. 'I'm so sorry, I need...' he got in before being cut off again.

This was ridiculous.

At least Emilia would know he was trying to get hold of her.

That was a good start. He glanced back at the file. There was also an address on the application form. He supposed he could actually write her a letter. There might be more chance she would read that, and by God he owed her an apology. He rummaged through his desk for some writing paper and found a pad his father had used. Lord Alfred had enjoyed writing letters. He would have used a good pen too. Rufus found a black Mont Blanc in a case, nestled on plush material and he slid it out.

It felt cool beneath his fingertips and Rufus felt an ache of loss, knowing his father would have been the last to touch it.

Two hours later, Rufus realised he'd written a love letter. There had been several false starts. The wastepaper bin under his desk now overflowed with scrunched-up balls of paper where he'd torn out pages and started again because he couldn't find the right words. Either he sounded patronising, or he sounded as though he was making crass excuses for his behaviour. But he'd finally ended up with something quite short.

My dearest Emilia

I'm so sorry for sending you away. I have no excuse, but that day is one I profoundly regret. All I can say in my defence is that I was lost in grief. Will you please accept my heartfelt apologies for my cruel words? They were not true.

The time we spent together feels like a bright warming sunshine and there has been precious little sunshine since you've been gone. I miss you more than I can say.

I would very much like the chance to apologise in person and I hope and pray that you will find it in your heart to forgive me.

Please will you get in touch, either by phone or by letter.

All my love

Rufus

He wondered if he should say he'd like them to try again, and to have a relationship, but he decided that would be too much. For all he knew, she despised the ground he walked on, and after the way he'd treated her, he certainly wouldn't have blamed her if she did.

In the end, he put the letter in an envelope, sealed it, downloaded a postage label online and then went straight to the nearest letter box and posted it before he could change his mind.

As he drove home, he felt a new lightness. It was out of his hands now. He had done his best. Emilia might tear the letter up without reading it, but he had written it. He had told her how sorry he was. He could do no more.

* * *

Phoebe and Sam finally left the wedding reception around 10 p.m., having first helped with the clearing up, along with several other members of the Dashwood family.

Eddie and Maggie were spending their first night of married life at Puddleduck Farm, and were off on their honeymoon to the Caribbean the day after. Having spent so long sleeping in different houses, they'd wanted to sleep under the same roof for at least one night before they dashed off anywhere new.

Sam had driven Phoebe back to his place in her car – he'd been on sparkling water all day – the AA had collected his Subaru and taken it to the garage, and now Sam and Phoebe were finally home. They trudged up the stairs to Sam's flat with an exhausted Roxie in tow.

'That was the best wedding I've ever been to,' Phoebe told him.

'Me too. Or at least what I saw of it. Sorry again about the slightly shaky start.'

'You are totally forgiven. You missed it for all the right reasons.

Oops.' She somehow managed to trip over the threshold into his flat and would have gone head over heels if he hadn't caught her.

'Are you drunk, Phoebe Dashwood?'

'Maybe a little bit tipsy,' she confessed. 'Thank you for driving, and thank you for being so lovely, and thank you for helping with the clearing up and thank you for being you...'

'You're definitely tipsy.' He smiled at her. 'I'm glad you had a chance to let your hair down. You hardly ever do.'

'The night's not over yet.' Phoebe gave him a slightly unfocused look. 'That's if you're up for any more hanky panky. Are you? Or did I wear you out in the practice, earlier?'

'That was a practise! Oh, I see what you mean. And no, I'm not worn out. Nor am I the one who's been knocking back the Prosecco.' Sam laughed. 'Just give me two ticks to feed Snowball and put Roxie in her crate, and I'll be right with you.'

* * *

The week after Maggie's wedding would have been an anti-climax, Phoebe thought, if it hadn't been the run-up to Christmas, which was always busy. Especially as she was behind on her Christmas shopping and had gone into a flurry of present-hunting activity. She and Sam had haunted the Christmas markets in both Salisbury and Southampton, where they'd bought lots of locally made products, and had come away weighed down with presents for their families, friends and animals.

Phoebe had bought Sam some new riding boots, which he knew about, and also a couple of surprise horse-related gifts that he didn't. He had said her present was a surprise and had refused to even give her a clue as to what it was. Sam was quite good at presents so Phoebe hadn't pushed him too hard. It would be nice to have a surprise on Christmas Day.

She was also helping Natasha and Marcus, who'd moved into Puddleduck Farmhouse while Maggie and Eddie were away, because someone needed to be on site twenty-four hours for the animals. Sam was busy helping his mother to hunt down a therapist. Now Jan had finally confessed she was ready to face her demons, she was keen to talk to someone as soon as possible but the NHS waiting list was very long, so they'd been looking at self-help groups and online forums. Jan had agreed to see someone privately if she could find a good recommendation.

Then there was the Puddleduck Vets Christmas party, which involved all of Phoebe's staff and their partners being treated by Phoebe to a slap-up meal in Bridgeford's best Italian. That was a riotous evening, despite the fact that hardly anyone was drinking – they were either on call or driving – but by the end of the night, Phoebe felt light, not just in the purse department but in her heart too. She had such a wonderful team of people around her – she could have burst with pride.

And of course there was the excitement of Tori's baby. She'd had a false alarm a few days after Maggie's wedding, and then another false alarm eight days before she was due. But the second false alarm turned into the real thing.

It was actually midday on 13 December when Phoebe had a text from Tori.

We're on our way to hospital. This time it's for real. They've told me to come in. Wish me luck. I'm terrified.

Phoebe texted back.

Everything's going to be fine. Just take all the drugs you can.

I will!!!!!

Tori had already decided that a natural birth wasn't for her and she planned to have all the medical intervention she could get if it meant less pain. The two friends had laughed about it.

'Natural births are for heroines, and I'm a wuss,' Tori had said, and then added, 'Joking aside, I'm not planning to suffer in silence for some thirty-six-hour labour, that's for sure. You know what a low pain threshold I've got. And Harrison says he's going to fight my corner every step of the way. Not many people argue with Harrison.'

Phoebe couldn't imagine they did. She'd warmed to Harrison lately. Considering he'd been as anti-having a family as Tori, he'd adjusted to the idea wonderfully. She thought about the wooden crib he'd made his daughter, and the way he'd looked at Tori so adoringly at Maggie's reception. She knew she'd be going to their wedding next.

To everyone's amazement, Tori ended up having such a short labour that there hadn't been time for many drugs.

Phoebe had been astounded to get a second text from Tori's phone at just after 7 p.m. on 13 December.

Vanessa Rose has arrived. She's 8lbs 5oz. Mother and baby are doing great. Visitors welcome from 8.30 p.m.
This is Harrison.

Phoebe had whooped with excitement and she and Sam had been the first visitors at Tori's bed. They were armed with a teddy, with a pink vest, embroidered with the name Vanessa Rose, which Phoebe had got from Etsy, as soon as she'd known Tori was definitely having a girl.

Tori was sitting up in bed, grinning from ear to ear, with her daughter, who already had a thatch of dark hair and tiny pink rosebud lips, sleeping soundly in a cot beside her.

'We won't stay long,' Phoebe said, gazing into the cot and cooing at the baby. 'We just wanted to say hello to Vanessa Rose, and well done, darling. How are you feeling?'

'Amazing. Stay as long as you like. Mum and Dad won't be here for another half hour. We've only told you and them so far – oh, and Rufus, but I doubt he'll come in. He hates hospitals.'

'How is he?' Phoebe asked idly.

'Harrison thinks he's been suffering from depression. But he doesn't help himself. Isolating from the world. At least Archie's back for Christmas. Hopefully that will cheer him up. Anyway, never mind about Rufus. How do you and Sam feel about being godparents?'

Harrison smiled, first at Tori, and then across at them. Phoebe thought it might be the first time she'd ever seen him smile, and it transformed his face. She smiled tentatively back.

'Of course we'll be godparents, won't we, Sam?'

'Absolutely,' Sam said. 'We'd be honoured.'

33

'Sam, would it bother you if I went up to Beechbrook House and gave Archie and Rufus a Christmas card?' Phoebe asked.

It was the night after they'd visited Tori in hospital and Tori's words about Rufus being depressed had been playing on Phoebe's mind.

'No, of course it wouldn't. Why would you think it would?'

'Because I might bump into Rufus. I'm planning to ring the bell. I'd like to say hi to Archie if I can.'

'I'd have thought that would bother you more than it would bother me,' Sam said idly and Phoebe met his steady gaze.

'I don't bear him any resentment, Sam. He always was a tortured soul, which sounds a bit melodramatic, I know. But it's true. I know he's a lord and wealthy and has had a life of privilege, but he's also had quite a tragic life. It wasn't just his wife he lost young. He lost his own mother young too. It can't have been easy, growing up with Lord Alfred in that big old place. The man was always iceberg cold towards me and he didn't seem much warmer towards his own son.'

'Yes, I guess you're right. I can't pretend I've ever really taken to

Rufus, but at least we had the privilege of growing up in loving families.'

'We're so lucky, Sam. And at least your ma was brave enough to ask for the help she needed. How's it going with the therapist she found?'

'She's getting there.' Sam's eyes warmed. 'Baby steps but I know she's going to be OK. She's got all of us in her corner.' He hesitated. 'I don't think I ever told you, but it was Rufus who gave Pa and I a lift to Maggie and Eddie's reception when my car conked out. So if you do see him, could you pass on my thanks? We'd have frozen to death and missed even more of the day if it hadn't been for him.'

'Of course I will. Thank you.'

But in the end it wasn't Rufus she bumped into when she went up to Beechbrook House. The first person she saw was Emilia.

Archie's nanny was just walking away from the door when Phoebe pulled into the wide drive that opened out at the front of Beechbrook House. She hesitated. That was bad luck. She hadn't known Emilia was back on the scene.

There were no other cars in situ, so presumably Rufus was out, but it was too late for Phoebe to make her escape. Besides, Emilia seemed to be waiting for her. She was now standing by the fountain, clutching a festive-looking bag to her chest. It was the only festive thing in sight. There were no Christmas lights. No tree visible through any of the downstairs windows. Not even a Christmas wreath or a sprig of mistletoe adorned the great old oak door.

Phoebe tensed as she got out of the Lexus and walked towards her former adversary. The last thing she wanted was a row.

'Good morning, Phoebe.' Emilia's greeting was formal, but she looked strained and pale.

'Hi, Emilia. Is anyone in?'

'No. I think maybe they have gone away for the festive season.'

'Right.' Phoebe didn't know what else to say. She was about to go and post the Christmas cards she'd brought with her through the door, but for the first time she realised there was no letter box. She had a vague memory of there being a post box at the bottom of the drive. Of course the postman wouldn't want to waste time driving up here every day.

Emilia blinked a few times. She looked so stricken and sad that Phoebe felt a surge of sympathy, despite herself. She leaned forward and touched the younger woman's arm.

'Are you OK?'

Emilia shook her head and, to Phoebe's alarm, a tear ran down her face. 'No. I am not OK.'

Phoebe knew she couldn't walk away. Whatever had happened in the past between them no longer mattered. Emilia looked utterly bereft.

'Would you like to talk about it?' she asked gently and after a few seconds' hesitation, Emilia nodded and began to walk back towards her own car.

Feeling committed now, Phoebe followed her slowly, and a few seconds later they were both sitting in what Phoebe realised must be a hire car, because it had a sticker on the windscreen: New Forest Luxury Cars.

Emilia was frozen in the driver's seat and for a moment she didn't look at Phoebe, just stared out of the windscreen. Then she finally spoke.

'I love him,' she turned her tear washed blue eyes towards Phoebe and said, 'but he does not feel like this. *Unerwidert*, I think the English word is "unrequested". You have this feeling before, ja?'

Phoebe took a breath. 'It's unrequited. And no. Not for Rufus. I liked him very much. But I wasn't in love with him.'

So this was why Emilia wanted to talk to her. She had assumed they were – or at least had been – in the same situation.

'But he asked you to go away, Phoebe, he did this same thing – ja?'

'No. Well, yes, he did. But I think it was more mutual when we split up. You understand mutual.'

'You both feel the same way,' Emilia said. 'But not love.' She sighed. 'Rufus and I – we do not feel the same. I love him, but he say I am only for sex. That he use me just for sex.'

Phoebe looked at her in shock. 'I can't believe he would say such an awful thing. Are you sure that's what he said? Were you arguing? Was he angry?' She couldn't imagine that Rufus would have been so cruel. He'd been arrogant, spiky, and on occasions icily distant towards her, but he'd never been cruel. On the contrary, he'd always been gentle, and sensitive and pretty perceptive too.

In the small space of the car, she could smell Emilia's faint perfume and she could feel the waves of pain radiating off her.

'He did not say this same thing to you, Phoebe?' Emilia looked at her with haunted eyes. 'Please will you tell me?'

'No, he didn't. But Rufus and I weren't lovers.' Despite her best efforts and at least two carefully planned seduction attempts, Phoebe thought somewhat ruefully, but she wasn't about to tell Emilia that Rufus had rebuffed her completely on that front.

'You did not sleep with him?' Emilia looked disbelieving. 'This is the truth?'

'Yes, it's the truth. Rufus and I were good friends. Nothing more.'

Emilia held her gaze for a few seconds before shaking her head. 'I did not know this.'

There was a small silence. The windows had begun to steam up with their breath. They were in their own little closed-in bubble and all Phoebe wanted to do was to make the young woman, who was clearly in such pain, feel better.

'I'm sure Rufus didn't mean what he said. He's grieving for his father.'

Emilia nodded and then she went on softly, 'Do you think that Rufus say these things because I am Archie's nanny? Because he thinks I am not of good enough family to be *freundin*?'

Phoebe hesitated. She guessed that *freundin* meant partner or girlfriend and an echo of what Tori had said flashed into her mind.

'Harrison said he couldn't square it with his ancestry, the fact that he's a lord and she's a nanny.'

She saw immediately that Emilia had read her expression.

'This is what you think is true, ja?' Her shoulders began to shake and Phoebe thought that she was sobbing. It took a few seconds before she realised to her utter amazement that Emilia was actually laughing. Mystified, Phoebe sat waiting patiently for her to stop. Maybe she was hysterical. Either way, she didn't feel able to leave her to it.

Phoebe rummaged in her bag for a tissue and found a pack, but Emilia brushed them away and produced her own yellow and blue handkerchief from the pocket of her coat.

The windows were now totally fogged. Emilia switched on the ignition and turned on the demister to clear them. She glanced back at Phoebe.

'I am not a nanny,' she said, and there was a blank detachment in her voice.

'You're not?' Phoebe queried.

Emilia shook her head. 'I have qualification as nanny. It's hard to explain in English. I love children. I love Archie, but I am not only a nanny. I was born in Lichtenstein – I am related to the Lichtenstein monarchy. My father is prince's second cousin – you understand?'

Phoebe felt her head spinning. For a moment, she thought she had stepped into a parallel universe.

'You're related to the prince of Lichtenstein?' she repeated.

'More complicated than this. But ja. My parents have title. I have title.'

'Jeez!' was all Phoebe could come up with, she was so shocked. 'You have to tell Rufus,' she urged. 'This may change everything.'

'Pfff,' Emilia said. 'I do not tell Rufus. He cannot love me as child's nanny. He cannot love me as monarchy. Pfff,' she said again and shook her head. 'But now you see why I laugh.'

'Yes,' Phoebe said, thinking that she did actually have a point. Tragic though it was. She looked back at Emilia with a new respect.

'When did you last see Rufus?'

'Many weeks ago. When he told me to leave his house.'

'So have you been back home to Lichtenstein?'

'No. My family now live in Geneva. But I stay in England. I have big bust-up with my family. Long time ago.' Her eyes sparked with anger. 'They tell me how to live my life. Do this. Do that. Do as we tell you. But I ignore them. I live my life how I choose to live it. So we finish family relationship.' Her chin jutted out in annoyance and for a second Phoebe caught a glimpse of the old haughty Emilia she had met before. Suddenly it wasn't hard to imagine her as some Lichtenstein princess.

She nodded slowly. 'I wish you would tell Rufus,' she repeated. 'I think he could learn a lot from you.'

That was the understatement of the century.

'No. Rufus must also choose to live the life he wishes. He follows his family rules. Fine with me.' Some of the fire had gone out of her voice and Phoebe nodded.

'I do understand,' she said slowly.

'I think that you do.' Emilia gave the faintest of smiles and sighed.

There was a pause. Then, remembering why she had come over in the first place, Phoebe got the Christmas cards out of her bag. 'I was going to give these to Archie and Rufus. Do you think you'll stay and see them? Can I leave them with you?'

Emilia shrugged. The festive bag she'd been carrying when Phoebe had first spotted her was in the footwell by her feet. 'I can keep them with mine if you wish. I have to go soon. I can leave by the back door in garden.'

'That would be great. Thank you. I have to go too.' Phoebe reached for the door catch. 'I really hope you can work things out with Rufus, Emilia.'

The other woman met her gaze. 'Thank you,' she said softly. 'Happy Christmas, Phoebe.'

'Happy Christmas to you too.'

'Phoebe.' Emilia caught her arm, her eyes suddenly panicked. 'You must promise me you will tell no one this secret I have shared with you.'

'OK,' Phoebe said. 'If that's really what you want.'

'It is.'

'Then I promise.'

Emilia let go of her arm and Phoebe got out of the car and walked slowly back towards her Lexus. This would be a really good time for Rufus and Archie to turn up, but she had a feeling that Emilia might be right about them having gone away for Christmas.

It would explain the lack of decorations. Not to mention the total lack of life around the place. Harrison would probably know. She resolved to ask Tori when she got home. She itched to tell Tori about Emilia's secret too, or at least Sam, who she knew wouldn't tell a soul. But having promised Emilia, she knew she couldn't.

It was so sad, but it wasn't her business. It wasn't anyone else's business either. But as Phoebe drove slowly down the long drive of Beechbrook House, beneath a moody grey December sky, she hoped fervently that Emilia would change her mind and tell Rufus the truth herself.

She had a feeling this wasn't going to happen. They were both too proud and Phoebe was terribly afraid that their pride would deny them both the happy ending they could so clearly both have done with, not to mention giving Archie a happy and loving family home. What a tragedy that was.

34

Several times over the next forty-eight hours, Phoebe came close to reneging on the promise she'd made Emilia. It was Christmas. The time for reunions, not senseless break-ups. The time people were supposed to come together, not cause each other unnecessary pain. She was desperate to tell Sam, who she knew wouldn't breathe a word to anyone, but she was even more desperate to tell Tori and Harrison because she knew Harrison *would* say something. Harrison was the one person who might actually be able to talk some sense into Rufus.

Phoebe was eager for a happy ending. But however much her heart told her the end justified the means, her conscience stopped her. She had given her word to Emilia, and she would do her best to keep it.

Tori and Harrison were spending their first Christmas with their newborn daughter at home while various relatives of Tori's popped in and out to welcome the new arrival. Apparently Harrison was cooking for them all. He was a dab hand in the kitchen. There was even talk he might be softening towards the idea of contacting one or two members of his own family to meet Vanessa Rose – but Tori had told Phoebe she was leaving this entirely up to him. 'They treated him pretty shabbily in the past,' she'd explained, 'so any reconciliation has to come from him.'

It was this throwaway line that convinced Phoebe she'd made the right decision about keeping Emilia's secret. If Rufus and Emilia were to have a future, the first move had to come from one of them.

The Dashwood family, in a departure from what usually happened at Christmas, were all descending on Puddleduck Farm on Christmas Day. Louella and James usually hosted the whole family in the home Phoebe and Frazier had grown up in, but it had been a squeeze last year and that had been without the addition of Sam and his folks, who'd been invited for Christmas dinner this year too. Jan might not be able to make it – she had said she would do her best – but everyone was rooting for her.

Maggie and Eddie had welcomed the idea of hosting because it meant they were on hand for all the animals. Most of the preparations for the meals had taken place in other people's kitchens, Maggie had been told in no uncertain terms that she was hosting, not cooking, but Phoebe knew she'd been baking batches of wonky mince pies because when she'd popped in on 21 December, just after she'd locked up the practice for the evening, the kitchen was full of the delicious smell of baking. And Maggie was laying some out on a wire rack to cool.

'They aren't wonky on purpose,' Maggie said. 'I was in a rush, that's all. My feet have only just touched the ground. Even if the floor does feel like it's still rolling about like the sea.'

'Well, if you will go swanning off on Caribbean cruises. What was it like? You haven't told me properly.' Phoebe looked longingly at the pies.

'It was great. But I'm glad to be back. So's Eddie. There's only so much sitting around stuffing your face you can do.'

'Talking of stuffing your face.' Phoebe made a grab for a mince pie. 'I think I should test a wonky mince pie.'

'They don't need testing.' Maggie snatched the tray away from Phoebe's outstretched fingers.

'How do you know without an independent tester trying them?' Phoebe pouted.

'Because I have absolute confidence in my baking skills. That's how I know.' Maggie held the tray high, which wasn't a very effective way of keeping them out of Phoebe's reach, as her granddaughter was quite a bit taller than she was.

'OK, I won't pinch one. Relax.' Phoebe made a gesture of surrender with her hands and stood back from the counter and Maggie put the tray back cautiously.

'You can do your independent taste test thingie when they're cooler,' she promised, her eyes sparkling with humour. 'After I've shown you my wedding photos, very thoughtfully printed out and put in an album by your brother.'

'Oooh, has he done it?' Phoebe clapped her hands with excitement. 'Why didn't you tell me?'

'I just have, haven't I?' Maggie rolled her eyes.

For the next ten minutes, they oohed and ahhed over the album, which was a mix of entertaining animal photos and pictures of people in posh frocks and suits, including some lovely ones of Maggie and Eddie, clearly madly in love and enjoying every minute. In almost every photo someone was smiling. There was even one of Phoebe and Sam smiling, with not a trace of puppy paws or donkey slobber visible on her dress, Phoebe was pleased to see.

'They're wonderful,' she told her grandmother.

'Aren't they? So are you looking forward to spending your first Christmas with Sam?'

'And the rest of our growing extended family. Yes, very much.'

'Gosh, yes, I know. And next year we'll have another one.' Maggie arched her eyebrows. 'I'm assuming Alexa will be making a Christmas announcement.'

'Did she tell you? She swore me to secrecy because she wasn't yet three months.'

'She didn't need to tell me. I do have eyes in my head.' Maggie paused meaningfully. 'It'll be your turn next.'

'I'm far too busy for a family. Anyway, I'm a traditional kind of girl.'

'Marriage first and babies second. Is that it?' Maggie went on before she could answer. 'We'd wait forever if we left it to the men.'

'I don't *want* to ask him.'

'But you *do* want to marry Sam.'

'Yes. Of course I do.'

Maggie laughed.

'What's so funny?'

'You, my darling. So independent and modern and yet so old fashioned and traditional.'

'I must take after you. Anyway, you waited for Eddie to propose. He got down on one knee and everything.'

'Yes, and look where that got us. He almost got stuck down there. It was a good job you came along at the right moment and helped me haul him up.'

'So I should wait for Sam to propose then?'

There was a sudden odd atmosphere in the kitchen. Phoebe wasn't sure what it was about, but she felt as though she'd stumbled inadvertently into some kind of secret. Even Maggie now seemed flustered. She'd turned away and gone to the sink and was busying herself with some pots and pans.

Phoebe took a step towards her. 'Or do you think I should propose to Sam? Is that what you're saying?'

'I'm not saying anything. I'm keeping my beak out. Well, mostly

I am,' she amended, and a reflective look came into her eyes. 'Don't ask me anything, love. I'm not getting involved.'

'OK, I won't.' Phoebe abandoned the idea of cross-questioning her further and changed the subject. 'Gran, I really need to get something off my chest. Can you keep a secret?'

'Keeping secrets is my superpower,' Maggie said, brightening. 'Whose secret is it?'

'Emilia's. Archie's nanny,' Phoebe added when Maggie gave a frown of puzzlement. 'But you really must promise not to pass it on. Not even to Eddie.'

'This sounds serious,' Maggie said, pulling out a chair at the kitchen table and gesturing they sit down. 'Go on. I'm all ears.'

Phoebe poured out the whole story of bumping into Emilia and all that she had said. At the end of it, she added softly, 'I want to help them. For Archie's sake if not Rufus's. That little boy deserves a happy ending, even if they are too pig-headed to speak to each other.'

'I agree. He does. But I don't think you need to do anything.'

'You don't. Why not?'

'Because I have it on very good authority that Rufus and Archie have gone to Switzerland for Christmas.'

'To see Emilia. How do you know that?'

'I told you just now. Nothing gets past me.' She paused. 'OK, OK,' she capitulated. 'I know because Archie himself told me. He came down to drop off Christmas cards for us all, bless his little cotton socks. And he told me he and his father were going to Geneva for Christmas to hand deliver Emilia's cards personally.'

'Jeez, I didn't see that coming. So Rufus does have a heart.'

'Indeed he does. Archie was full of it. He said his father had written to her but not got an answer, so they were heading out to make sure they had the right address.'

'Yes, but Emilia's not there, she's here. She didn't say anything about going back to Geneva. What if they miss each other?'

'Darling, we can't control everything in this world, no matter how much we would like to.' Maggie's eyes were soft. 'Trust me, it's one of the few things I have learned in my long years on the planet. Would you like to try one of the wonky mince pies? They should have cooled down enough by now.'

* * *

Rufus and Archie were at that very moment riding in a taxi through the Christmas lights of Geneva. They were on their way to the address where Rufus had sent the love letter. A hypnotic swirl of snow fell softly from the dark sky and Rufus mused that the Swiss were so much better set up for snow than the UK. The taxi driver had told him that in Switzerland it wasn't a legal requirement to have snow tyres on your vehicle but if you caused an obstruction because you didn't have them, you were heavily fined.

Rufus had given up waiting for Emilia to answer his letter, he wasn't even sure it would have arrived in the Christmas post snarl-up, so he'd decided to call on her personally. And maybe it was cowardice to take Archie along because Emilia wasn't so likely to slam the door in both their faces, but he was past caring. Besides, Archie could hardly just stay at home.

Fortunately, one of the gardeners was looking after Enola. His daughter was a keen horsewoman and had her own, so Enola would have some equine company. Archie had agreed to this on condition they got back to England in time for the Boxing Day Pony Club meet and that Rufus accompanied him.

It was a high price to pay but Rufus had agreed without hesitation. Something fundamental had altered in him since the day he'd sat sobbing like a child in the Land Rover. He needed to move on and this time he needed to do it properly. He could no longer be shackled to the demons of his past. He had to focus on the future.

The address, Rufus had discovered, as they drove through the twinkling festive lights and dressed-up trees, was three kilometres from the centre of Geneva, in an area which was more expensive than he'd expected. He wondered if it was Emilia's family house and, if so, who had answered the phone when he'd rung. She had sounded young.

As he and Archie crunched their way through virgin snow to the gate of the property which was surrounded by high hedges frosted with a shimmer of white, Rufus felt his stomach crunch with anxiety. He'd come here on a crazy whim. No, not a whim. He was sure about this. He was surer than he'd been about anything ever – even Rowena.

The house itself was white pebbledash with large windows, a tiled roof with a lip of snow and a sprinkling of sparkle on its copper-green finials. A row of glassy stalactites dangled from the eaves. Rufus assumed there must be a driveway somewhere for cars, or maybe an underground garage. A house like this would surely have parking.

There were wooden planters alongside a floor-to-ceiling window on one side of the house which had a small terrace, he realised as they got closer, their breath puffing out like smoke.

'Wow,' Archie said. 'This is a cool house.'

'It's very nice.' They'd reached the front door, also white, with a zigzag pattern on it and a doorbell which Rufus pressed.

After a few moments, there was movement behind the door and then it opened and they found themselves looking at a girl, a similar age to Emilia. But she had dark hair and wore big-framed glasses. The word chic could have been invented for her.

She launched into German, but 'Hallo' was the only word Rufus understood.

'Do you speak English?'

'Yes. Good afternoon. How can I help you?' Now he recognised her voice. She was the woman he'd spoken to previously.

'My name is Rufus Holt. I'm looking for Emilia.'

'And I'm Archie.'

Her face softened as she glanced at Archie. 'You have come from England?'

'Yes, we have. It took hours and hours,' Archie told her. 'Our plane got delayed. Then it got cancelled. Then we got another one. We should have been here yesterday. But we only got here today. And it's freezing.' He stamped his feet and rubbed his hands for good measure.

'I see.' She looked slightly taken aback. 'I am sorry but I think you have had a wasted voyage. Emilia is not here.'

'Are you expecting her?' Rufus bit his lip. 'We're very anxious to see her.'

'I'm not expecting her.' She blinked a few times behind the glasses. 'My name is Sofia. I'm Emilia's friend. She occasionally stays here, but she mainly uses this as her postal address. You'd better come in.'

They stamped off snow on the doormat and followed her into a large modern room full of light, with wooden floors and white furniture. It was the room with the floor-to-ceiling windows, Rufus could see the wooden planters outside. It smelled faintly of something cinnamon, air freshener or polish maybe. A huge Christmas tree, bedecked with gold and silver stars, its branches laden with Santa Claus chocolates, sat in a gold tub in the corner.

Sofia invited them to sit on the pale green leather sofa, which was scattered with faux-fur cushions. She offered them drinks and disappeared to get them.

Archie and Rufus looked at each other. 'We should probably have told her we were coming, Dad,' Archie said in a disappointed voice.

'I know, son.' He'd tried hard enough. But if Emilia didn't want to see him then, other than stage a stake out, there was very little he could do about it. And even a stake out was useless if he didn't know where she was.

Sofia came back with hot chocolate for Rufus and apple juice and biscuits for Archie and set them on a low white table. Apart from the tree, the room was sparsely furnished and looked more like a show home than a young woman's apartment.

'I think Emilia is still in England,' Sofia said. 'Why are you looking for her?'

'Are you in touch with her?' Rufus answered her question with one of his own.

She nodded slowly, and he felt himself sag with relief. 'I can't get hold of her. I've tried phoning and I've written – I posted a letter here,' he murmured, looking around, in case it was anywhere to be seen. 'I just want to talk to her.'

'They were dating,' Archie piped up, 'but they had a misunderstanding and Dad wanted to apologise.'

Sofia looked startled, although not as startled as Rufus felt. He glanced at his son, feeling genuinely lost for words.

'I am right, aren't I, Dad?' Archie looked at him expectantly.

'Er, yeah, you're right. But how did you know?'

Archie clapped his hands. 'Because Emilia's *in lurve* with you.' He drew out the word lurve, smiling self-consciously. 'She's been in *lurve* with you for ages and ages. But you're not very good at noticing things like that. My friend Jack said you'd probably notice in the end. But I wasn't so sure.'

Rufus shook his head in bemusement. Talk about out of the mouths of babes. He was torn between a rush of supreme embarrassment and a huge relief that his son hadn't inherited his locked-down attitude towards feelings.

'Is this true?' Sofia asked Rufus.

'Yes, but it was a little more than a misunderstanding. I said some terrible things to Emilia.'

'I know you did. Emilia told me this. She told me I must not tell you where she was. However much you begged me to say.'

'Right,' Rufus said weakly. 'I see. And is there no negotiation at all on that?'

'She also said you would probably not do any begging,' Sofia added with a glint in her eye. She folded her arms. 'I see that she was right.'

'He is begging on the inside,' Archie said, leaning forward. 'Aren't you, Dad?'

'I am,' Rufus said. 'I really am begging.'

This time, Sofia laughed. 'Wait there. I will try to contact her.'

While she was gone, father and son stayed side by side on the sofa. Rufus was trying to resist getting up and pacing the room and Archie played with his phone.

Sofia was gone a few minutes. Maybe she couldn't get hold of Emilia, Rufus thought, or maybe Emilia wanted nothing to do with him. He wouldn't have blamed her. He was bracing himself for disappointment. For Archie's disappointment too, he realised, because Emilia was the reason that Archie was so well adjusted. Archie might complain and whinge about his nanny's strictness, but Rufus knew he also loved her. Emilia was the closest thing he'd had to a mother for coming up to half of his life.

But then finally Sofia came back into the room. Rufus and Archie both stood up – there were some habits he was glad he'd inherited from his father, and then Rufus realised that Sofia was not alone. Emilia was standing just behind her.

As Rufus met her eyes, she stuck out her chin and put her nose in the air. 'I do not think very much of your begging,' she said in her haughtiest voice.

Rufus's reply was drowned out by a squeal as Archie shot across the room into a delighted Emilia's outstretched arms.

35

A little while later, in Sofia's kitchen, while she and Archie watched a Christmas movie in the other room, Rufus had told Emilia that he loved her. That he didn't care that she was a nanny. That he wanted to spend the rest of his life with her. To be with her and his son, to start a new life with them, either in Beechbrook House, or somewhere else. Once he'd begun, he couldn't stop. The words, the love, they had poured out of him.

She had listened quietly, tears in her eyes, and at the end of it, she'd told him about her background, and how she'd fallen out with her family because she wished to make her own way in the world. Even if it meant leaving behind her life of privilege.

The two of them had looked at each other in a kind of awed amazement. Then they'd hugged each other tightly and gone into the lounge to tell Archie and Sofia the wonderful news.

'I'm glad you've seen sense,' Archie said matter-of-factly. 'Does that mean you're going to come and live with us again? But forever and ever this time?'

'Oh, yes.' Rufus squeezed Emilia's hand in one of his and Archie's in the other. 'That's definitely our plan.'

They'd stayed at the Geneva house that night, which was luckily big enough to accommodate them all, and Rufus had fallen asleep with Emilia in his arms, feeling as though he'd wandered into some kind of magical Christmas fairy tale.

They'd been unable to get Emilia an extra seat on the same flight back to England as them. Every Christmas flight was full. But Rufus had refused to leave without her. So they'd driven back to the airport anyway, through the twinkling lights of Geneva, and then sat in a hot airport lounge looking out at the endlessly swirling snow against the plate-glass windows waiting for a cancellation.

In the end, the magic that had enveloped them all since their big reunion had made a reappearance and Rufus managed to get tickets for all three of them on a midnight flight two days before Christmas Eve. Archie had the window seat and he'd spent most of the journey with his nose pressed to the glass. 'Look out for the Santa Claus sleigh,' Emilia had told him. 'He must have started on his deliveries if he's to get them all done in time. We're in the same airspace. You might see it.'

Archie had shot her a look over his shoulder. 'I don't believe in fairy tales, Emilia.'

Although he'd turned back to the window pretty sharpish, Rufus noticed.

And his son might not believe in fairy tales, but by God, Rufus did. Because he was in the middle of his own fantastic fairy tale. A part of him was scared that if he pinched himself hard enough, he would wake up.

* * *

Rufus still felt as though he was living in some wonderful dream, when back at Beechbrook the next day, he took Archie out onto the estate in search of the perfect Christmas tree. They dug one up, and dragged it back to the house, to find it only just fitted through the door, despite Rufus's careful measurements. Emilia teased them mercilessly, and Rufus couldn't ever remember laughing so much.

When the tree was finally in situ, its top grazed the ceiling. The three of them spent a happy hour dressing it with tinsel, baubles and painted wooden decorations that were generations old, and Rufus found a set of lights that worked and twined them around it. Then they all went shopping for presents, food, and all things Christmas. They'd decided to go out on the 25th so no one had the stress of cooking, but there was a mass of other stuff to buy and it was excellent fun mingling with the festive crowds, and then later, going to the carol service in their local church.

Rufus, Emilia and Archie shook hands with the vicar. Then they stood side by side in a pew at the front of the church and no one batted an eyelid and Rufus felt as if it was the beginning of a new era. There would be no more kowtowing to the tight pretentiousness of the past, from this day forward he would hold his head high, proud to be with the woman he loved.

The most ironic thing of all was that when it came to nobility, Emilia outclassed him by a mile. He might have an hereditary title, but she was actual royalty.

'Not that you are ever to tell anyone this,' she had warned him. 'I wish to be accepted for who I am, not because of the family into which I was born.'

Rufus had agreed he would respect her wishes absolutely. It was a wonderful feeling that he no longer cared what people thought. The new lord was going to change a few things around here. The chains of snobbery, pretentiousness, and pomposity no longer bound him. For the first time in his life, Rufus felt totally free of them all.

* * *

On Christmas morning, Phoebe and Sam had arranged to head over to Puddleduck Farm at around eleven, which had given Sam time to see to Ninja. Phoebe and Roxie went with him to the stables. Roxie already adored going to see the horses. They had just got back, loaded up the car with presents and food and a very excited Roxie, who knew something was going on and had already been sick on Sam's kitchen floor.

'I'm not sure that was excitement, I think she ate Snowball's Christmas catnip,' Sam told Phoebe as he guided the pup safely into her crate in the back of the repaired Subaru. 'Is catnip safe for dogs?'

'Yes, it's fine. But she probably ate the packaging too.' Phoebe shook her head. 'At least one of them is participating in Christmas.'

Snowball, when presented with his gift, had stuck his black fluffy tail in the air and stalked out of the kitchen, although he'd been quite keen on his smoked salmon breakfast.

'Snowball's idea of a great Christmas Day is to go mouse hunting and then spend the afternoon asleep lying along the back of the sofa in the patch of sun that comes through the big window,' Sam said. 'To be honest, that's his idea of a great day whatever time of year it is. He'll be relieved we're all going out.'

'Are you worried about your mum?' Phoebe asked him as they got into the car because he was definitely tense about something. She could feel it in him. 'Or is it the prospect of spending Christmas Day with my entire family?'

'I am a bit worried about Ma. I'd hate her to feel disappointed if she can't make it over to Puddleduck.'

'But she knows there's no pressure,' Phoebe said.

'Christmas Day is full of pressures. We usually have a really quiet one at home. Not that I'm not looking forward to today,' he said, starting up the engine and putting the car in gear. 'It's our first Christmas together too. Properly together, I mean.'

'There's still time to change our minds and turn around.' Phoebe put her hand on his knee.

'No. We can't do that to your folks. And we can't miss watching Ma walk in. Turning up at Puddleduck is the equivalent of climbing Everest for her.'

'I do love you, Sam Hendrie.'

Roxie gave a small whine from the back.

'I love you too,' she called back to her.

'I love you both too,' Sam said. 'We'd better get going.'

At Beechbrook House, a roaring log fire, made up and lit by Rufus, burnt in the inglenook. Dozens of cards, opened and put out by Emilia, jostled for space on the mantelpiece and Christmas music belted out from a speaker on the sideboard.

Rufus had just made Emilia and Archie breakfast. They had both tried to dissuade him. Emilia because she said she was much better at making porridge than he was, this was true, and Archie because he'd arranged to go riding in the forest with the gardener's daughter, Leah, and he was in a hurry to get outside.

'It's not porridge,' Rufus had said, bringing in a plate of deliciously scented pastries. 'It's something more Swiss themed.'

'The Swiss don't have a traditional Christmas breakfast,' Emilia said, looking at him suspiciously.

'But you love pastries, and so does Archie.'

'Thanks, Dad.' Archie grabbed a pain au chocolat. 'Is it OK if I eat it on the way?'

'No. You'll give yourself indigestion.'

'Sit down and eat half with us,' Emilia suggested. 'And then you can have your Christmas present.'

'OK.' Archie wolfed down the pastry and wiped the crumbs

from his mouth. 'That was pretty good, Dad. Can I take one for later? Can I have my Christmas presents later too?'

'Go on then,' Rufus gave in.

Emilia rolled her eyes. 'Make sure you're back by lunchtime. You know we're going out.'

'OK. I promise. Happy Christmas.' And he was gone.

Rufus and Emilia looked at each other.

'Just the two of us then,' he murmured. He still couldn't believe he had persuaded her to come back with him. Especially as she'd only just got back to Switzerland herself and had planned to spend it with Sofia and her partner Rudi. Sofia, being the good friend she was, had said she wouldn't hear of it – that she and Rudi would be glad to have the house to themselves.

'She is very happy she played a part of our reconciliation,' Emilia had told Rufus when they were on the plane back to England. 'She is a very good friend.'

Now they were alone again in his lounge, Rufus took Emilia's hands in his and he dropped to his knees.

'Will you marry me, Emilia? Will you do me the very great honour of becoming my wife?'

She looked down at him. 'I will, Rufus, yes. On one condition.'

'What is it?'

'You marry Emilia the woman. Not Emilia the titled girl.'

'It's Emilia the woman I want.' Rufus offered her a ring. 'This belonged to my mother. I would love you to wear it. But if you would prefer a new one, we can do that too.'

She shook her head, and he saw her fingers tremble as he slid the ring, which glittered with rose-cut antique diamonds, onto her finger. It was slightly too big, and she had to hold her hands to stop it falling off.

Emilia drew him to his feet, and they held each other tight in a patch of sunlight that poured through the window and encircled them. And in the amazing warmth of that embrace, Rufus felt as though the long dark shadows of the past had finally, and completely, loosened their grip.

* * *

At Puddleduck Farm, there was a buzz of excitement in the air. Eddie had just seen Jan get out of a car outside, holding tight to her husband's arm, but everyone was pretending not to notice, because they didn't want to frighten her straight back into it again.

In the end, it was Sam who went to the door to welcome his parents in.

His mother looked pale, but resolute. He leaned in and kissed her cheek, 'Hi, Ma, there's a mince pie with your name on in the back room. Shall we rescue it before one of the dogs gets there first?'

'I'd like that, son.'

Moments later, Sam and Phoebe and Jan and Ian were sitting by the huge Christmas tree that glittered with lights and sparkled with baubles and Jan was slowly getting a hold on her breathing while Phoebe and Sam chattered to Ian about the Christmas weather. It was one of the mildest UK Christmases on record.

One by one, the dogs came into the room, first Roxie, then Tiny, then Buster. They seemed to know Jan was feeling fragile and they sat protectively close to her, and slowly Sam watched her relax. It was going to be a different kind of Christmas this year. A more hectic one than he liked. But he was looking forward to it too. He knew he'd feel more relaxed after they'd all sat down for dinner and until then he'd just have to fake it.

* * *

The huge old farmhouse table was made for family celebrations. It could seat twelve people comfortably, fourteen at a push, and today it sparkled with tinsel, and the best silver cutlery gleamed in the light of a dozen red candles, held in candelabras at intervals.

There were silver and gold crackers on every plate, although Phoebe knew that Maggie would soon be issuing warnings about not pulling them too near the dogs because they were scared of the bangs.

Today there were also name tags by each plate, held by animal-themed clothes pegs, and right at this moment people were checking their names and jostling each other as they found the right chairs. Phoebe's name was held in place by a rearing brown horse – where on earth had Maggie found that? – and Sam's by a black and white spotted dog. Her grandmother had clearly had fun.

Three bottles of champagne waited in ice buckets on the work-top. Someone had pushed the boat out; champagne wasn't usually part of the Dashwood Christmas celebrations. But then again, this one was special on so many levels. Alexa was probably going to announce her news, that deserved champagne. So did the fact that Jan had managed to get here.

In fact, it looked as though Alexa was going to announce her news right now because Frazier was tapping a spoon against a wine glass.

'We have an announcement to make,' he said. 'Listen up, guys.'

The table hushed miraculously, except for Flo, who was never very quiet. 'Mummy, I need to pee.'

'You've only just been,' Alexa said in exasperation.

'I need to go again.'

'And to think we've signed up for another one of these,' Frazier said as there were giggles around the table. 'Yep, that's right. We're expecting another baby, everyone.'

A cheer went up, and then everyone was congratulating Alexa

while Frazier took his daughter along to the downstairs bathroom. There were more congratulations when they both came back again; Flo was smiling, and Frazier was rolling his eyes. 'Kids have such great timing, don't they?'

Phoebe stole a glance at Jan, who finally had some colour in her cheeks, and their eyes locked across the table. 'You OK?' Phoebe mouthed and Jan nodded.

Frazier was tapping the glass again. 'I think Sam wanted to say something too.'

The table hushed again, as Sam cleared his throat. 'I did. I do.' He glanced at his mother. 'I'm so proud of you, Ma. I'm not going to go on about it, but I am.'

She acknowledged this with a nod and blushed furiously, and Sam blew her a kiss. There was more clapping.

'And also,' Sam went on when they'd stilled again, 'I wanted to do this.' He stood up and then walked around to Phoebe's side of the table. She was sitting opposite him at one end, and when he reached her, he dropped down on to his knees. 'Phoebe Dashwood, you're the love of my life. You have been since the moment I first laid eyes on you, and I can't imagine growing old with anyone else. Oh, heck, I'm just gonna say it. Will you please marry me, Phoebe?' He held something out, a small box, on which nestled the most beautifully classic ring Phoebe had ever seen – three sparkling diamonds, their light catching in the sunlight that filled the room.

Phoebe felt in that moment as if there was a great rushing in her ears. Or maybe that was the adrenaline pounding through her body. She just knew that the whole world stilled. Even Flo stopped talking, as everyone waited for her answer, and the moment drew out in an exquisitely lengthened silence.

They were all smiling. They'd all known, she realised – that had been part of the excitement she'd been feeling all day, and probably part of the reason for Sam's tension too. And Maggie's odd behaviour in the kitchen when she'd baked the wonky mince pies. They had all kept the secret of Sam's Christmas Day proposal.

She wondered – had he been the only one who hadn't known how she would answer? He still looked pretty tense now.

But there was love in his face too. The kind of love she knew was going to last a lifetime. No matter what. Her mouth felt so dry it was hard to speak, and when she did, her voice came out in a not very romantic squeak. 'Of course I'll marry you, Sam Hendrie. Of course I'll flaming marry you.'

The applause this time was deafening. Phoebe felt as if they were lifting her up on their excitement, as she and Sam both stood up and hugged and kissed in the middle of the kitchen.

Her father had stood up too. He headed for the champagne buckets. 'I think we've got enough for quite a few toasts,' he said, sounding more excited than Phoebe had ever heard him. 'So who's going to help me open all of these bottles then?'

EPILOGUE
NEW YEAR'S EVE

'I'm actually finding this all quite surreal,' Phoebe whispered to Tori, as Harrison drove Tori's car with herself and Tori wedged in the back with food and drink, and Sam in the passenger seat beside him, up the quarter-mile drive to Beechbrook House.

'So am I,' Tori said. 'A lot's changed since the old Lord Holt died, God rest his soul. I can't imagine Alfred would ever have thrown open his house for a New Year party, can you?'

'He wouldn't,' Harrison said cheerily from the driver's seat. 'He'd have hated strangers trampling around the grounds and then wandering willy-nilly through the house leaving doors open, causing draughts, nosing in rooms they had no business to be in.'

Sam chuckled. 'And possibly nicking the silver?'

'He'd have locked all that up,' Harrison said. 'Not that Rufus has a lot of silver.' His dark eyes caught Phoebe's in the rear-view mirror. 'He's happy, though. Happier than I've ever known him.'

'I'm so thrilled for them both,' Phoebe said. She had kept Emilia's secret and she'd not heard anyone else say a word about it, so she assumed that either no one knew, or that the new couple had sworn everyone to secrecy. She strongly suspected the former. Tori would have found it impossible not to run such a romantic fairy tale headline – 'Widowed Lord Meets His Princess' – if she'd known.

They drew up outside Beechbrook House, which was ablaze with lights and looked like something out of a Richard Curtis movie. Twelve dancing reindeers pulling a sleigh galloped over one wing and every cherub on the fountain sparkled with fairy lights: one wore a Santa hat and the others sported red and gold tinsel. The front door was open in welcome, spilling an oblong of golden light and the sounds of festive tunes out into the chilly evening. There were already several cars parked.

'I'm glad we left Vanessa Rose with Maggie,' Tori told Phoebe. 'Rufus offered us a bedroom for the night, but I don't think she'd have slept through this lot.'

'Maggie loves kids, and she's got my parents and Alexa and Frazier to help. They'll have a great time. Stop worrying.'

'I know they will.'

Moments later they had disembarked, no mean feat, when they were carrying four bottles of wine, a crate of soft drinks, a tub of mince pies and half a Christmas cake which Tori had made for the buffet.

'Not that Rufus said he wanted us to bring anything, but we don't want to be eating it all year,' Tori quipped.

They went into Beechbrook House, to join what appeared to be half the residents of the New Forest, none of whom had wanted to miss out on a society party. Never before had Beechbrook House flung open its impressive doors for a party to which the whole neighbourhood was invited.

Everyone was keen to see how the lord of the manor lived and it seemed he was just as keen to show them.

Rufus's office door was closed tonight, Phoebe noticed. In another lifetime, Rufus had told her there that he didn't think they had a future. Every other room was packed with people, although the staircases had ropes clipped across them at the bottom. Parts of the house were clearly out of bounds.

Phoebe spotted Marcus and Natasha talking to a stunning blonde in a figure-hugging gold dress that sparkled with sequins. Not far from them was a group of volunteers from Puddleduck Pets.

Rufus and Emilia were in the kitchen. Rufus was serving mulled wine from a cauldron that simmered on his enormous range oven. He was dressed casually, as he often was, in jeans and a polo shirt, 'designer casual', Tori called it, and when he saw Phoebe and Sam, he smiled and beckoned them over and Emilia, who was beside him, waved.

A few seconds later, the four of them were standing by the oven, chatting easily, Sam complimenting the house and Phoebe complimenting Emilia on her outfit, and it wasn't long before Emilia and Phoebe were comparing engagement rings. Never in her wildest imaginings had Phoebe thought things would turn out like this but she was so happy they had. Emilia was glowing and there was a new confidence about Rufus that Phoebe had never seen before. It was very heart-warming.

Phoebe and Sam had only planned to stay an hour or so, they were sleeping over at Puddleduck Farm, where Maggie and Eddie were babysitting Roxie as well as Vanessa Rose. They planned to walk back home across the fields when they were ready. But there were so many people they knew that they stayed longer.

Phoebe caught up with Archie, who was a delight, and he filled her in on everything that was going on at school. He clearly loved it. She had never seen him so energised. So far, he'd joined the chess club and had contributed a feature on woodland birds to the school newspaper, and of course there was all the news on Enola and how fantastic she was. Phoebe let his bright chatter wash over her. Archie had inherited none of his father's social phobia. Not that there was much evidence of that in Rufus tonight.

At around nine o'clock, Phoebe and Tori were chatting in the main lounge, a huge room split in half by an enormous inglenook fireplace, and Tori was discreetly pointing out various dignitaries who she'd met through her work. 'That's the new Lymington and Pennington mayor, he's the youngest ever one, and he's very into social media.'

'Wow.'

'And that's the new Lord Mountbatten.'

'Gosh. Who's that very posh-looking couple by the tree?'

'They're Harrison's parents. It's really early days but there's a bit of a reconciliation going on, because of the baby.' Her green eyes softened. 'It's amazing how a new baby can bring people together.'

'That's really good news, Tori, I'm so pleased.'

'Me too. Life's too short for falling out with family.' She hesitated. 'You see that stunning blonde just to their left with a crowd of male admirers?'

'Yes.' Phoebe spotted woman in the sequined dress from earlier. 'I was wondering who she was.'

'She's an animal behaviourist; she mainly sees dogs. Her name's Destiny Dolittle.'

Phoebe spluttered on the sip of Prosecco she'd just taken.

'*Destiny Dolittle*. That can't be her real name. You're making it up.'

'I'm not. It's her real name. I interviewed her for a feature in the mag. She owns Dolittle Animal Magic, and apparently she's stunningly good at her job, as well as being – well...' Tori narrowed her eyes speculatively. '...stunning. Not that I'm jealous,' she added quickly, 'although it is hard not to be when someone's that beautiful and talented. And she's only twenty-seven. Mind you, I'd definitely like to be that slim.'

'You've just had a baby,' Phoebe reminded her. 'And you are beautiful.'

'Mmmm.' Tori sounded despondent and Phoebe suddenly felt the same. Just looking at Destiny, who exuded beauty, like some people exuded wealth, made her feel underdressed and inadequate. And she had her best togs on. What was that about!

'Well, I'm sticking with Paula's Puppy Pals,' she told Tori. 'That's where we're taking Roxie in January. Paula is motherly and mid-sixtyish. Judging by the photo on her website anyway. Marcus recommended her.'

'Sounds perfect.' Tori brightened. 'Anyway, New Year's Eve is not a night to fret about what we haven't got. It's a night to look to the future. The year of the wedding,' she said. 'Yours and mine. And Rufus and Emilia's. I wonder if we'll get an invite to that one?'

'Oh, I think that's a given,' Harrison said. He and Sam had just materialised beside them.

The four of them were soon immersed in talk about the future. For Harrison and Tori, it was the joy of watching their daughter grow.

For Phoebe and Sam, it was the hope that Jan would make a full recovery from the agoraphobia, the continued prosperity of Puddleduck Vets and the excitement of choosing their own home together and planning their wedding.

'I'm hoping Ma will be well enough to come and look at places with us,' Sam said, slipping his hand into Phoebe's. 'She was brilliant when I bought my flat. I think we looked at about fourteen properties. I'd have settled for a few of them but Ma insisted that we'd know the right place when we saw it. And she was right.'

It was ten thirty when they decided to head for home. Tori was missing Vanessa Rose; it was the first time she'd left her. Phoebe was tired and Sam had an early start, as always, for Ninja. Harrison promised he'd see them back at Puddleduck before midnight but he'd talk a bit more to his parents first, and the other three took the shortcut back to Puddleduck Farm across the fields.

'This reminds me of when we were kids,' Tori said, laughing, as they all linked arms, Sam flanked by the two girls, and made their way over the uneven ground towards the twinkling lights of the farmhouse. 'It was such fun being out at night, do you remember?'

'Oh, yes,' Sam said. 'Especially when we weren't supposed to be. They were the best times.'

'If we could have looked into the future twenty years ago, we'd never have predicted this,' Tori murmured, putting her head on one side. 'Me all grown up with a little one, and Phoebe with her own vet practice.'

'You've always been a hopeless romantic,' Phoebe said, 'so actually I'd say that was completely predictable.'

'And Phoebe's wanted to be a vet from day one,' Sam put in, 'so that was pretty predictable too.'

'I'd definitely have predicted that you and Sam would get together.' Tori shot a playful glance at Phoebe. 'I knew that long before you two did.'

'Fair enough,' Phoebe said happily. 'We could have predicted most of it.'

Sam stumbled on a dip in the uneven ground and the two women stopped him from falling flat on his face. 'Cheers,' he said breathlessly, and for a second, they all paused midway between the blazing lights of Beechbrook House and the softer, more muted lights of Puddleduck Farmhouse. Somewhere close by, an owl called to its mate across the starlit darkness.

'So, what kind of predictions would you make going forwards twenty years from now?' Tori asked as they hesitated, their breath puffing out into the night air.

'I'm not sure I'd even dare guess,' Sam answered.

'Well, I'm going to predict that we'll all still be best friends,'

Phoebe said, feeling suddenly emotional and joyous and certain she was right. 'Frazier too, of course. And our kids, all the ones we have and all the ones that aren't yet born. They'll all be great friends too.'

'I don't think I can add anything to that,' Sam murmured.

'Me neither,' Tori said happily. 'Here's to a future of friendship and fun. Should we have a group hug or is it too cold in the middle of this field?'

'It's never too cold for a group hug,' Phoebe said, and so they hugged while high above them the moon chose that moment to slip out from behind a cloud and bathe the three of them and Puddleduck Farm and Beechbrook House in a soft silver glow.

Twenty seconds later, they broke apart and ran, giggling like children, the rest of the way down the gentle slope to Puddleduck Farm. Midnight wasn't very far away and Phoebe wanted to see in the New Year with her friends and family, the rest of whom were at the farmhouse. She was looking forward to chatting until the early hours about all the fun and adventures in the fast-approaching New Year. She couldn't remember the last time she'd looked forward to a year so much. Bring it on.

ACKNOWLEDGEMENTS

Thank you so much to Team Boldwood – you are amazing. Thank you to every single one of you who works so hard to bring my books to my readers in paperback, audio and digital.

As always, my special thanks go to my fabulous editor, Caroline Ridding, and also to Cecily Blench, Debra Newhouse, and to Alice Moore for the gorgeous cover.

Thank you to Rhian Rochford for her veterinary knowledge, without whom this book would be a lot harder. Thank you to Hannah Buteux, Millie Byrne and Diana Kimpton for helping with my research about horses. Thank you to Dunford Novelists and especially to Annie Probin. Thank you to Susan Luetolf for guinea pig research and fabulous photos. Thank you to Liz Meyer, who generously shared her puppy journey and whose own dog Darcie was my inspiration for Roxie. Thank you to Mark Winwood, who won the competition to name my dalmatian character. I loved the name Roxie, and my fictional Roxie sends love to the real Roxie.

Thank you to Gordon Rawsthorne for being my first reader.

Thank you, perhaps most of all, for the huge support of my many readers – without whom it would be pretty pointless writing novels. I love reading your emails, tweets and Facebook comments. Please keep them coming.

ABOUT THE AUTHOR

.

Della Galton is the author of more than 15 books, including the *Bluebell Cliff* and *Puddleduck Farm* series. She writes short stories, teaches writing groups and is Agony Aunt for *Writers Forum* Magazine. She lives in Dorset.

Sign up to Della Galton's mailing list for news, competitions and updates on future books.

Visit Della's website: www.dellagalton.co.uk

Follow Della on social media:

 facebook.com/DailyDella

x.com/DellaGalton

instagram.com/Dellagalton

bookbub.com/authors/della-galton

ALSO BY DELLA GALTON

The Bluebell Cliff Series

Sunshine Over Bluebell Cliff

Summer at Studland Bay

Shooting Stars Over Bluebell Cliff

Sunrise Over Pebble Bay

Confetti Over Bluebell Cliff

The Puddleduck Farm Series

Coming Home to Puddleduck Farm

Rainbows Over Puddleduck Farm

Love Blossoms at Puddleduck Farm

Living the Dream at Puddleduck Farm

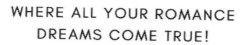

WHERE ALL YOUR ROMANCE DREAMS COME TRUE!

THE HOME OF BESTSELLING ROMANCE AND WOMEN'S FICTION

 WARNING:
MAY CONTAIN SPICE

SIGN UP TO OUR
NEWSLETTER

https://bit.ly/Lovenotesnews

Boldwood

Boldwood Books is an award-winning fiction publishing company seeking out the best stories from around the world.

Find out more at www.boldwoodbooks.com

Join our reader community for brilliant books, competitions and offers!

Follow us
@BoldwoodBooks
@TheBoldBookClub

Sign up to our weekly deals newsletter

https://bit.ly/BoldwoodBNewsletter

Printed in Great Britain
by Amazon